Initiate of
Darkness

Novels by Barb Shadow

A Step Into Darkness
Shifting to Black
Invitation to Darkness
Touched by Darkness

Anthologies

True Ghost Stories and Hauntings, Vol. 1
True Ghost Stories and Hauntings, Vol. 2

Poetry Collections

Among the Dying Violets

Initiate of Darkness

Barb Shadow

From the Shadows Publishing
Forestburgh, New York

To Kathleen,

for Dunkin' runs, late night talks,
bad movies (no Oxford comma)
and keeping me grounded.

I love you, girl.

Drive safe.

He heard the front door open.
The shadow-thing in the corner of his room
woke
and commenced a buzzing in his mind
like flies in a bottle, shaken to a frenzied pitch.

Chapter 1

Olivia sat in the kitchen, her mind churning. She'd been up since the crack of dawn, going over every scenario she could think of regarding the new kid in the house. New *foster* kid. Was he abandoned? Left at a fire station? She sipped her hot cocoa, savoring the steamy chocolate, and stared out the glass doors to the patio. Every foster had a tale and she wanted to know his.

She watched Elaine at the stove, whisking eggs and milk as if she'd done it a thousand times and was happy to do it a thousand more. Humming. Appearing every bit as if she'd stepped out of a 1950s Ladies' Home Journal. Dress freshly ironed. Makeup applied. Light, but not obvious. As if she were moments away from stepping out the door to church. Not that they went to church. Olivia cracked a smile. They were a prim and proper house of heathens.

"What's funny, O.?" Her foster mother glanced over her shoulder, then continued stirring the eggs, turning down the heat under the pan.

"Oh, nothing." She shifted in her chair and took a mouthful of cereal. She chewed, brushing a stray crumb off the tablecloth. It was a tasteful beige embroidered with autumn-colored leaves. Matching towels hung from the oven handle. She swallowed. "So, what's the kid's story?"

"Story?" Elaine kept her tone light. She had known Olivia would be asking. The girl always wanted to know, figure the angles, get to the heart of things. And once she sunk her teeth into a story, she didn't like to let go. But this was a sensitive topic.

"Backstory. Why he ended up a foster. Why he ended up here." She leaned forward, elbows on the edge of the table, chin resting in her hands. "Showing up late on a Saturday night. The kid must have a backstory."

Elaine shut off the stove and scraped the scrambled eggs onto a serving plate next to bacon that was cooling. She glanced down the hallway to make sure he wouldn't hear them and placed the plate in the middle of the table.

"Just between us, O. You and me. His mom killed herself yesterday. He's got no dad that they can find. No relatives." She broke eye contact. "Poor thing."

"Whoa."

"Whoa is right. We've got to be extra understanding with him. He's too young to understand what happened and why he's not home with her. And, unless they find some distant relative somewhere, he'll probably be with us a while."

A hundred thoughts raced through Olivia's mind. "He'll be the brother I always wanted."

"Thank you." Elaine reached for the orange juice as Seth sauntered into the room. Hair unbrushed. Puffy, half-closed eyes. He yawned.

"And here's the one I never wanted."

"Don't start." Elaine turned toward her son. "Morning, hon."

Seth stuck his tongue out at Olivia. "I know you are but what am I?"

"How does that even make sense?" Olivia arched an eyebrow. "What are you, seven?"

He held up his middle finger and opened the refrigerator door. "Anything to eat in this place?" He didn't feel like being nice or participating in cheery morning conversation. His brain had been on fire all week and, since the night before, ached like a knife through his temple.

Elaine took a plate from the cabinet. "Breakfast's on the table and the tea kettle's hot."

He grabbed a Coke.

"Really?"

He shrugged, popped the top. The tab broke and he dropped it into the garbage.

"Any word from Blake?"

Seth struggled to keep his composure. Everything inside him trembled into a sick, guilt-ridden shudder. "No." To the outside world, his best friend was missing. Lost. Alone. But he knew what had happened. Knew Blake's body would be found, slumped over a bench in the mausoleum they'd broken into. He choke-cleared his throat. "Nothing yet."

His mother mouthed the words, "I'm sorry," as he chugged a mouthful of soda. His eyes burned as his head throbbed, but the sound of little feet coming down the hallway took his mother's, and Olivia's, attention. Tommy, in bright red footie pajamas, padded into the kitchen rubbing his eyes.

"Morning!" they greeted in unison. Except Seth. He took a drink.

The little boy crossed the kitchen and climbed into a chair across from Olivia. "Morning." He stretched.

Seth gripped the metal can and shut his eyes as the butcher knife in his brain twisted and his headache intensified. It eased long enough for him to open a cabinet and rummage through the various bottles of cold medicine, cough drops and vitamins until he found the ibuprofen. It rattled as he grabbed it, and he started down the hallway.

"No food?" Elaine called after him.

"Later."

They heard his bedroom door close, his music rumble to life.

"How's he do that if he's got a headache?"

Elaine shook her head, her brow furrowed. "Your guess is as good as mine." Switching her attention to Tommy, she asked,

"How'd you sleep, little man? Would you like some breakfast?" She picked up a plate and gave him a child-sized portion of bacon and eggs.

"I slept good," he said. "Yum, bacon." He fiddled with the zipper of his pajamas as he chewed. "Who was that?"

"That," Elaine said as she folded her dishrag, hanging it over the faucet, "was Seth."

A Beagle appeared at the sliding glass door and gave one sharp bark. Olivia jumped from her seat to let him in. "Iggy!" she said, scrunching the puppy's ears and giving him a kiss on the forehead.

Tommy watched the pup circle the table, sniffing. "I like your pumpkins." A row of jack-o'-lanterns perched at the edge of the patio, facing the house.

"I carved the spooky one in the middle," Olivia said. "The one without a face is Seth's."

"I like spooky." Tommy picked up a piece of bacon and scooped up some of the eggs. He took a big bite. "Can I have a drink?"

"Sure." Elaine smoothed her apron and stood. "What's the magic word?"

Tommy swallowed. "Please!"

She took a small glass out of the cabinet. "Milk or orange juice?"

"Juice, please." Another slice of bacon, another scoop of eggs. "When are we going trick or treating?"

Elaine put the cup on the table and took a moment to pour while she considered his question. "Do you want to go?" She hadn't expected him to want to do anything, let alone eat, and she thought she had prepared herself for the different scenarios . . . a sullen, contemplative little boy, sad, depressed, scared being in a new home with strangers. Withdrawn, broken. Yet here was this child, happily munching on his breakfast, chatting about Halloween as naturally and normally as someone out of a Norman Rockwell painting. Not the kid whose mother killed herself the day before. Not the kid with no family in the world and nowhere to go. She shivered.

"Yesh," he said, holding the bacon in his cheeks. "I want to be a skeleton."

"I see a trip to Walmart in our future," Olivia chimed in. "The very, very near future."

Before Elaine could comment, the phone rang.

"You know," Olivia said, "if you want to carve that pumpkin, we can. Seth won't care."

Tommy chased the last bit of egg across his place, trying to scoop it onto the last bite of bacon. "Can we make it scary?"

"We can make it really scary."

"Okay!"

Elaine was listening intently on the landline, the color draining from her face. "Beverly, oh my God, Bev. I don't even know what to say."

Olivia quieted and held her finger to her lips, signaling to Tommy. There were long pauses in their foster mother's end of the conversation, and she was holding the receiver with both hands.

"Yes, yes. He'll talk with the police. I don't know what he can tell them, but of course he will. He and Blake were," her voice cracked, "best friends." Another pause. "Please. When you know the arrangements. Oh, Bev, if there's anything I can do. Anything you need." Elaine hung up the phone and stood, facing the wall. "O., I need you to take Tommy for a little while."

"I thought maybe we could carve a pumpkin?"

"That would be fine. I need some time with Seth." Elaine left the kitchen and walked down the hallway to Seth's door. She stood in front of it for a minute, as if she were engrossed in the detail of the wood grain, then knocked. "Seth? I need to talk to you."

He unlatched the door, pulling it ajar, and broke out in a sweat. A clammy fear-sweat. A knowing, fight or flight ten-ton weight on his chest anticipation. Surprised it took this long, sick it hadn't been sooner. His heart was beating a crescendo and threatening to explode. He knew what words were going to leave his mother's lips. He knew. As dizziness took over, his legs turned to rubber.

"They found Blake."

He gripped the door jamb.

"I'm so sorry." She averted her eyes, trying not to cry. Wanting to be strong for her son. "He's dead."

Seth crumbled. He collapsed at his mother's feet before she could react. Blake's death was final now. Not a nightmare he could wake from. And the demon they called from hell that night hadn't left his side since. He took a shuddering breath.

Elaine dropped to the floor and wrapped her arms around him as he sobbed. "I know it's hard, hon. Try to pull yourself together a bit, throw some cold water on your face. The police will be here soon."

"W-What?" he pushed away from his mother.

"They want to talk to you. Piece together what happened."

"I didn't kill him. Mom, I wasn't even there." He could barely contain the panic rising in his mind. The dark thing brushed against his shoulder, and he recoiled.

Elaine touched his arm. "Of course not, Seth. Of course not. No one thinks that. Beverly believes Blake committed suicide."

Seth winced. If only that were true.

"They're not coming to interrogate you. They're gathering information."

They heard the whoosh of the kitchen door and shuffling sounds, giggling. A thud on the table. "Let me get a marker and you can draw on the face," Olivia was saying.

Seth stood and held out a hand to help his mother up. "Can you send the kids outside? Get them out of here?" He needed the house still to compose his thoughts. Solidify his lies.

"Sure, honey. When the police get here. Whatever will make you more comfortable."

Chapter 2

Seth stood at the kitchen window, waiting for the squad car to pull up. His nerves were raw. Headache roaring. Maybe they'd think he did it. Did they know he was there that night? Were they coming to nail him for murder?

Fingerprints. There'd be fingerprints. That damned planchette! And the blackout paper on the windows of the mausoleum, he'd put that up. He and Blake sliced their palms to drip blood onto the spirit board, too. Seth ran his fingers across the scab. Still rough. Sore. He rolled his eyes, a new panic erupting in his chest. Screw fingerprints, there'd be DNA. Would they test for that? It'd been almost a week, did that matter? His mind spun.

"Seth?" Olivia laid her pumpkin-carving knife on the table.

"What?" He continued staring outside, unable to break his gaze from the driveway.

"Sorry about your friend."

He swallowed. "Me, too."

The police cruiser parked, and, for Seth, time stopped.

Detectives Burns and Henderson exited their vehicle and took a moment to assess their surroundings. Burns, the younger of the two but still pushing fifty, scanned the area. The neighborhood seemed a typical, middle-class suburb. Key word seemed. Manicured lawns, no trash in sight. He was sure the only time there'd been a bag of garbage anywhere other than in a tall, heavy plastic receptacle, was when it was in the homeowner's hands on the way to the bin. There was the occasional basketball hoop or bike in a driveway. Nothing out of place, the flower beds weeded, and probably every neighbor within a hundred yards was peeking from behind their curtains, curious as hell as to why they were there.

Henderson adjusted his hat and moved closer to his partner. They started up the short walk.

"You think he knows anything?" Burns asked.

"They usually do."

Henderson rang the doorbell.

Iggy barked and danced as Elaine answered the door. "Ssh, Iggy." She hooked her fingers into his collar and, with her other hand, opened the screen door. "He's really a good boy," she said. "He doesn't bite."

"Not a problem, ma'am." Henderson waited until Iggy calmed before he said, "Detectives Henderson and Burns." They showed their badges and ID. "We're here to speak to Seth."

"Yes, yes. Come in. Beverly, Mrs. Calhoun, called to say you were coming." She held the screen while they stepped inside, taking off their hats. They were older than she'd envisioned. Too many crime shows under her belt. She'd pictured a young, coffee drinking detective who solved homicides in under an hour, butting heads with the disgruntled, rough about the edges, chain-smoking sergeant.

"They're here, hon," she called.

Seth entered from the living room.

"These are Detectives Burns and Henderson."

The men stepped forward; Burns taking in the atmosphere of the home. Clean, well kept. The generic painting of a seascape over the sofa, family photos on the mantel above the fireplace. Henderson greeted Seth. "We're very sorry for your loss but we'd like to speak with you about your friend."

"Okay." Handcuffs. They'd be taking him out in handcuffs, and he'd be lucky to ever see his family again. The thoughts were an avalanche through his mind, with him at the bottom, bound, gagged and left for dead.

"Please, sit down, officers," Beverly said. "Can I get you some coffee?"

Henderson spoke for them both. "No, thank you, ma'am." He sat on the sofa, flipping through a spiral notebook, and motioned for Seth to join him. He took a pen out of his shirt pocket. "You were a good friend of Blake?"

"Yeah." Seth rested his hands on his knees. Shifted. It was awkward; he was awkward. He envisioned this was how the guilty sat.

"What can you tell me about him?"

"What do you what to know?"

"His personality. Did he have a lot of friends? Was he outgoing? An introvert?"

A lot of friends? Hah. It'd been him and Blake against the world for as long as he could remember. And, sometimes, Blake would shut him out. "I guess you could say he was an introvert. He was a good guy. Kind of dark."

"Dark? How so?" Henderson made eye contact with him, as if he was trying to draw the answers out of Seth's mind. Cop telepathy.

"I don't know. Music and stuff."

"Okay." He jotted something in his notebook.

"Are any of these photos of him?" Burns indicated the framed photos at the fireplace.

"Yeah. That one on the far end." Seth pointed.

Burns picked up a shot of two young boys, dark haired and smiling at a county fair. "Nice memory," he said, returning it to the mantel.

"Yeah."

"How about other friends?" Burns asked. He was standing beside Elaine, acting as an observer but taking in every word. "How long did you know each other?"

Seth shook his head. "Mainly just the two of us. We've been friends since kindergarten."

"And what did you do together? Any places you liked to go?"

Something was laughing inside his mind. Yeah, they liked to get high in cemeteries and summon things these guys wouldn't have believed, let alone want to hear about. Or understand. They'd take him in, for sure, and lock him away in the psych ward. "Nowhere in particular. We'd go to his house, sometimes here."

"Was he happy? Depressed? Did he have any problems at school?"

"Problems?" Seth's mouth tasted like sawdust, tongue as dry as sand. Yeah, he had problems. But he found a way to deal with them through the Ouija board. He'd gotten special help with his problems.

"Bullying. Anything that would've maybe driven him to hurt himself?"

"There were some tough times here and there. But things were getting better." Better enough that when Pete Munson shoved Blake's face into the school lockers, something grabbed Pete's steering wheel that afternoon. Something. He remembered Pete's broken arm and heard him say that just after he hit the tree, he saw Blake. And a shadow standing beside him. Scared him shitless. Yeah, things had been getting better.

"You know, often when someone is coming out of a depression is when they can take a turn for the worse," Detective Burns said.

Seth wanted to tell them it wasn't suicide. It was confidence. Cockiness. Arrogance. And pulling in demons from the depths of hell that they couldn't control. He understood it all too well and had the talons sunk into his soul to prove it. "That's what they say."

"Did you know he was going to the mausoleum that day? Did he talk to you about any of it?"

He exhaled, glancing at his mother and then at the floor. "He mentioned wanting to break into one. Had talked about it for a while."

"Oh, Seth, really?" Elaine wrung her hands. "Really."

Detective Burns motioned for her to let him continue. "And?"

Seth shrugged. "Blake was into Ouija and wanted to do it in a creepy place."

"Did you do it with him? Were you with him that day?"

"No," he said. "No, sir. I told him it wasn't for me." He pressed himself backward into the sofa and patted his lap. Iggy jumped up, laying his head across Seth's thigh. He scratched the pup's head, ruffled his ears. He inhaled. Let the lies commence.

His mother said, "Thank God," under her breath. "Why didn't you say something?"

Seth turned toward her. "Like what? Who tells their mother something like that? I didn't know he was going that day. I didn't know he'd go alone." Lies upon lies upon lies.

"And you missed school last week because?" Henderson asked, pen hovering.

"He had the flu," Elaine interjected.

Henderson studied her expression, Seth's.

She smoothed her blouse. "What are you implying?"

"Nothing, ma'am. We're just trying to establish the facts. Get a clear picture of what was going on around Blake when he made his unfortunate decision."

"Well, Seth had the flu. He was here all week and most of it with a fever."

The detectives faced Seth.

"Yeah. Stomach flu." Or the fact that something evil had attached to him and filled him with a hate-bile that made it nearly impossible to eat sometimes and fever-burned his nightmares. Yeah, stomach flu. His hands were shaking as he shoved them into the kangaroo pocket of his hoodie. "I don't know what I can tell you. I didn't know it was going to happen. I didn't know." He began an almost imperceptible rocking back and forth and said more quietly, "I didn't know." Tears welled in his eyes, and he blinked them away.

"We'll wrap it up here," Detective Henderson said to his partner. "I think we have all that we need." He unbuttoned his chest pocket and took out a business card. "Seth, if you remember anything or something pops into your head that might add some clarity to this situation, even if you think it's insignificant, give me a call. It might be nothing to you but could help Blake's family."

Seth examined the card briefly before tucking it into the pocket of his jeans. "Yes, sir."

The detective stood, holding out a card to Elaine. "If you think of anything. Feel free to call. It can really help the family."

Elaine glanced at it, running her thumb along the smooth edges. She showed the detectives to the door.

"Goodbye, Seth. Thank you for speaking with us."

As the officers turned to leave, Seth called out, "What happens to his things? Blake's things . . . from where it happened?"

Henderson said, "Anything personal would be returned to his parents once the investigation is complete."

"The Ouija board, too?" Maybe if he could get his hands on it, tell them it was his, he could close the thing. Send the demon tormenting him back to the shit hole it crawled out of.

Detective Burns scratched his head. "Ouija board? There was no Ouija board at the scene."

Seth fell back into the sofa cushions, a punch to the gut. No board? Had someone gotten there before the police? Taken it? No, that wasn't possible. Something from the darkness had.

Detective Henderson stood on the porch and pivoted. "Mrs. Resnick."

Elaine joined the officers outside. "Yes?"

The detective lowered his voice. "You know, Mrs. Resnick, Seth might benefit from some counseling. Situations like this can be awfully hard on teens. It's not just the death of a friend. A self-inflicted death can be very hard to process. Feelings of helplessness, depression, even guilt over not being able to help, not knowing their friend was troubled."

"I would love to see Seth get some help." Her voice caught and her chin wavered.

"The school will be setting up grief counselors in the next day or two. Let him know they can help with anything he's feeling."

"I will. Thank you."

Burns climbed into the passenger seat of the cruiser, tossing his hat onto the dash. "What do you make of the kid's story?"

Henderson pulled his seatbelt across his chest and clicked it into place. Turning the key in the ignition, he said, "There's something more to this. I'd bet on it."

Burns watched the house as his partner put the car into reverse and backed onto Wilson.

"My gut says we'll be back."

Olivia flopped onto her bed while Tommy wandered the room, examining her things. Her desk, books, stuffed animals. Makeup. He wrinkled his nose. "Smells like chalk."

She agreed and dumped her eyeshadow pallets into the bucket with her nail polish.

He peered in. "They're all black."

"No, they're not," she said. "Well, not all. A lot are, I guess."

"I like black."

"Yeah? What's your favorite color?"

He thought for a minute, running his hand along her desk, checking out her highlighters. "Black." Taking the cap off a yellow one, he drew a face on a piece of paper.

"Mine's purple. People think it's black, because I'm into ghosts and stuff, but it's actually purple."

"Why do you like ghosts?"

"I like to find answers. Why are they here? What can they do? Can we talk to them? Things like that. I'm into the unknown. Come here, I'll show you something special." Olivia stood at her bedroom window. "Be careful of my stuff. My room's a little messy."

Tommy skirted a basket of laundry and pressed his toes under the baseboard, wiggling them in the heat.

"It's all clean. I just haven't put it away. Look out there." She pointed to the side yard. A metal garbage can lid was upside down on the grass.

"Where's the pail?"

"Doesn't have one. That, my friend, is a bird bath. Made it myself."

Tommy giggled. "Birds don't take baths. Friend."

"Sure, they do. And I have a bird I've been making friends with for a few months now. He's a crow named Milo and he's very smart."

"I like crows."

"Then you'll like him. I'll show him to you the next time he visits. I'm trying to get him to bring me little trinkets. Did you know they can do that?"

"Oh, yes. I've known that for years and years."

Olivia eyed him. "Well, I've been leaving Milo peanuts and things and he's getting pretty comfortable around me. We'll start slowly with you, but I bet he'll be your friend, too, in no time."

"I'd like that."

"So, do you like it here? I mean, I know you haven't been here long." She regretted asking the question, but the reporter in her had taken over. Again. Asking too many questions too soon. "I mean, you don't have to tell me." She fumbled for words.

"I like it. New Mommy is nice." He pulled up the bed skirt and peeked under. "Dust bunnies."

Olivia was happy he changed the subject. "What are you looking for?"

"What's this?" He spied a box with the picture of a Ouija board on the side and slid it out from between puzzle boxes and books piled at the bottom of Olivia's bookshelf.

"Oh, that's my spirit board."

"I had an A-B-C board once. It was fun."

"Well, this is a little different from that, I'm sure. This one's for talking with ghosts."

"I like ghosts."

"Do you?"

He shook his head up and down. "I do. Ghosts and crows, crows and ghosts." He climbed onto her bed to get a better view of her headboard. "What's this?" He picked up a small, white crystal and rolled it in his hands.

"That's a selenite point. See how it's shaped like a little tower?"

He rubbed it across his palms. "What's it for?"

"Some people just think they're pretty. I like it because it soaks up negative energy. It's for protection from things unseen." She widened her eyes.

"Oh." The stone felt smooth as he passed it from hand to hand. "Spooky. Like magic."

"Like nature. There's magic in nature. I'm into all that."

"Cool."

"Let's go see if Mom and Seth are done."

"Okay."

As Olivia passed through the doorway, Tommy laid the crystal on her headboard and followed. Neither noticed that the point was now a smoky grey.

"Hey, Mom?" Olivia asked.

Elaine put the last dish into the cabinet and shut the door. "Yes?" She used her foot to close the dishwasher with a soft thud.

"Do we have today's paper?"

"You know, with all the commotion this morning I never brought it in. It must still be on the porch."

Olivia was off in a shot. "Thank you!"

Elaine followed her into the living room. "Kind of late to be starting homework, isn't it?"

"Oh, no, it's just right." Her lips curved upward in an innocent smile. "It won't take long." Outside, she shivered, watching her breath condense and dissipate, then saw the newspaper resting on the deck chair to her left. As she picked it up, she noticed old Mrs. Harper sitting on her porch four houses down across the street. The woman waved and Olivia shifted the paper under her arm to wave in return. She went inside.

"Current events due tomorrow, eh?" asked Elaine.

"Yeah. I figured it'd be easier to concentrate with Tommy in bed." Olivia divided the paper into sections on the living room floor and sat in the middle.

Elaine stirred her tea. "Probably. But that's something you'll get used to in time."

"I guess." Olivia poured over the categories on her homework list and thumbed to the Community News section. She ran her index finger down the column. "Whoa."

"What?"

She read the headline out loud. "Local Ghosthunter Found Dead." She bent closer to the paper, elbows on the floor, head in her hands.

"You probably can't use that."

"Listen to this. 'A team member of Out of the Dark Paranormal was found dead in her home in Montgomery yesterday. Police are investigating the possibility of foul play.'"

"How sad."

"I wonder if it was something demonic."

"What?"

Olivia sat upright. "You know, whatever killed her. I wonder if it had to do with a case she was working on, something evil that popped up in the night. Maybe even stalked her."

"Olivia, really."

"Well, it could have. You never know with the paranormal."

Elaine smiled. "And it could very well have been an accident or a flesh and blood person that broke in or . . . something."

"I suppose, I suppose." She reread the short article. "How far are we from Montgomery?"

"About fifteen minutes."

"We should go sometime."

Elaine cocked her head to the side.

"Just to drive by. I'd like to see the house. Get a feel for the area, you know." She picked up the page, reading the article again. Another pause. "Wilson Lane."

"They published the address?"

"Just the street."

"We're not going, O."

"We might."

"Maybe in a year or two."

"Maybe next week?" Olivia hopped onto the sofa beside Elaine. "Maybe we'll have an errand there. Just have to stop by and pick up toilet paper or something and we'll happen to be a turn or two from Wilson. I bet I could pick out which house it is just from the atmosphere."

"Or the police tape?"

Olivia rolled her eyes. "That'll come down as soon as they have all the forensics they need."

Elaine chuckled. "Get to work, you CSI-paranormal maniac."

She went back to her spot on the floor and began scanning the police blotter.

Chapter 3

Olivia straightened her orange sweater and tied her hair into a ponytail with a black scrunchie. She was ready. As she walked into the kitchen, she poked the on-switch of the little television her mother kept on the side counter, and it came to life on the local news channel. Olivia liked to keep abreast of the events of the day before school. Grabbing a chocolate doughnut out of an Entenmann's box, she held it in her teeth. The newscaster caught her attention as she took a mug out of the cabinet.

Tragic events in Montgomery Township last week. A local Paranormal Investigator was found dead in her home. This is an ongoing investigation into the death and an apparent suicide on the same block. Police are asking anyone with any information related to these deaths to contact them at the number below.

"Whoa," she said. She took the coffee pot off its warmer and watched the steam rise from the mug as she poured. "Whoa." She sat at the table, muting the television as the station went to commercial. She dunked her doughnut.

"What's up?" Elaine stepped in from the living room. "Something going on in the outside world?"

"Yeah. More on the murder in Montgomery. How weird is it that a ghost hunter dies questionably at Halloween? With a suicide on the same street. At the same time. I wonder what she was investigating when it happened."

"Who says she was investigating? Wasn't she found in her home?"

Olivia had a mouthful and, before she could answer, Seth wandered in. He lifted the top of the box and took a doughnut, dropping powdered sugar across the floor. Licking his fingers, he said, "I bet it was a fall." He rubbed his forehead, leaving a white trail across it. Olivia narrowed her eyes.

"Most home deaths happen from falls." He shrugged. "Heard it somewhere." He didn't want to say that he'd seen it. Dreamed it. Watched it happen over and over in his nightmares, waking before he could see who the killer was.

"That's for the elderly. She wasn't old."

Almost out of nowhere, Tommy appeared at Olivia's side and climbed up onto the chair beside her. His yellow pajamas were fuzzy, and he snuggled into her. "She fell."

"What?" She looked at Tommy, picked up the remote and hesitated before unmuting the news. "What did you say?"

"Got more doughnuts?"

"Sure." Olivia put the box in front of him. "What kind do you like?" Odd that he'd said she'd fallen. He must've been echoing Seth, latching onto that big brother role model thing.

Elaine set a glass of milk in front of Tommy and addressed Olivia. "You and your friends are taking him tonight, yes?"

"Yes," she said, washing down a mouthful of doughnuts with lukewarm coffee. "They'll be here at 5:30 pm."

"Perfect. I'll have a couple of pizzas waiting and you can all have a slice before you set out." She tousled Tommy's hair. "You do like pizza, right Tommy?"

He shook his head yes, wiping his mouth on his sleeve. Crumbs fell into his lap and Iggy was waiting. The dog devoured them, then ran his tongue along the floor. "Silly puppy."

"Good. That settles it. Better get moving, O. Homeroom's not going to wait for you."

Olivia placed her mug in the sink and slung her backpack over one shoulder. "What are you and Tommy doing today?"

"We're going to get right over to Walmart and find a Halloween costume."

"Skeleton!" Tommy beamed at his new family.

Chapter 4

Dom's shaking hands balled into fists, crumbling the newspaper he was reading. His heart jackhammered in his chest, every thud like its last. Tears cascaded down his cheeks. He squeezed his eyes shut, hoping to rid himself of the headline. Of the sadness. The despair.

A strangled cry escaped his throat. Amanda shouldn't be dead. Shouldn't have had to fight a demon. Ever. It was his fault. His cross to bear for eternity. He'd brought her in on the case at Jack Barnes' house. Then, the converted asylum. The prison. Instead of feeding her passion for the paranormal, he'd handed her over on a platter. Her brother, too. Depression and anxiety fought in his stomach, desperation in his mind, waging a war he knew he couldn't win alone.

He reached for the phone, knocking a small lamp off the end table. It crashed to the floor, breaking into three chunky, sharp pieces of ceramic. It didn't matter. Nothing mattered. And that was why he had to make the call. There'd be nothing left at this time tomorrow. He'd make sure of that. With the smallest bit of his remaining will to live, he thumbed through his contacts for Dr. Ryan. Dr. Michael Ryan, Hemmingway Hospital, in Newcomb. And he chose the number marked "personal."

He clenched his fists as it rang. If it hit four rings, he was hanging up. Done. Gone. At three he held his breath, ready to drop the phone and end it all.

"Hey, Dom. What's doing?"

Relief and terror flooded him, hysterical tears nearly choking off his words. "Doc," he said. "I need help," and then he broke.

Chapter 5

Tommy was on his knees, holding onto the back of the sofa, watching intently out the front window. "Is she here yet? Is she here?" He was dressed in black with white felt bones along his torso, arms and legs, beside him a plastic pumpkin waiting to be filled with candy. He was ready. It was Halloween and Olivia would be taking him trick-or-treating. He couldn't wait. Why did school have to take so long?

Olivia turned off Orchard at the corner of Wilson and could see Tommy in the window. She waved and continued up the steps into the house. He ran to her with Iggy at his heels.

"Are you ready? Are we going? Look at my costume!" He spun so she could get the full effect.

"Very nice, little man. I like your bones!" She reached past him to drop her book bag in the corner of the entryway and scratch Iggy's ears. "But we're not going yet."

"Not yet?" He held his pumpkin bucket close to his chest.

"Soon. I need to get changed and we'll eat when my friends get here. Plus, I've got a little homework to do before we go."

Tommy balanced his pumpkin on top of his head. "Okay."

"First, do you want to come with me to feed Milo?"

"The crow?"

"Yup," she said. "Come on."

He trotted after her into the kitchen and watched as she took a bag of peanuts from the cabinet beside the sliding door to the patio. "Can I give him a peanut?"

She almost said yes but reconsidered. "You may have to just watch for a few days. It took a long time for Milo to trust me, and he may not be ready to trust another person. We'll work on it, though."

They stepped out into the chilly air. Tommy waited beside his jack-o-lantern and admired its scary face. He'd had Olivia cut crooked eyes, and a mouth with jagged teeth. When it glowed, it looked like a goblin about to eat your feet. He giggled. Eat feet. If it had been on the table or deck railing, it would've looked like it was going to eat a face.

Olivia crouched next to the metal can lid.

"Where's Milo?"

She touched a finger to her lips. "Ssh."

Tommy wrapped his fingers around the rough stem of his pumpkin, lifted the lid and sniffed, watching the sky where Olivia pointed. She sat, still, next to what she called the bird bath. In her outstretched hand was a peanut. They waited.

From a tall pine tree at the edge of the property, a black bird emerged. It flew to within a few feet of her, edging closer to see what she had in her hand. Quietly, she said, "Hello, Milo." It jumped onto her hand and took the peanut.

"Hello, Milo!" Tommy echoed. The bird flew into the sky, toward the pine. "Oh."

"That's okay. It was your first time saying hi. He'll get used to you. When there's someone new, he's very wary."

"Does wary mean scared?"

"More like concerned and careful. He wants to make sure it's safe to be near you. That you're not going to hurt him."

"He's a scaredy crow."

"Maybe a little. He just needs to know he's safe. Here," she handed him some peanuts. "Leave these in a pile by his bath. He'll be back for them later."

Tommy arranged the nuts in a small pyramid, taking great care not to let any topple over.

"Great. Now, homework and then we'll get ready to trick or treat."

"Yay!" He followed her inside.

# # #

The doorbell rang as Elaine deposited boxes on the kitchen table. "Would you get that, O.?" She ripped the plastic off a stack of paper plates and set them beside the pizzas.

"On it!"

Christie and Jules stood on the doorstep, fully decked out in their costumes. Jules was in a wispy grey dress, hood pulled over her eyes, while Christie was in a sleek armored suit with black knee boots, a bow in hand and arrows slung over her back.

"Oh, my God, you both look great! Did you bring them?"

"Of course, I did!" Jules lifted the side of her dress to dig into the pocket of her jeans, pulled out a stack of bangles and handed them to Olivia.

"This is exactly what I needed." She slid them onto her arm. "All I need now is this." She grabbed a top hat off the back of the sofa and adjusted it in front of the mirror by the door. She turned. "Am I the quintessential Rose the Hat?"

"You are amazing!" The girls tittered for a moment admiring each other.

"Let me see," Elaine said, coming into the living room. "Well, now." She squinted over the top of her glasses. "Turn around, Christie." She pretended to scrutinize the girl's costume. "You must be Katniss from The Hunger Games." She folded her arms.

Christie bowed. "Mockingjay, to be exact."

"Very nice."

Christie stepped back, motioning to Jules that it was her turn.

Elaine twirled her index finger in a circle. "Turn around, dear."

Jules put on the hood of her shrug and, arms outstretched, pirouetted. The dress flared outward and the tattered mesh hanging from her arms floated through the air. Her eyes were outlined in black eyeliner.

"You passed away waiting for your loved one to return home from the sea. A dead bride?"

"A haunting beauty, if you please." She bowed.

"Ah, yes! Lovely. In a disturbing, ghostly sort of way," Elaine said. "And Olivia." Her foster daughter placed her hands on her hips. "I still haven't watched Doctor Sleep, but I've seen pictures of Rose the Hat. You do pull off the villain quite well." She shook her head. "You and your horror. Stephen King would give me nightmares."

"Mr. King is an icon," Olivia said. "He rocks."

Elaine clapped her hands. "Pizza, everyone. Get your rear ends to the table. Can't trick or treat without pizza in your gullets."

Tommy peered from his bedroom and meandered over to join the girls.

"This," said Olivia, "is my new little brother, Tommy." She stepped aside, showing off the little skeleton standing behind her.

Christie dropped to one knee, exuding the aura of a strong teen defender. "Hi, Tommy. Olivia's told me about you."

Jules gave a little wave. "Hey, kid."

Tommy tugged on Olivia's arm and whispered something into her ear. She held back a laugh. "He thought you'd be sparkly."

Jules tilted her head to the side.

"Jewels."

She laughed. "Come here," she motioned to Tommy and kneeled. "Check these out." She closed her eyes. Her lids were covered in black shadow with shimmery glitter.

"Oh!" he said, happy again.

"Come on. Let's get pizza before we go out."

It was twilight. The house across the street lit a strand of orange and purple lights twisted around their railing, leading to their porch. In the distance, they heard the amplified howl of what could only come from the werewolf animatronics of her neighbor, ready to pounce if you stepped on his trigger plate. They'd have to see how Tommy did when they got close to that house.

The girls and Tommy stood on the front step of Olivia's porch and took stock of their options. "Which way do you want to start? Left, or right?"

Elaine flickered the porch light to get their attention and tapped on the small side window. "Are you dressed warmly enough? Do you want jackets?" Her voice was muted by the glass.

"We're good, Mom. Long sleeves under the denim." Olivia pointed at her arms and gave Elaine a thumbs up.

"Thermals under the dress, Mrs. R."

Christie shrugged. "I'm in armor. Nothing can penetrate."

"Does Tommy need a hat?"

Olivia observed the little boy, excitedly shifting from one foot to the other. He was holding her hand with his left and had his pumpkin in his right. "Do you want a hat?"

"Nope!"

"He's good, Mom. We'll get home before it gets too cold."

"Okay, have fun."

"Let's go left. We'll do the houses till Chestnut Street, go up Chestnut, cut around the block to Amsel, up Orchard and back here."

"Sounds great!"

They crossed the street and waited on the sidewalk as groups of trick-or-treaters passed. A pack of six squeezed past them, all dressed as pirates, and wandered up the street to their next pillaging.

Christie and Jules stood to the side at their first stop to let Olivia go to the door with Tommy, then filed in behind.

"Ring the bell," Olivia said, "and when they come to the door, you say, 'Trick or treat.' Okay?"

He reached for the button and gave it a fast push, falling into place beside Olivia. An elderly man in a gray wool sweater greeted them. "Well, well, well. What do we have here?"

"Trick or treat!"

"My, my. What a lucky little man to have three young ladies out with him tonight. Here, here." With a shaking hand he held out an orange plastic bowl with candy bars and lollipops. "Take a few, take what you like," he said.

"I like lollipops."

"Then I'm happy I have some for you."

Tommy dug through the candy, trying to find the perfect one. He held up a grape Tootsie Pop and dropped it into his pumpkin.

"What do you say, Tommy?"

"Trick or treat!"

Olivia smiled. "It's his first time." Then, to Tommy. "When someone gives you something, what do you say?"

"Thank you."

The old man laughed. "You're welcome. Enjoy your scares tonight!" He went inside and shut the door.

"That was fun. Can we do another?"

"We have a lot of stops to make. Are you up for it?"

"Oh, yes!" Tommy dropped Olivia's hand to reach into the pumpkin to touch his prize. His fingers toyed with the waxy wrapper as they walked.

They continued, Christie explaining to Tommy that you only stopped at houses with their lights on, and that some people left out bowls and expected kids to be honest and only take one candy each. As they approached the old, pale green Victorian at the end of the street, Christie and Jules quieted. They moved on ahead, watching the sidewalk, focused on getting to the streetlamp at the corner. Olivia slowed, staring at the columned porch. Mrs. Harper was there, as she always was, sitting in her favorite wicker chair. She was in a faded yellow summer dress and Olivia was concerned she might be cold.

They made eye contact. The woman now had a sweater on, yellow, with little pearl buttons adorning the front. Mrs. Harper reached over to a small wicker table and picked up an empty glass next to a pitcher. She raised it to offer Olivia lemonade as she always did when they visited.

Olivia mouthed the words, "Thank you, but I can't . . ." and glanced at Tommy.

The old woman put the glass down and set her gaze on the small boy. Her colors darkened with her frown. She picked up the tray and faded through the wall into her house. Olivia wondered what had upset her, but then caught up with Christie and Jules at the red house on Chestnut.

Tommy, straining to get another glimpse of the Victorian, said, "Did you see that?"

Olivia was startled. "What? What did you see?" But his answer was lost in the cries of trick or treat and the handing out of candy.

"Wow. Look at all that loot!" Elaine cleared the pizza boxes off the kitchen table, so they'd have space to lay everything out. The girls dumped small piles of candy from their bags, while Tommy's mound was huge. He sat, cross-legged, in awe.

"Can I have this one?" He held out a Twix bar.

"Absolutely, you can. And we'll store your candy in your pumpkin so you can have a little every day."

He ripped off the wrapper and broke the bar in two. "Okay," he said between bites.

Jules and Christie were busy sorting candies and listening to Pop Rocks fizzle in their mouths.

"Did you have a good time tonight?"

"Yes. I love trick or treating."

"Were there a lot of kids? Any spooky costumes?" Elaine asked. Nightmares sprung from trauma and fear, in her opinion, and he'd had enough to last a lifetime. She still wasn't sure if letting him go tonight was the best decision.

He nodded as he chewed. "I saw a ghost."

"That's great. Was it a scary ghost?"

"Nope. Just an old lady."

Olivia kept her ears on Tommy, a slight chill running down her spine. It wasn't often that other kids could see what she saw, if ever. And she never expected it from him. Maybe she should have. She'd read that children are sensitive to the paranormal, little kids the most, but they outgrow it. "Must've been some good makeup.".

"There's so much out there these days. When I was a kid, we had these awful masks that were held onto our faces with elastic cords. They never fit right. Now, you guys have access to cool prosthetics, movie-type makeup. It's a different Halloween world."

"It wasn't makeup," Tommy said, starting on his other piece of chocolate. "It was a ghost."

Elaine winked at Olivia. "I see. And you weren't scared?"

"I'm not scared of anything."

"Well, you're a very brave boy."

"I am."

Iggy nuzzled Olivia's thigh. "Hey, pup." He balanced on his hind legs, mouth agape, and barked. "Nope. No chocolate for you." She patted him on the head.

"Why not?" Tommy asked.

"It makes dogs sick."

"Oh." He scooped the remaining candy into his pumpkin and said to Iggy, "None for you."

"Tommy, hand me his toy. That yellow duck tucked under the cabinet."

He picked it up, turning it over in his hands.

"Squeeze it."

It let out a long, slow squeak that perked up Iggy's ears. He sprinted to Tommy's side, wagging his tail.

"That's his favorite."

Tommy squeezed it again and Iggy jumped.

"Here, watch this." Olivia took the duck and swung like a baseball player, pretending to lob it down the hallway. Iggy ran. He scrambled to return when the toy didn't land. Tommy belly laughed.

"Throw it, O." Elaine's eyes crinkled at the edges.

She wound up again and this time threw it as hard as she could. The duck hit the floor and slid to the side, coming to rest at the mudroom. Iggy looked like the Road Runner from Looney Tunes as he tried to dig in and take off on the linoleum. He made it almost to where his duck lay and put on the brakes, skidding to an abrupt stop. He beelined to the girls empty mouthed.

"Silly dog," Olivia said. "Why didn't you bring it back?"

Iggy laid under the table as if he'd been reprimanded, head on his paws.

"I'll get it!" Tommy leapt from his chair and was off in a shot. He picked up the duck and stared into the mudroom. The shadow beside the boiler caught his attention. It was tall. Familiar. It was home. Tommy gave a tiny wave and ran back to the kitchen.

Once the girls said their goodbyes and left, Elaine tucked Tommy into bed. The house was finally quiet. She sat on the sofa and clicked the remote to turn on the television. It'd been a long two days, and it was time to unwind. Olivia sat beside her.

"Mom?"

"Hmm?"

"Is Tommy from Montgomery?"

"Yes."

"What was his address?"

"I'm not one hundred percent sure, but I think it was on Wilson Lane somewhere. Why?"

Olivia toyed with the pencil in her hands, as if she wanted to write the information down, but didn't have a pad. "I think he and his mother lived next door to Amanda Harper, the ghost hunter who died."

"Okay. They may have."

"Well, Amanda died Halloween weekend."

"And . . ."

"And Tommy's mom committed suicide Halloween weekend."

"Where are you going with this, O.?"

She tapped the pencil against her temple, then pointed it at her foster mother. "Don't you think it's strange? Blake died. A ghost hunter died. A mom next door to the ghost hunter, died. What if it's all connected?" She settled, resting the pencil in her lap, and whispered, "What if there's a thread that ties it all together?" Olivia's eyes were wide.

"Blink, girl. Take a breath. Not everything is paranormal or part of a grander conspiracy. I would say it's all coincidental. Things happen. Life happens. Death, too. Blake didn't live in Montgomery, you know."

"I know, but . . ."

"The news is saying now that they believe it was a home invasion gone wrong. That the Harper woman was in the wrong place at the wrong time and maybe surprised a robber. Not something otherworldly. And Tommy's mother," Elaine angled closer, speaking quietly, "hanged herself. She must have been a depressed, tortured soul who took her own life, even when she had that wonderful little boy to live for."

"That's another thing."

"What?" Elaine sat back, clicking the television off, and dropping the remote into its holder.

Olivia lowered her voice. "Shouldn't Tommy be upset? Or something? It's like he walked in from a vacation. I'd think he'd be bawling over his mother, scared to be living with strangers . . . I don't know. Shy. Something different from the way he's been acting."

Elaine's shoulders sagged. "I've been watching him, too. Waiting for that little break in his demeanor, that welling up of emotion we know must be churning inside him. But we all react differently to trauma and everyone, even a little boy, grieves differently. He may seem fine, but I'm sure on the inside he isn't. He might break down in an hour, a day or next month. God only knows. We just need to be here for him when it happens."

"I suppose you're right."

"Absolutely."

"And maybe he doesn't even realize she's dead. I mean," Olivia straightened the fringe on the afghan behind her, "what dead is. You know? He's just a kid. He may not have a concept of death meaning gone. Forever."

"It's very possible. We're going to have to take things with him day by day."

"Day by day, for sure. Hey, Mom?"

"Hmm?"

"Are you bringing him to Blake's viewing? The funeral?"

"Oh, you know, I hadn't even thought that far."

"We all have to go. I'd offer to babysit him, but it's only right that . . ."

Elaine cut her off. "Yes, we all need to be there. We all do . . ." she let her voice trail off. "But Tommy."

"Maybe Christie or Jules could watch him?"

"I'm sure they'll be in school or attending themselves."

"I don't think they knew him."

"Exactly." She tapped her fingers on the end table. "We'll have to bring him. But you and I can run interference."

Olivia lifted an eyebrow.

"I'll go in with Seth, you stay outside on the porch with Tommy. We'll come out and take him and you can pay your respects. I don't think he should see a dead body."

"Will the coffin be open?"

"I don't know. Probably not. But why chance it?"

"True. And what about the funeral? It's only right we all go, with you knowing his family for so long. I can only assume we'd be going to the cemetery with the family?"

Elaine looked over the top of her glasses at her foster daughter.

"I'll make up whatever schoolwork I miss, and I'd be the most respectful kid you've ever seen."

"You're a great kid. But I also know you'll be peeking at every gravestone, waiting for some sign of a ghost."

Olivia flicked the fringe once more. "It's in my blood. And there'll be a hearse."

Elaine laughed the first good laugh she'd had in days, setting free the nervous energy and upset they'd been living. "Just remember why you're there and don't let anyone catch on."

Chapter 6

Elaine pulled her Camry into a parking spot behind Emerson's Funeral Home. Seth was stoic in the front seat, eyes unwavering from the side window. He stared hard at nothing, not wanting to think. Not wanting to look into the side mirror. Or to feel the blood seeping from the wounds on his back. He'd stuffed a couple of paper towels in his shirt before they left in the hope it wouldn't stain and his mother wouldn't notice it in the laundry. Maybe he'd burn it later.

Elaine touched his knee. "Are you ready?"

"No."

A sad smile crossed her lips. "Let's go in."

He reached for the door handle and realized there were no other cars in the lot. "Are we the first ones here? I'm not going in if we're the first. I won't."

"There are others inside, I'm sure. We're not early. Come on."

The world stretched and flexed, and everything went silent. Seth stumbled, legs weak. Unsure if he was awake or dreaming. He stood at the base of the three steps leading into Emerson's and didn't know if he could go on.

"Seth?"

His mother's voice was a thousand miles away, yet at his shoulder.

"Seth?"

She came into focus, but her features were wrong, somehow. As if the lighting had shifted and the setting sun cast fiery shadows, sharpening the angles of her face.

"Yeah."

They walked inside, to the room on the left. It was packed with people milling about. Some older, suited gentlemen were gathered off to the side. Family. Friends. He recognized some kids from school, Bud Tyler and Glenn Wakins, both out of place in suits and not their jeans and Giants jerseys. He acknowledged them with a nod.

They turned their backs.

"There's Beverly." Elaine made her way through the throng with Seth trailing behind, wondering what the hell was up with his friends. Maybe they hadn't seen him? But he'd looked into their faces.

"Oh, Elaine." Beverly put down her drink and continued to grasp a handful of crumpled tissues as she hugged his mother. Beverly stared at him over her shoulder.

"I'm so sorry. So very sorry," Elaine was saying.

Beverly's eyes never left his own, her mascara smeared into dark bags beneath them. She let go of his mother and reached for him, pulling him into a tight embrace. She whispered in his ear, "I know the truth."

Seth recoiled.

Beverly eyeballed him with a controlled insanity and backed away to stand beside her husband. She picked up her drink.

Elaine took Seth by the hand and pulled him toward the closed coffin. Tommy stood on a chair at its head, surrounded by bouquets of black roses. He was in a tuxedo with a baton in hand. Tapping the coffin with the tip of the baton, he yelled, "Let the show begin!" The beast Blake had summoned leapt atop it, its maw open in what could only be construed as a grin, curled a lip and snarled at the boy. Echoing laughter spilled out of it like poison and, with a cadaverous fist, it banged on the lid.

Seth jumped, scrambling to see if anyone else had seen it. Heard it. But they were all talking, laughing. The sound of the crowd rolled and mixed with the crowing of the demon until he had to cover his ears to shut it out. It pounded on the lid again.

A knock answered from within.

Blake.

In a panic, Seth tried to run, but his feet were mired in a black muck that filled the room. Bud Tyler opened his mouth to laugh, and a pool of green spittle dripped down his chin. He wiped it on his sleeve and his skin rippled. Glenn twisted his neck to get a better view of Seth and the breaking bones snapped with a sickening intensity. What the hell was going on?

With the creak of coffin hinges, everything went black.

Seth woke in a fear-sweat, with the beast of his nightmares sitting on his chest. An anchor of ice, like a spear through his heart, pinned him to the bed. It slowly eased, the wraith backing off, retreating to its corner. He shivered. The sheets were soaked, and their dampness chilled him. He yanked the
m from the mattress, balled them up, and threw them into the corner of the room. His hands were shaking as he grabbed a hoodie from the laundry basket. At this point he didn't know if they were clean or dirty. He didn't care. He needed to be warm.

A pair of jeans was slung over the back of his desk chair, and he pulled them on. He cast his gaze away from the thing now nestled in the corner of his ceiling and spat, "This wasn't how it was supposed to be. This was never how it was supposed to be. You were supposed to obey us."

It shifted, a slight downward tilt of its chin, and sludge-whispered into his brain.

Never

Seth's skin crawled.

Never

He sucked in a lungful of air and made himself put one foot after the other to meet his mother in the living room.

"Oh, honey," Elaine was exasperated. "Can't you wear something nice?" She was putting on her coat. She wore a long-sleeved, navy-blue dress. Not a mourning black, but close enough to convey her sadness. Olivia was in jeans and a black sweater, a silver pendant. "You need to be respectful."

"Blake won't care, will he?"

"His mother might."

"I think she has bigger things on her mind right now."

Tommy ran into the room with Iggy barking at his heels.

"Shut up, dog." Seth kicked the air in Iggy's direction.

"Hey!" Olivia yelled. "Quit it." She scooped the wiggling puppy into her arms.

"Stupid dog."

"Stupid you."

"Enough," Elaine said. "Don't take your emotions out on the pup. It's a tough day and we've all got to give a little. If that's what you're comfortable wearing, fine. Time with the family is more important than what's on your body." She grabbed her purse and car keys. "The next few days will be a blur to them anyway."

She clicked the remote on her keychain and the Camry's doors unlocked.

"Shotgun!" Olivia said.

"Like hell."

"Fine." She acquiesced. She'd have to give him this one, even if he did kick at Iggy.

Tommy climbed into the back and Olivia buckled him into his car seat while Seth slumped at the window in the passenger seat.

Elaine started the car. "Chilly morning."

After a pause, Tommy called out, "I like winter."

Seth slouched deeper into the seat and tugged his hood to cover his face.

"Do you, honey?"

"I do."

"Do you like snow?"

"No. Just the cold."

"It's coming, that's for sure." Elaine hit the defog button for the windshield. "At least it isn't a long drive."

"Right," said Seth. He watched the scenery, house after house, driveway after driveway. A meaningless repetition that ticked the seconds by. Almost by accident, he glanced at the side mirror and immediately regretted it. The face of the fiend was there, superimposed on his own and his stomach lurched.

"Are you okay?"

He cleared his throat. "Yeah. I'm all right." The déjà vu of his nightmare made his heart skip a beat. Damn Blake for wanting to bring demons from the other side. Damn him for ruining everything. Damn him for dying and leaving him to go on. To pretend life was normal and the sun would come up every morning. But it wasn't normal. The sun still came up but only after nights of torment. There was no moon for him, no beacon in the darkness. No light at the end of the proverbial tunnel. Only a well of despair with a fall into infinity.

Tommy unclicked his seatbelt and scooted forward to rest his hand on Seth's shoulder. It went numb and Seth jerked away. Olivia looked up from her book and said, "Little man! Back in your seat." She re-buckled him.

Seth recognized that bone-searing cold and his throat tightened. "Don't do that again. Don't touch me."

Tommy frowned.

"He didn't mean it, Tommy."

"Yes, I did. Don't fucking touch me again."

"Seth!" Elaine gripped the steering wheel. "I understand you're upset. More than upset. This is horrible for both families. But you've got to get a grip."

His voice came out as a low moan as he shrank against the side of the car. "Leave me alone. Please. Just leave me alone."

No one spoke again until they could see Emerson's Funeral Home in the next block. Elaine hit her signal bar to turn. Seth straightened, alert.

"No. Please, Mom. Park in front."

"I don't see any spaces."

"Even if we have to walk. Please, Mom. I need this."

"Okay," she said, confused. But whatever would help him be calm and remain in control, she'd do it. She drove past the funeral home and found a spot in the next block. "It's a little way."

"That's okay. I just needed to be out front. Really. Thank you."

"Of course."

Seth scuffed his feet along the sidewalk, head down, and made his way toward Emerson's. A temperate breeze blew but he was bone cold. It could've been ninety degrees and he didn't think he'd crack a sweat.

His family, plus one, caught up and they stood at the steps, waiting to see who would make the first move. Elaine said, "All right. Let's do this."

Olivia took Tommy by the hand and started up the steps behind Elaine and Seth.

Seth said, "It smells like death."

"It smells like the bakery down the street."

He stared in the direction of Branson's Bakery. Fresh baked rolls did not smell like decay. Week old roadkill had a better aroma than what was creeping into his nostrils. "Nope."

Elaine ignored him. "I think there's a small waiting room to the right when you first go in," she said to Olivia. "Take Tommy there and we'll trade off in a little while."

"You got it."

The group parted as they crossed the threshold of the building.

Elaine watched as Olivia ushered Tommy to the right. She soaked in the solemnity of the foyer, the cloying smell of a thousand lilies permeating the peaceful, death-quiet greeting room. Wood paneled, with wall-to-wall padded carpeting and faint Muzak in the background. Voices drifted in from the room on her left. She pointed her son to a pedestal where a spiral bound book perched under a small light.

"Sign the book and take a memorial card."

"No and no."

"Seth," she admonished.

He shrugged. "You sign."

Elaine wished she could help him through it all, but grief was personal. "Okay," she said. "I'll put both of our names. And Olivia and Tommy, too."

She wrote their names, read those who had come in before them. Taking a card with Blake's photo and a bible verse, she steeled herself and walked into the room on the left.

Beverly Calhoun stood at the archway, her back to the chairs and the visitors chatting. Visiting. Paying their respects to the family, stopping at the coffin to cross themselves and shake their heads. Say a prayer. The coffin itself was a pale wood, in stark contrast to Blake's dyed-black hair. The death-room a stark contrast to his age. Carnations and lilies adorned each end of the coffin, with a spray of roses and a banner that said "Son" laid across the top.

"Oh, Beverly, I'm so sorry," Elaine said.

The other woman's eyes were red and swollen, and she hugged her friend. "I- I," she stammered, uncomfortable, and absently smoothed the belt of her dress. It was lavender with flowers, low cut. "It was all I had." Her voice broke. "Who has funeral clothes? What do you wear to your son's funeral?" She seemed lost as she dabbed at her face with a wadded-up tissue, scanning the crowd like she was searching for a seat in a movie theater. Then, she saw Seth. She held up her arms and motioned for him to come closer.

"Seth," she managed to say before a sob cut through her words. She clung to him as if he was a life preserver in a turbulent sea. As if he himself wasn't going down the for the third time and dragging everyone along. "Seth."

He fought tears, blinking, and scanned the room. Everywhere but at Mrs. Calhoun. He was taller than she was, and her hair kept catching on his chin. Guess he hadn't shaved in a while.

"I'm sorry," he whispered.

Beverly Calhoun leaned back, taking his face in her hands. "We all are, Seth. We're all sorry and sad. But it's going to be okay. It will be." She was shaking nearly as much as he was, her makeup blotchy, mascara smeared. She squeezed his hand and left to greet the next person in line.

Seth saw a shadow pass between him and the front door, but

then it was gone, and his mother was motioning him toward the coffin. His feet felt like lead. Everything was the same. Surreal images from his nightmare with subtle changes. Mrs. Calhoun's dress wasn't red; the flowers weren't black. But it all was arranged exactly the same.

Bud and Glenn stood with their backs to the wall and nodded when they saw him. He wondered if they were going turkey hunting later. Bury your friend, go out and chug a few beers while you shoot at birds. Go on with your lives. He envied them. Envied the hell out of them. He'd be going back to his room. And his tormentor.

The coffin lay ahead of him. His mother was already on her way back from paying her obligatory respects.

"Take as long as you need, hon. It's not easy to say goodbye."

He wanted to tell her this was all a sick formality, that he'd said goodbye and go to hell a thousand times in the last two weeks. Every time the guilt rose in his chest like a bomb, he'd said goodbye. The guy he loved like a brother, he was sure he hated now. And that brought with it a whole new kind of guilt.

"Hey, man," he said under his breath. "Asshole. We both know you're not in there. But maybe you're watching from somewhere. Thanks for not Jacob Marley-ing me. Guess we'll see what Christmas brings. If I'm still alive by then." His hand brushed the wood edge of the coffin and he cringed.

Seth turned to leave and saw his mother rush to the back of the room. Olivia had run in on Tommy's heels, as he climbed onto a folding chair. He was holding a flower and began waving his arm as if conducting an orchestra. Seth stared as Elaine scooped him up and escorted Olivia outside.

Bud Tyler shoulder-bumped Seth to get his attention. "You want a ride home? Get away from everybody for a while?"

"Maybe? They don't get it, man."

"We're going to get high. This," he inclined his head toward the coffin, "sucks."

Seth gave the place another once-over. "Yeah, it does."

"Tell your mom we just want to chill for an hour or two and then we'll have you back."

They bumped fists and Seth went to find his mother. He waited behind her while she buckled Tommy into his seat. Olivia was already in the front of the car with a shit-eating grin.

"Mom?"

She pressed a hand into the small of her back as she straightened. "Must be getting old," she said. "This back of mine. What's up?"

"The guys said they'd give me a ride home."

"Oh?" She peeked past Seth and waved at Bud, who was waiting at the bottom of Emerson's steps. "You won't be too late?"

"Nah. Just kind of de-stress everything. Shake off the feeling of the day. It was awful in there."

"Okay, hon."

"Thanks, Mom." Getting high might take the edge off this butcher knife of a day.

Elaine watched as he stuffed his hands in his pants pockets and jogged to the rear of the lot where an old GM pickup was waiting.

Seth got home, red-eyed and worn out. He could sense the tension inside the house. Elaine was still asking Olivia, "Why didn't you watch him?"

"He got away from me for ten seconds and he didn't do anything bad, really," Olivia was saying. "He stood on a chair with a flower, for God's sake."

"Don't get huffy with me, Olivia Mulvey. We were in a funeral home. It was embarrassing."

"I said I was sorry. He said he was sorry. It's not like we recreated the scene from Pet Sematary."

"Don't bring it up if I haven't seen it. I can only imagine what horrible funeral scene Stephen King must have written if you're mentioning it now."

"I don't think you can. It was pretty unique."

"Olivia, I'm about done with this conversation. You know how I feel."

"I do and I am really, you know."

"I know." Elaine sat at the kitchen table, sorting through bills, moving from one stack to another. Busy hands, accomplishing nothing. "I know and I don't mean to bark at you. It's just been an extremely long, horrible week."

"You're fine. You're being a mom and that's a good thing." Olivia gave her a one-armed hug and went to find Tommy.

Seth peeked his head in. "All okay out here?"

"Yeah, it's good. How're you holding up?"

"Tired. Think I'll go lie down."

Elaine put her face in her hands and rubbed her eyes. "Seth?"

"Yeah?"

"I spoke with Beverly while you were at the coffin. She said you don't need to go to the funeral if you're not up for it." She paused. "I'm going to go, and Olivia. If you want to stay home, I'd just ask that you watch Tommy."

"Sure, Mom. Thanks." He didn't know about watching the kid, but he was sure as hell wasn't going to the funeral.

He hesitated at his door and touched the knob. Icy. He took a deep breath and went inside.

Chapter 7

The phone rang. Again. The red numbers on the clock read 7:35 am. Elaine groaned. She reached for her phone on the night table, almost spilling a cup of water from the night before, and squinted to see who was calling. Unknown number. She yanked the charger cord out of the phone and rolled onto her back. "Hello?" Her annoyance was thick, but she tried to veil it.

"Mrs. Resnick? Elaine Resnick?" a gruff voice asked.

"Speaking. Who's calling?"

"I'm sorry to have contacted you so early, ma'am, but I own the property at 235 Wilson, where Ms. Lilith Anderson resided."

"Okay?" Nothing clicked in Elaine's sleepy mind. Ambulance chaser? Salesman? She shoved her hair off her face and sat up. "I'm not interested in buying any property."

"And I'm not selling any. I was told that you were the temporary guardian of Ms. Anderson's son."

Elaine sat up, swinging her feet out of bed and into slippers. "Well, yes, I am. What can I do for you?" She held the phone with her shoulder and slid on a light blue terry robe, tying it at her waist. The sun was barely up, but it was going to be a beautiful day. She frowned. For a funeral.

"As I said, I'm the landlord of 235 Wilson. The little boy's home. From what we can ascertain, there were no other relatives. Adult relatives."

"As far as I know, that's accurate."

"Well, there are quite a lot of possessions in that home that need to be moved."

"Oh, my God." She fumbled for her glasses.

"Yeah."

"I never even thought of that. We've only had Tommy a few days."

"I get that, ma'am. And I am deeply sorry for his loss. But I hope that you also understand I need those possessions moved or I'll have to dispose of them. I'm sure the boy has things there that he would want. I don't know about the rest. Someone needs to go through it. I can give you until the end of the month, but then anything remaining will be disposed of. I need time to clean it up so that I can rent again."

Elaine took in everything he was saying. One more straw on top of the camel's back they had going on. "Yes, yes. I understand. How long do we have again?"

"Till the end of the month. That's as long as I can go."

"No, no. I get it. I do. The timing's rough. Not that that's any fault of yours. We have a funeral today. A friend of my son's."

"Seems to be a lot of that going on. I'm sorry for your loss as well."

"Thank you. I'd like to get over there as soon as we can, just to see what Tommy might need or want. And anything we leave you'll take care of?"

"Yes, ma'am."

"That works for me. How's Saturday? I'd like to go through, get what he needs and leave you with ample time to do what you have to do with the rest."

"That would be much appreciated. I can meet you with the key at 9:00 am, if that works."

"It does."

"See you then."

Elaine clicked to end the call and added it to her mental list of things to get done.

Knocking brought Seth out of a deep sleep and into a biting

headache. "Yeah?" he called out.

"We're leaving for the funeral, hon. Tommy's at the table having some cereal. I let him know you'd be out in a few minutes and the two of you will spend the morning together."

Seth rubbed his temples, the dull roar in his head muting his mother's words. His skin prickled like the bites of fleas, but he knew if he opened his eyes, there wouldn't be any bugs. Nothing to swat to free himself from the swarm. It was in his mind. Or in his tormentor's, to be exact. Another plague dumped on him.

"Seth?"

"Yeah, Mom. Yeah. I'll be out in a few."

"Okay, dear."

His mother walked away, and he heard the front door latch shut. The mass of hornets in his head went wild when he thought of the boy alone in the house. They buzzed and stung, and he buried his head under his pillow to escape. Quiet them. He clenched his teeth and slowly relaxed as they eased, and he fell into an exhausted sleep.

He watched from the graveside. The minister and pall bearers setting the scene. Emerson's was unfolding chairs for the family, friends. The hearse was to the side, parked off the dirt road far enough to not be in the way of the incoming cars, yet close enough to have brought in the coffin without much trouble.

They'd suspended the box over the hole in the ground and were arranging flowers across it. Make it seem pretty so folks don't think about what we're doing, where we're depositing the body of their loved one. He shook his head and rested his hand on the coffin. Carefully, though. Didn't want to disturb the dead. Damn it, Blake.

The cars filed in, his mom's first, with Olivia and Tommy.

Wait.

Why would they be first? The family of the deceased always parks first, out of respect. Maybe the Calhouns got held up in traffic or something. Sent his mother with a message for the minister. That had to be it.

But the other cars continued. His aunt and uncle, cousins. His. HIS. They drifted in, heads lowered. His mother clutched a tissue, sobbing, while Olivia solemnly watched over the kid.

Then they were gone.

It was dark and he was enclosed. It was hard to move, his arms at his sides. He was in the coffin. The coffin! Panic set in. But how was it HIS funeral? He'd get out. Tell them he wasn't dead.

Mom! Mom! Someone!! I'm here!

He rocked, side to side. Tried to kick the ceiling of the box, the sides, but could barely bend his knees. You can't bury me!! It was Blake who died! Blake called up the demon who killed him. Someone, anyone. Let me out!

He screamed until his voice was gone, his throat tight and painful. Vocal cords torn. Fingers bloody from digging into his wooden confines. Why didn't they hear him? He wasn't in the ground yet. Yet. Oh, my God.

Writhing, his stomach sick with fear, he slid his cheek as far as he could to the edge of the satin pillow and let a sour stream of vomit pour into the space beside him. The stench of orange juice and eggs permeated the tight space, making him fight the urge to puke again. Fight with all he had. Another slippery bucketful of sludge escaped him, covering the side wall and ceiling of his crate, dripping back into his face.

He rolled back and forth, trying to escape the vomit, the foul-smelling batch of puke, his putrid internment. A final wretched yell pushed past his lips.

And he felt it. The coffin lurched and began its descent.

Thud

Thud

Thud

Handfuls of soft dirt hitting the lid. Burying his body and sending his soul to oblivion.

Thud, his mother's

thud

Thud, Olivia's

thud

Thud, Tommy's

that boy's

No

That boy

that boy was burying him alive

The screaming of the hornets in his mind intensified, as if they were using their stingers as burins, engraving their hatred into his skull.

Thud

thud, and before he lost his mind

thud

thud

An echo? What was that added sound?

He took a breath and listened. A milder handful of dirt, hitting like a ricochet. A rebound.

He came to consciousness and the noise continued. Pulling the pillow off his head, it still didn't register. Thud, thud, like water torture, muffled. He stumbled to the door and whipped it open. Tommy caught the blue rubber ball he'd been bouncing off Seth's door. "Aren't you supposed to be watching me?"

A jagged, shimmering light hit Seth's vision hard enough that he winced. "Yeah, sure. Just let me get something for this headache."

"Your head hurts?"

"Yeah."

Tommy followed him to the kitchen and watched while he searched a tall, thin cabinet for some medicine.

"Why do you stay in there?" the little boy asked.

"Where?"

"That room." Tommy bounced the ball against the sliding glass door.

Thud

bounce

"It's my room. I like it."

"No, you don't."

"What do you know about it?" Seth popped the tab on a can of Mountain Dew and sat at the table with a bottle of Tylenol.

Tommy climbed onto the chair across from him. He dropped the ball into a coffee mug, watching the splash as it hit the bottom. "I know you hate it there. But you keep going back."

"You don't know what you're talking about." Seth swallowed three pills, washing them down with the soda.

Elaine made the turn onto Elmwood and rechecked the map on her phone. Harmony Hills Cemetery. She'd driven by it a handful of times throughout the years, but when push came to shove, she relied on her app. "Three-quarters of a mile, left on Main." A pleasant day, but most of the leaves were on the ground, thanks to a pounding rainstorm a couple of days before. "I hope the grass isn't too soggy."

Olivia watched the side streets go by. "Shouldn't it be dry by now?"

"Hard to say."

"Do you think there'll be many people? School kids and such?"

"I don't think so. They'd be more likely to come to the viewing. This is more family and close friends."

"Weird thing, a viewing."

"Is it?" Elaine waited. With Olivia's fascination with all things ghost and death related, she had a pretty good idea of what was coming.

"Think about it. A viewing. Of a corpse. It's like, 'Hey, come on over to my house and hang with my dead father. Gather 'round and take pictures.'"

"People don't take pictures with the dead person."

"Some do, yeah." Olivia shifted in her seat. "Did you know in Madagascar they dance with the dead?"

"No. Dance?"

"Well, they uncover the bodies and rewrap them, then play music and dance."

"Interesting tradition."

"They believe it'll help the dead decompose faster, so they can move on to the next realm or heaven or whatever awaits."

Elaine pressed her turn signal and waited at the light for traffic to lessen.

"And." Olivia strained against her seatbelt to face her foster mother. "Did you know that in Tibet, Buddhists send their loved one's soul to heaven but leave the bodies outside for the birds to eat?"

"I didn't know that."

"Fascinating stuff. And don't get me started on cremation." She settled into her seat, taking in the scenery.

"No worries there. You know an awful lot about death customs."

"Well, it does go hand in hand with the paranormal. Death, dead, ghost. It's all related. Everything we are, were, will be. It's so cool."

Elaine pulled into a parking space outside of the Harmony Hills gates. English ivy had grown up the gate, almost obscuring the name.

"We're not driving in?"

"I don't want to get stuck behind the family cars if there's not a lot of room. We can leave when we're ready." She unhooked her seatbelt. "Hey. Do you know why cemeteries are so popular?"

Olivia loved riddles, especially dark ones. "No. Why?"

"People are dying to get in." Elaine chuckled as Olivia let out a long moan. "My dad used to say that every time we passed a graveyard."

They left the car behind and crossed the threshold of wrought iron fencing. It was a huge cemetery, with headstones as far as they could see, up and over hills. Peaceful. Following the dirt road, more like a worn-in path, they saw several cars and people setting up chairs beside a canopy.

"This must be the place."

A sound distracted Olivia. "What's that whistling?"

"I don't hear anything," Elaine said. "Maybe you heard a mockingbird. They can mimic a lot of sounds."

"No, wait." Olivia tilted her head to listen. "It's human."

"You look concerned."

"You never whistle inside a cemetery."

"Why?"

Olivia shook her head. "It's a thing. Whistling in a cemetery summons spirits to you. And not necessarily nice ones."

Elaine exhaled. "I'm sure it must have been a bird."

Lost in thought, her analytical mind seizing the paranormal possibilities, Olivia asked, "Why would someone want to draw negativity to themselves?"

Her foster mother began walking once more, the heels of her pumps wobbling over the uneven ground. "You shouldn't get caught up in all those superstitions. Really, Olivia."

They continued on, approaching the hearse and mourners. Blake's mother had propped herself against a car. Cigarette in hand. Out of place. His father was seated, alone, in front of the coffin.

"Bev," Elaine started. The women embraced.

"Thank you for coming." She saw Olivia standing behind her foster mother, reached out and gripped her hand. "And you, Olivia." She sniffled and let them go. "I would've asked Seth to be a pallbearer."

"I know. I wish he could've come, but he's breaking, Bev. I almost don't know what to do."

"We all are. It's unfathomable."

As the two women spoke, Olivia fixed her gaze across the headstones, searching for the source of the sound. She knew it wasn't a bird and it nagged at her. But then she saw. At the far end of their section, at the tree line, was the faint outline of a woman. Far enough away that Olivia could only make out a few features, the shoulder length hair. No one else saw the figure. No one noticed or even paid attention to the whistling. The woman made eye contact with Olivia and disappeared.

She was sure it was a message. Or a warning. And meant for her alone. She wanted to slip away, go feel the area the woman was in, touch the ground. The ground! What if there was a marker in that spot that would give her a clue? She needed to get over there.

"Come," Beverly took a final drag on her cigarette, then snuffed it out with her shoe. "Let's sit. The reverend's about to begin."

Elaine and Olivia sat behind the Calhouns, Bev and Jim, some aunts, uncles. Cousins. A few other family friends. The folding chairs were black metal and uncomfortable, but Olivia figured you shouldn't be comfortable at a funeral. A man stood at the head of the casket, Bible in hand, wearing a sport coat and slacks. Not what she pictured as a minister. This guy looked like he was going yachting in an hour. Trendy.

"Let us bow our heads and pray. Matthew 11:28-30. Come to me, all you who are weary and burdened, and I will give you rest . . ." The words fell away from Olivia. She was intent on seeing the spirit again. She studied the tree line, tracing it, memorizing it. She needed to get back to that spot to find her answers.

She shut her eyes and went over every detail of the spirit's image in her mind. A wisp of familiarity plagued her, but nothing she could put her finger on. A word at the tip of her tongue, a face without a name.

At least this spirit hadn't startled her the way Mrs. Harper had. But that had been the first time she'd seen a ghost, and that's not easy for anyone. It wasn't long ago, either. Eight, maybe ten months. Maybe she'd always seen them but never realized it until Mrs. Harper was standing, clear as day, on her front porch. Offering her lemonade. The woman had settled into her wicker rocking chair and Olivia hadn't thought anything was out of the ordinary until she reached out to take the glass off the tray. It dissolved through her fingers and the old woman chortled. Olivia's eyes had widened, and her jaw fell.

Mrs. Harper stopped her rocking. "It's all right, child. Don't worry. It's our secret."

Olivia didn't blink. The old woman was translucent.

"Close your mouth, honey. You'll get flies."

She shut her mouth.

"Blink, child. Good Lord, I certainly didn't want to scare you."

"I- I'm not scared."

"Of course, you're not."

"I'm not."

"Good. Now just relax and spend some time with a lonely old woman." Mrs. Harper sat beside the girl as if it was as natural and normal as anything for a ghost to spend an afternoon with the living. It didn't take long for Olivia to accept that she was, almost, having lemonade with a spirit. That was how it started. She didn't know how or why she was able to see her, but from then on, she could.

A Calhoun relative got up to speak, bringing Olivia's attention back to the here and now. He was a cousin of some sort, once removed or step-by-marriage or blood something. She was more interested in watching the crow that had settled on the stone nearest the foot-end of the coffin. He was a sleek black and slightly larger than Milo. A male. And a cat was stalking him. A tabby by the looks of it, large and rather ratty. Like he'd lived outside and been in more than his share of fights. Feral, maybe. Scrappy, for sure. And absolutely after the bird.

The crow, self-sure and unconcerned, faced the crowd. Intent on deciphering what all these humans were doing in his neck of the woods. The cat, eyes beaded on the bird, was statue-still and crouching. There was no way Olivia was going to let this happen. Not to what could be a distant relative of her Milo.

"Tss!" She tried to capture the cat's attention. Warn the bird. Something.

Elaine glanced at her, mouthing the word, "Stop," and went back to listening to the minster.

Olivia set her jaw, bent down, and pretended to tie her shoe as she scooped up a pebble. She threw the stone with all her might in front of the cat, startling it and sending the crow to the treetops. A satisfied smile overtook her.

"Olivia!" It was a whisper, but sharp.

She basked in the metal chair. Reprimanded, but happy.

The minister rose. "Please join me in reciting Psalm 23 and know in your hearts and minds that God has an ultimate plan for each of us, though we may not be aware of what it is. Blake is wrapped in God's love and unending grace and though we may miss him, he is with his Father in Heaven." Dropping his hands to his sides, he began. "The Lord is my shepherd . . ."

"What were you doing anyway?" Elaine asked as they got up, letting other people make their way out ahead of them.

"A cat was stalking the crow. I had to stop it."

"In the middle of a funeral service."

"It would've been worse to have a murder in front of everyone."

Elaine watched the ground as they followed the path to the street. "I suppose. Watch the puddle."

Olivia hopped over it. "Still a little wet."

"Yeah."

"Hey, Mom?"

"Yeah?"

"Would it be okay, I mean, would you mind if, there's a spot at the far end of that section of the cemetery that I'd like to check out."

"Not today. It wouldn't be respectful if we started wandering in among the stones while the Calhouns are grieving."

"Right. I understand. Maybe another day? Maybe you could bring me back? It isn't far."

"We'll see, okay?"

"Thanks." She was determined to see if there was anything in that corner that would give her a clue to the spirit she saw. Let her know why a ghost would be whistling to call other spirits. The why of it all was the puzzle. Or maybe the spirit wasn't bringing them to herself. Maybe she was luring them away from someone else. Away from her. Olivia's detective mind and journalistic nature started churning.

Chapter 8

Seth ripped the Alka Seltzer packet in half and dropped the two tablets into his lukewarm coffee, listening to the fizz.

"You know it doesn't work like that," Olivia said, shaking her head.

"Why wouldn't it? Kill two birds with one stone."

"I'm not sure hitting a sour stomach with caffeine and fizzy medicine is your best choice."

He raised his shoulders, picked up the mug and gulped the concoction. Letting out a contented sigh, he burped.

"See?"

"Maybe. But give it five minutes. Smooth as silk."

Elaine fished in her purse for her car keys, then dropped them onto the counter. "Have you thought about coming with me?"

Seth slumped farther into his seat, running his fingers along the sides of his coffee mug. It was the photo mug they'd made for his mother last Christmas, the one that changed from solid black to a picture of Olivia and himself. The warmth of the coffee illuminated their bodies, their heads a blurred mass of muted tones. "Not really."

"I could use your help. And company. And it'd be-"

"Good for me to get out of the house." He set the mug down to punctuate his words.

"Well, yes. And you know I'm right." She waited, hands on her hips.

Another shrug, another slouch. She had a point. And it might help to get a little time away from his tomb. The days were getting darker lately. He didn't know if it was the time of year, his vision, or the fog in his brain since that thing moved in. The pain made his eyes sensitive, and he lived in a solid-state migraine much of the time.

"We'd get a few hours out together, just the two of us, and who knows what we'll find in that house? Might be worth it. Even as just an explore." Elaine pulled a couple of contractor bags out of the box under the sink and dangled her keys in front of him, like a carrot in front of a stubborn mule. "You can drive."

"Well," he said, giving in. "Now you're talking."

The navigation app announced their arrival at 235 Wilson and Seth guided the Camry into the short driveway. The house could have been any one of seven other Victorian homes on the block. Its lawn was mowed, and the edges of the walkway had recently been weed whacked. They sat, seatbelts still buckled, half expecting something to jump out at them, or some obvious marking that screamed a tragedy had occurred within its walls. A passerby wouldn't have a clue to the home's newfound dark history.

"It's so normal it squeaks."

Elaine squeezed her eyebrows together and stared at her son. "What?"

"You know, squeaky clean. So normal it's creepy. I at least thought there'd be some police tape."

"Gotcha. And I agree with you." She gathered the bags at her feet. "Let's do this."

A heavy man in denim overalls exited a rusty pickup truck parked along the street. "You must be Mrs. Resnick." He approached, hand outstretched.

"Yes. And my son, Seth."

The man nodded at Seth, his comb-over swaying. He brushed it out of his eyes with the back of his hand. "I'll be working at another property a few houses down. You can text me if you have any questions." He stopped on the steps to catch his breath, then unlocked the front door. "It's hell to get old," he said. "Aching bones. Rain's on its way."

Elaine and Seth glanced at the cloudless sky, then at each other.

The landlord stopped to admire the doorframe. "Good wood." He exhaled. "Well, you'll be wanting to get to business. Just turn the lock and shut the door when you're out. I'll make sure it's tight as a drum before the day's out."

"Thank you."

"Thank you," he said. "You're making my job a little easier."

He held onto the railing and made his way down the driveway. "Yup," they heard him say. "There's rain on the way."

Seth stretched, arms high over his head, and took a deep breath. He cracked his neck. "It smells." He'd noted the odor when his foot touched the curb. Pungent, like rotting meat with decayed fruit. It was more a sense than a smell, and it burned his thoughts. Permeated his mind. He tugged his shirt over his nose.

"What? No, it doesn't." She sniffed. "Damp leaves. Really, Seth." She rested her hand on the doorknob and twisted. The door swung open without a creak or complaint. "Really."

Crossing the threshold, she dropped the plastic bags and said, "Where do you want to st-" but was struck by a print to her right, hanging on a wall in the living room. A crow on a tree branch, unmistakable with its straight beak, opalescent feathers and black feet. And it was stunning. "Olivia would love that."

Seth was caught up in the grim reaper figurines that filled the room. Everywhere he turned, there were more. On top of the television, every shelf and empty spot seemed to own a reaper. "Mom."

Elaine broke her gaze at the picture. "Yes?" Then, she saw. "Oh, my God." They stood in silence as they took it all in. "There must be forty or fifty. What was with this woman?"

"She had a thing for Thanatos." Seth snorted. "It's kind of cool."

"It's entirely not. And don't think any of those are coming home with us. She must have been troubled."

"Well, that's kind of obvious. She killed herself."

"I mean more than a depression. She must've been into the occult."

"It's no worse than stuffed animals or jigsaw puzzles." Seth picked up one of the figures, its face obscured by a shroud. "They're just a collection. It's not like she was worshipping Satan. I don't think they give out ceramic angels of death at the monthly meetings."

Elaine cracked a smile. "I guess not. But it is a little weird." It felt good to joke with her son again. Normal. She hoped it was the beginning of him healing from all that had been going on the last few weeks.

Walking through the rest of the first floor was the same. Clean, and cluttered, with reapers. "So far, there's nothing I can see that a little boy would want or need."

They continued to the second floor.

Olivia arranged her pillows so they framed her purple comforter and she laid across her bed. "What do you want to do?"

"I don't know." Tommy meandered through the room, checked under her bed and sat next to her. "Where did New Mommy go?"

The corners of Olivia's lips turned upward. It was sweet and sad that he called Elaine "New Mommy," as if that was her name.

"She went to get some of your things." She bit her lip. Maybe she shouldn't have said anything. Shouldn't have reminded him of his prior home.

"That's what I thought."

"You did?"

"Yup." Tommy laid his head on her pillow and stared at the ceiling. It was white and bumpy. He walked his bare feet up her wall. The sun shone through Olivia's window creating dusty beams, and he made shadow puppets with his fingers.

"Here." She positioned his fingers to make a dog shadow. As he worked its mouth, she barked.

"I like cats better," he said. Tired of the game, he rolled onto his stomach. "Will she bring my toys?"

"I think so."

"Good."

She relaxed. He wasn't upset. Somehow, for now, he was okay. "She'll probably be gone for a while. We've got the whole house to ourselves. How about something fun like hide and seek?"

Tommy's face brightened. "I'm good at that."

"Great. I'll count to ten and you go hide. Bet I find you fast."

Tommy scrambled off the bed and out the door. "No, you won't. I'm the best hider."

"One, two, three."

"Slower!"

Olivia heard him dash down the hall and Iggy barked from the living room. Oh, yeah, she thought. Right behind the recliner. An obvious choice. "Four. Five."

"Ssh, Iggy. Stop."

"Six. Seven. Eight, nine, ten. Ready or not, here I come!" Sliding off her bed, she stopped first in Elaine's room. "Could you be here?" She made a show of searching behind the door. "Nope. Not there. Where could he be?" Tapping her chin, she walked toward the front of the house.

Tommy snickered behind the chair.

"Could you be here?" Olivia ran into the kitchen, looking under the table. "Nope. Not there, either."

Another giggle. Iggy pounced from behind the chair and barked at Olivia, his floppy brown ears wiggling.

"What's that, pup? Did you find something?"

"Me!" Tommy jumped up and tackled her at the knees.

"Wow. You are a great hider."

"I know." He sat up. "My turn to count." Tommy covered his eyes and sunk his face deep into the soft fabric of the chair. "One."

Olivia was off like a shot, grateful for the tread on the bottom of her slipper socks against the wood floor. She made a beeline for her closet. The sliding door was half-closed, and she wiggled past it, dodging another pile of laundry. She wedged herself between the side wall and her dad's old survival pack. It was a canvas backpack, filled with everything for a long trip into the wilderness. She didn't know why she'd kept it; she'd never gone camping a day in her life.

"Eight, nine, ten! Here I come!"

She scrunched behind the pack and held her breath. She may have only been playing with an "almost five" year old, but she was a lover of the game.

Tommy called out. "Are you here?"

He was still down the hallway, probably checking Elaine's room. Olivia shifted her weight to her other foot. There wasn't a lot of room, but she ducked down. Sacrifices had to be made for the best hiding spot in the house.

She heard movement. Scampering. Olivia squeezed her eyes shut. Iggy. He was at the door, nosing and snuffling.

"Iggs," she whispered. "Quit it."

Tommy burst in, flinging aside the closet door. "Found you!"

She shielded her eyes so she could see him in the light and worked her way out and into the bedroom. "You sure did. And that's one of my favorite hiding spots."

"It is?" He peered into the tiny space.

"Yeah. Most people don't think to look behind the backpack. It's like a shield."

"Wow."

"My turn to count." She covered her eyes with her hands. "One." She figured she'd hear him sneaking into her closet and climbing to the back. That's what little kids liked to do, copy what worked. But she didn't hear it. She didn't hear him at all. "Two. Three."

Tommy left Olivia's room, destination in mind, and when he got to Seth's door, he glanced back before turning the knob. Without a sound, he sneaked in.

The room was in disarray. The bed was an unmade mess. Old plates and cups were on the floor, the computer table. A heap of clothes sat at the end of the bed. The computer, left on in the middle of a game, gave off a dull glow. And the room was cold.

Tommy stared at the ceiling.

A shadow surrounded him, coalescing as if a hundred thousand flies buzzed into solid form. Protective. The thing in the corner recoiled with a shudder. It'd been seen. Sniffed out. It wanted to bolt, dive through the portal in the board and hide itself in the hell it'd been summoned from, but it was bound to the human and close to possessing him. Nothing would take that away. It gnashed its foul teeth, fangs bared like a cornered badger.

"Hey, kid." Olivia touched Tommy's arm and broke his concentration. "Tommy." She tugged him by his arm into the hall. "I don't think you should be hiding in there."

"Why not?"

She shook her head. "I don't think Seth would like it. And it's really messy. You might step in something nasty."

"Eww. Like what?"

They walked into the living room.

"I don't know. Old food. Bugs. Maybe food that's been there long enough maggots and worms have taken over the floor!" She chased him to the sofa, tickling.

"I'm done with hide and seek." He put his heels on a cushion. "Let's do something else."

"Like what?" Olivia sat up, brushing off her jeans. Keeping a little kid occupied was fun but tiring. Iggy bounded in, climbed onto her lap and wagged his tail. "Want to take this monster for a walk?"

At the word, Iggy jumped to the floor.

"Can I hold the leash?"

"Sure."

Olivia opened the top of the ottoman, pulling out a rhinestone studded navy-blue leash. She clipped it onto Iggy's collar. "Grab our jackets. I'll make us some lunch when we come back in."

Tommy ran to get his coat off the hook on the back of his bedroom door, then stopped in Olivia's room. She had a denim jacket and hoodie over the back of her desk chair. He drooped them over his arms and returned, slowing to a near stop in front of Seth's door. He glared as he stepped past it and handed the pile to Olivia. "Here."

"Thanks, Sport. Now, the important decision I'll leave up to you." She shoved her arms through the snug sleeves of the double jacket. It was cumbersome, but definitely worth it on days like this. Even the midday sun didn't quite push them above fifty degrees and, when the clouds blew by, it dipped. They stepped outside.

"What's that?"

"Which direction do you and Iggy want to go?"

Iggy had his nose to the ground and didn't care which way they went as long as he could sniff and pee along the way.

"Left."

"Sounds like a plan. Left we go."

They walked along, trailing Iggy as he spied squirrels, birds and the occasional stick that was bigger than he was. "ADHD pup," Olivia muttered. Iggy glanced at her feet, mouth agape with puppy glee, and pounced on a rock.

When they'd gotten about three houses down, Olivia noticed Tommy watching the house across the street. The paint was time-faded and in spots had peeled away, leaving it forlorn. He fingered the leash.

"You saw her the other night, didn't you?" Olivia searched every window but saw nothing except reflections.

"Who?"

"Mrs. Harper. The old lady who owned that house."

A leaf stuck to the side of his sneaker, and he wiped it off in the grass. "I don't know. What's she look like?"

"Like a grandma."

"Whose grandma?" Tommy squinted at Olivia, using his hand to shield his eyes from the sun, then whirled to stomp on his shadow.

Olivia narrowed her eyes at him, and thought it was an odd question to ask. Or maybe not for a little kid, but it felt dodgy to her. "All right for now, shadow boy. Let's walk on."

Seth reached the top of the stairway to the second floor and waited for his mother to catch up. A good-sized sitting room was in front of him with toys strewn through it.

"We've struck the mother lode," he said.

"Oh, good." She licked her fingers and worked to open the contractor bag. "Get the best ones. I don't want to inundate him with everything."

Handing the bag to her son, she walked through the hallway, taking it all in. It was weirdly intriguing. Every knob to every door was different. Crystal shapes, handles. Nothing matched. She tried the door closest to the playroom.

She caught her breath. "Oh, my God," she said, walking inside. "Oh, my God." Was there nothing normal or appropriate in this house? Hanging on the walls of what had to be Tommy's mother's art room, were paintings. Not that she would have hung any of them in her own house. Or anywhere, for that matter. Paintings of broken porcelain dolls. It was the strangest thing. "Seth."

"Yeah?"

"You have to come see this."

He walked in, shuffling through the things he'd put in the bag. "I thought he'd like th-" He gazed at the walls. "Wow."

"Wow is right," Elaine said. "What was wrong with this woman? I assume the artist is Tommy's mother, it would have to be, but . . . damn."

Seth set the bag beside a table covered in canvases and paint tubes and thumbed through a stack of paintings against the wall. "More of the same."

"I've never seen anything like it. Why would someone paint porcelain dolls? Broken ones at that."

He let the stack fall back on itself. "No idea." For now, here, his mind was quiet. There was no aching headache, no racing heartbeat. His tormentor had backed off. Maybe it was asleep, if demons slept. His stomach knotted and his anxiety blossomed. He had to talk to his mother. Had to tell someone who would listen before he went crazy. But she was out the door.

"I found Tommy's room. Across the hall," she called.

He grabbed the black bag and followed.

"Here," she said, at the dresser. "I want to get all his clothes."

Seth complied, catching sight of himself in the mirror. The lack of sleep was taking its toll, under his eyes it was puffy and dark, his hair stringy and unkempt. But that's what hoodies were for. Hide your downfall. For a little while.

"Earth to Seth."

He tilted his head toward his mother.

"Are you with me? We've got the clothes. I want to see if there's anything else he might need."

"Yeah, sure." He slung the bag over his shoulder and shadowed her. "Mom?"

"Hmm?" She bent down beside the bed. "What's this?" She hooked the corner of a wooden board with her finger and slid it out. "A Ouija board."

Seth wasn't impressed. He was crawling out of his skin.

"What would a little boy know of Ouija boards?" Elaine asked.

"I don't know."

"Would O. like this? Real workmanship."

"Yeah, she would. It's nice, Mom."

"Christmas." She handed it to him. "I don't think it'll fit in a bag. We can give a quick look in the other rooms, but I don't think they'll have anything Tommy'd be interested in."

"Mom." His voice was stern, a little louder than he'd intended.

She stopped in her tracks.

"I need to talk to you."

Elaine sat on the bed. Tommy's bed. "Of course."

He ran his fingers through his hair, knocking the hood back. "I-I'm dealing with so much." He paced. "I don't know what to do with how I feel."

"Oh, honey." She tried to take his hand, pull him close.

"No." He shoved her hand away. "Mom, I need you to listen." A shaky exhale, hands trembling. "I'm not doing well. In fact, life is sucking pretty hard. I can't seem to get it under control." His hands clenched and unclenched, tight fists with no release. "I can't sleep. When I do, it's nightmares. Awful nightmares. I can't eat. The headaches. Mom." He sat down, locking eyes with her. "The headaches." He inhaled and held it. "I feel like I'm being watched. Like something's after me."

"What can I do? I'll do whatever you need."

His jaw tightened. Ached. "I can't go back to school."

"But you're almost finished."

"You're not listening. I'm trying to tell you what I'm going through. I can't even maintain my emotions, how the hell do you think I can study?"

Elaine bit her lip. "Okay. Look, everything with Blake is still so fresh. The hurt. The upset. How about if I arrange for you to stay home, not worry about school right now. Take a break. It's understandable if you need time. But I want you to talk to someone. A grief counselor or . . . therapist . . . social worker. Someone. A doctor, too. Someone to help with the anxiety. Depression. With all that you're feeling."

Tears ran down Seth's cheeks. "I can do that. I can." Being able to let some of the steam out of the pressure cooker in his chest helped. A little. But he was going to explode soon, and it wasn't going to be pretty.

Elaine took Seth's hands in hers, a tear escaping her eye. She shook her head yes. "We can do that. Together."

A shadow at the doorway nabbed Seth's attention. "What was that?" He sprinted, surveying first one way then the other.

"What?"

"I thought I saw a cat."

"The landlord didn't say anything about any pets."

"I swear I saw a black cat go past."

His mother walked over to where he was standing. "Maybe you did see one. Maybe there's a window or door ajar. It doesn't mean you're crazy, you know."

He half-smiled. "I know." The truth was he didn't. Every ounce of his reality had been shredded in the last few weeks and he'd seen things that belonged in horror movies. Right now, he'd be happy if someone told him he was losing his mind. It'd be more comforting than the alternative, that a demon inhabited his bedroom and his brain. His being.

"Let's take that print and go home. I think we have everything Tommy needs."

As they loaded the bags into the car, Elaine waved to the landlord a few houses down. "We're done here! Sell the rest or throw it in a dumpster, we're set!"

Olivia held the screen door open, and Iggy dashed to the Camry, bouncing at Seth's feet. "What was it like? I can't wait to hear!" Elaine handed her a contractor bag to carry, and she dragged it across the floor to the sofa.

"Get away, dog." Seth lunged at Iggy to scare him and crossed the room to set the print, back facing out, against the wall.

"Don't do that. He was just happy to see you." Olivia scooped up the puppy and set him on the sofa cushion beside her.

"He needs to stop being such a pest."

"You're a pest." She stuck her tongue out.

Seth stuck his out, farther. Olivia crossed her eyes.

"All right, you two," Elaine said. "Stop. It's hard, O., to have our hands full and Iggy is a massive bundle of energy."

"He didn't have to be mean."

"I wasn't."

"You were." Olivia rubbed Iggy's ears, his tail wagging so hard he almost fell onto the floor.

"I'm going to go lie down."

"Close your door so Iggy doesn't come in and bite you."

"If he does-" Seth mumbled the rest and shut his door.

"Olivia, really."

"Sorry." She lowered her eyes, then with renewed excitement, said, "Tell me. What's the deal with the house? Did it feel different? Spooky?"

Elaine craned her neck to take in the hallway. "Where's Tommy?"

"I tired him out playing and he dozed off on my bed. He's been out five, maybe ten minutes."

Elaine squatted next to her, petting Iggy, then sat. "It was creepy."

Olivia's eyes widened, her mouth opening. "I knew it. I knew it would have a feel."

"Seems his mom collected grim reaper figurines. They were all over the place. Big ones, like a foot tall and better. Even a doorstop. Tiny ones, too. On shelves, on the television. Everywhere. Ugly ones, friendly ones."

"That's cool, actually. A death hobby."

"Death, hobby and cool in the same sentence. Not something I've heard before. Oh, wait. Yeah, I probably have, right out of your mouth." Elaine winked.

"Well, you aren't wrong."

"But that's not the oddest thing." She took Tommy's clothing out of the bag, stacking it into piles. Underwear, shirts, socks. Jeans. Everything needed to be washed and freshened.

"What? Come on, he'll be awake soon. What was there?"

Iggy climbed onto Elaine's lap and settled, trying to nip the occasional pants leg as it went by his nose.

"Paintings."

"Paintings?"

"Paintings. Of broken porcelain dolls. They were extremely realistic and what a disturbing subject. Very macabre."

"Wow."

"She had an entire room devoted to her art. Now, don't get me wrong. Tommy's mom was an amazing artist. But, geez-o-whiz, definitely not for me."

"Wish I could have seen them."

"I'm sure you can imagine."

Olivia peeked around Elaine, to the framed print against the wall. "What's that?"

"That is something Seth should've put in my bedroom. But," Elaine paused her folding and adjusted her glasses, "it may be a birthday present for you. I have to check with Tommy first."

Olivia raised an eyebrow. "A painting?"

"Nope. Not a porcelain doll, either. Now, here." She slid the plastic bag to Olivia. "Why don't you arrange these toys where he can find them while I get rid of that 'potential present' and put his clothes away?"

"Sure thing." Olivia took the bag, pondering what her foster mother could have possibly chosen for her out of that house.

Chapter 9

Dom pushed the metal bar and the door opened with a cha-thunk of metal. A small plaque to the side indicated the area was called Torrance Gardens, an unfortunate name if he ever heard one. Mr. Finley Torrance must've been quite the benefactor to have warranted an entire garden. He shivered and belted his robe over his scrubs, breathing in the autumn air. It was clean and sharp, with a smoky hint of burning deadwood.

The small park was enclosed by a cement wall, far enough away to not carry with it the prison vibe, yet it reminded you of where you were. Hemmingway Hospital. Not free to roam, always within sight of the orderlies. A stone path ran through the yard past wrought iron benches. Oak trees. Pines. The oaks were barren. The chaos of leaves gone, a stark clarity in the crisp air. He'd always loved the fall. Moreso for the lull in the world than anything else.

He waited on the path.

Another cha-thunk broke the stillness. The man of the hour had arrived.

"Hey, Dom." Dr. Ryan approached, rubbing his hands together. He watched his breath condense. "A little cold for a robe, wouldn't you say? We can still meet in my office, you know."

"I like it. Wakes up the senses."

"If you say so."

The men took the path to their right and Dom pointed out the plaque. "Torrance, eh? Specialize in topiaries and axes?"

"Tor-?" The psychiatrist furrowed his brow, then grinned, the movie reference clicking. "This is Hemmingway, not the Overlook."

He echoed his doctor's smile. They followed the walkway, the only sounds were their footsteps on gravel, stones crunching, and the rattle of keys in the doctor's pocket. Running his hand across the Boxwood hedge to his right, Dom said, "I'm ready to go home."

Dr. Ryan crossed his arms. "Ah."

"My stay was voluntary, and I know you'd agree that I'm sane. Rock solid."

The doctor considered his words carefully. "Well, I do believe that over the past two weeks, we've gotten your feet back onto steadier ground."

"Exactly. Which was what I needed to sort through everything. Have it make sense. Listen." He met the doctor's eyes. "I get it. I understand that none of it, Amanda's death, the caretaker at Forest View. Brian. None of it was my fault. It was never my fault. I had no hand in the events unfolding other than living through them." He did get it. And now it was time to act. To execute a plan.

"True."

"Survivor's guilt, doc." Dom averted his eyes. "It's a bitch."

"It certainly is. But the emotion of it doesn't go away that quickly. We both know what words to say and what makes sense logically. Rationally. But emotions aren't rational, and we have to make sure that what you're feeling, what might be brewing beneath it all, is under control. That we're here to deal with it."

"Definitely."

"I think you're ready. We'll keep some regular appointments once you're home, make sure all is going well. I can also give you information on a support group or two that you might want to pop in on. They can really help."

Dom nodded.

"Well, then," Dr. Ryan said. "Let's get inside and start some paperwork." He clapped Dom on the back, and they turned toward the building.

The flapping of wings caught their attention as a large, black bird perched in an oak tree on the path.

"Would you look at that," Dr. Ryan said. "A raven?"

Dom stared at the bird, knowing full well what it was and where it came from. "No," he said. "It's a crow."

"Huh. I didn't think they came that size."

They continued on and, as they returned to the Torrance plaque, the bird cawed. Three times. The doctor glanced at the tree while putting his code into the lock.

"Almost sounds like it's laughing, doesn't it?" he asked.

"Yeah." But it wouldn't be for long.

As Dom stepped into the building, he spied a late-season wooly bear crawling along the jam. It was fuzzy and mostly black, with a small band of brown in the middle.

It was going to be a harsh winter.

Chapter 10

Seth sat in a peach-colored chair. Or coral. The entire waiting room was decorated in nauseating pastels. Side tables with magazines fanned out, an empty coat rack. Plastic plants in large terra cotta pots beside windows that gave a view of the parking lot. His mother had already gone, grocery shopping and who knows what else. They'd warned her that his initial visit would take about two hours. He slumped deeper into the seat. There was no television to distract him, like in the doctor's office. He was alone with his thoughts.

"Fuck all."

He shifted again, crossing his heels. It wasn't what he expected from an office in a mental health facility. Hemmingway Hospital appeared more medical than mental when he walked in, and he'd had to stand in line at a hub to ask where to go. Elevator, second floor, to the left. First door. He'd found it, dodging men in white coats. It reminded him of that old 60s song, "They're Coming to Take Me Away." He bent forward, trying to stretch his back. It was as if he'd carried someone piggyback the last five miles. Five days. With a backpack full of rocks. And knives. The scratches he'd found in the mirror after twisting like a contortionist showed his back was a mass of welts. Some scabbed, others fresh and weeping.

How was therapy going to change that? Tell him it was all in his head? He sneered. He'd told his mother he would do this, talk to someone, and he would. Maybe the guy would listen. And then throw him on some kick ass meds.

The receptionist's phone rang, and he could hear her lilting voice through the glass barrier. Got to keep the crazies separate from the staff. He was the only crazy, though. Maybe they shuffled everyone out the back door when they saw him coming. Keep the God-fearing people away from the demon oppressed.

He exhaled, checking his chewed-off fingernails, and picked at the skin on his thumb. At least he'd been able to do the intake form online, but that was a joke. Have I struggled to be myself lately? Have my worries increased? Have I lost interest in things I used to love doing? Have I not bounced back from something? It'd been pretty extensive, a laundry list of questions and "thought provokers." After that were the medical questions, have you ever had this or that, any prescription drugs or other. He'd smirked at that. And suicidal thoughts. Ever had those?

He moved to the next finger, tugging at a hangnail, and wincing a bit when the skin pulled up almost to his knuckle. Yeah, he'd had those thoughts over the last couple of weeks. After the third screaming migraine of the night and the bastard in the corner of the room slashed through his nightmares one more time. He'd thought about it.

Seth sucked on the cut; the blood was salty. Metallic. He'd probably walk out of there with a string of diagnoses and none of them representing what was actually going on. Anxiety, check. Depression, double check. Self-harm? Hah! Add a little schizophrenia and who knows what else. One from column A and two from column B, if you please. Is it a demon or a hallucination? You be the judge. He could host that gameshow.

Another ring of the phone. Popular place. He turned to see if there was a clock on the wall. It felt like he'd been there for hours. No clock. That figured. No doctor's office that he'd ever been in had one. They never wanted you to know how long you'd been waiting. He half-reached to grab his phone from his pocket and stopped. It wasn't there. It was on the floor of his bedroom, the screen broken into pieces, deader than dead. He'd smashed it against the edge of his desk one night to stop the ringing in his mind. Rational thoughts were hard to grasp lately, harder to hold onto for any length of time.

Especially in his room. Its lair.

Near a ceiling vent, a spider slowly descended. It worked and played, letting out its web, getting to within an inch of the top leaf of the ficus. Seth pictured it having the head of a person and having conversations with the patients that sat beside the plastic tree. Maybe the little arachnid was the actual psychiatrist and the rest of this was a ruse. *Let me write you a prescription on my teeny tiny pad.* His lip curled into a smirk. Maybe he was losing his mind.

Boredom set in. He pawed through the magazines on the table beside him. Psychology Today. *Really? Are we self-diagnosing now? Get a handle on what's wrong with you before walking in for your visit? Hard pass.* The New Yorker, National Geographic. *Geez.* Nothing he even wanted to pretend he was interested in.

"Seth?"

Somehow, he'd missed the sound of the door. The receptionist was standing there, chart in hand, waiting for him.

"That's me," he said. "Guess it's my turn." He followed her into a small office, this time in sage green. More plastic plants beside a large window. Some chairs, a couch.

"Sit wherever you'd like. Dr. Ryan will be right in." She disappeared behind the door they'd come through.

Doctor Ryan. Was that a last name or was he some soap opera, romance novel doctor? *Doctor Great-Big-Pecs will see you now. Seduce your bored housewife-life and show you how to love again.* The certificates on the wall said otherwise. Michael Ryan, MD. He read the diplomas, trainings, yadda, yadda, yadda, and sat on the couch. It was more therapy-esque than one of the chairs. They were suited for a job interview or funeral home. *Time to pick out Great Aunt Maude's coffin, dearie. The dark chocolate wood or the cherry?*

He pulled at a thread on the seat cushion and scanned the wall of books behind the chairs. Lofty psychological reference library, he assumed. Like when you see a law office on television, and it's stacked with books no one ever reads. Maybe it's a false wall. Something built to resemble books, so these guys come off smarter than they are. Raise those stats.

A knuckle-knock at the door, and a man in a light-blue collared shirt and navy tie walked in. No white lab coat as he'd expected. The man held out his hand. "Hi, Seth. Dr. Ryan. You can call me that, Dr. Mike, Mike. Whatever you're comfortable with." The man sat, setting his clipboard on his lap. He had a "pushing forty, not quite graying at the temples" look. One of those people who would still pass for sixty-five when they're eighty.

"Uh, thanks."

The doctor shut the laptop that had been up and running on the side table. "Hemmingway wants us to type notes directly into the system while we work with the client. Kind of speed things up. But I find that impersonal and distracting. I'm just an old pen and paper guy on the inside." He held up his Bic. "What brings you here today?"

The doctor reclined in his chair, hands resting on Seth's file.

"My mother." A nervous grin spread across his face, then dissipated.

Dr. Ryan smiled, with crow's feet in the making. "Then this is a joint effort? I saw you signed the consent form."

"Her idea, my follow through."

"Gotcha. Have you ever seen a counselor before? Any type of therapist?"

"Never."

"So, why don't we talk about what's been going on in your life that's brought you to this point? What's changed?"

Seth's hands were clammy, and he ran his palms along his pant legs. "I- I don't know how to do this." He leaned forward, resting his forearms on his thighs, not knowing how to condense his life into a therapy session. Not knowing if he'd be believed or cinched into a straitjacket for the rest of his life. Not knowing if he believed it himself.

Dr. Ryan noted Seth's discomfort. It was nothing new to him. He set his clipboard on the table. "What I want you to keep in mind is this." He pointed from Seth to himself. "This is a process. It doesn't have to come out today or next time, or in three weeks. We walk through whatever you're comfortable with and take it from there."

"Layers."

"Layers."

"Like an onion," Seth said. He let out a slow breath.

"You bet. Why don't you try to relax a little and I'll ask some questions?"

"Sure."

"Since Mom made the appointment, why don't we start there? How's your relationship with her?"

"Mom? We're fine. She's a typical mom. You know, the one who bakes cupcakes and brings them to school, is at every function. Star of the PTA."

"Very involved."

"Extremely."

"Overly so?"

Seth crossed, then uncrossed, his legs. "I don't think so."

"Any siblings?" He held up the file. "I did read through the form you filled out, but I'd rather talk with you. You took the time to come in and I want to hear what you have to say."

The guy was making an effort to set him at ease, and he almost believed he could trust him. At least until the word demon was brought up. Then, all bets were off. "A foster sister. Olivia. She's fourteen. Kind of a pain, but she's okay."

"I know what you mean. Teen girls can be a little trying."

"Yeah."

"Is that all? Just the sister?"

"Kind of? I mean, Olivia's lived with us a few years now. She's like a real sister. But Mom just brought home a little boy that she's fostering. Not sure if he counts. We've only had him a couple of weeks."

"How old?"

"I don't know. Four or five?"

"Ahh. Young children can disrupt a home when you're not used to having them around."

"He sure does."

"Takes a lot of your mother's time, I bet. Gets into your things?"

"All of the above." He made a checkmark in the air with his index finger.

"And how do you feel about that? Your mother being a foster parent?"

"It's okay, I guess. I mean, she's a good mom and these kids are in need, but . . ."

"But?"

Seth shrugged. "I think she has enough on her plate without taking in more kids."

Doctor Ryan picked up his pen. Seth raised an eyebrow.

"No worries. I do need to make the occasional note." He tapped his temple. "Age and the profession dictate."

"It's your job. I get it."

"Good." He folded his arms. "So, fostering takes up a lot of your mother's time."

"It does. But it's not even that. I don't know. Olivia is family now. I'm okay with that. But the new kid . . . there's something weird about him. Something off."

"Well, if he's being fostered, something in his homelife had to be pretty horrible. I'm sure it's affected him."

"His mother killed herself."

Dr. Ryan tucked his pen behind his ear. "There you have it. He's having to deal with death at an age where he doesn't have any coping mechanisms yet. He doesn't have a concrete understanding of death and its permanency. That could easily make him feel 'off.'"

Clouds rolled in, covering the sun. Seth stared out the window as flurries began and grew into larger flakes. "I guess." He dreaded they'd get into it all soon. That he'd have to somehow bare his soul.

"How's school?" Dr. Ryan noted the subtle change in Seth's

demeanor. The boy had tightened, sat a little straighter. He could almost hear the metal walls as they surrounded his patient. Slam, slam, slam.

Seth cleared his throat. "I haven't been in a while."

"How long's 'a while'?"

"I don't know," he ran his hand through his hair. "A little over three weeks? Close to a month, maybe." He was on the spot. The guy was going to grill him over not going to school and failing his senior year. Thoughts spun in his head. This wasn't going to work. This wasn't going to help.

"Is that why Mom's concerned?"

"Yeah."

"How was it when you were going?"

He didn't expect that and had to think for a moment. "Okay. Normal."

"Like any other senior."

"I guess." Like any other kid whose best friend was trying to summon demons. Wanting to connect with and control the unseen. And died for it. "I mean, mostly." It was boiling up inside him, but he couldn't get the words out. Couldn't do anything more than a silent scream inside his skull.

"What was different?"

"Is it okay if I walk around?" His heart was beating faster now, and he could feel it in his ears. The rush of blood, the pre-migraine ache.

"Of course."

In three strides he was at the window, looking out over the cars. A grey-green truck had backed up to one of the facility's dumpsters and was loading the week's garbage. A stray cat darted from behind the truck, jumping onto the fence then the shed roof. It arched and sat, watching him.

"Seth?"

"Yeah?" He glanced away from the window, then back. The cat was gone. But cats do that, right? Just like the one the other day.

Masters of disguise and deception.

"What was different?"

His mouth went dry. "How does all this work? It's confidential, right? Like you don't tell the cops or my mother?" His eyes were hot, and he was going to spill his guts then and there, no holding back. Like the acid bile that churns before you projectile vomit, his mind was rolling.

"Everything that gets discussed here is between us. The only time anything would be disclosed to anyone would be if I thought you were going to harm yourself or someone else."

"Even if I was a witness to something? Something bad? Really bad."

"Even if."

"You're going to think I'm crazy." He laughed at that. Higher pitched than he was comfortable with, and he heard himself outside his head. Awkward and uncomfortable. "God, you're going to put me away." A low moan escaped his throat. He collapsed onto the couch, covering his eyes with his arm. Tears flowed as the dam inside him burst.

"Sorry," he said when he'd calmed. "Sorry."

Dr. Ryan passed him the box of tissues he'd been holding in his lap. "Don't apologize. Seems like you needed it."

"Yeah." Seth wiped his eyes, now red and puffy. He blew his nose and wadded up the tissue, tucking it into the pocket of his hoodie.

"So, why don't we talk about what you've been bottling up?"

Seth sized up the room, the plants, the chairs, and tried to focus on anything but the conversation he knew he had to have. He tugged at his sleeve. "Blake."

"And Blake is?"

"My friend. He died about three, four weeks ago."

"I'm sorry for your loss."

Seth nodded.

"That was the event that changed everything?"

Seth hesitated. "It was." He pulled once more at the thread poking out of his cushion, creating a small hole. "We were friends for years. Mom fostered him when we were little. We were better than friends. We were brothers." The upset was returning, but this time with anger. At Blake. The demon. At his life. His voice tensed. "And he died."

"How?" He was surprised at how quickly they'd gotten to the heart of the matter. But some walls weren't made of bricks.

Seth stared at nothing, a direct empty gaze. Almost a hypnotic avoidance of the question. But he had to tell someone. Had to let it out before he lost his mind.

"I was there. I was there when he died. And it wasn't supposed to happen. It wasn't supposed to be this way." His throat went tight, and his voice held a desperation he couldn't control. "I watched him die." He balled his hand into a fist and punched the arm of the couch, then locked eyes with the doctor, unblinking. "I watched him die. And then I ran." Dirty. Cowardly. A sick truth that made his guts burn.

"It's not abnormal to be afraid when confronted with something so terrible."

Seth shook his head. "No. You don't get it. No one will." His mouth worked as he tried to find the words. "Blake was troubled, you know? Rotten homelife." He pushed his hair out of his face. "There were some guys who bullied the crap out of him. Made life a living hell. And he decided he'd find a way out. He needed a way out." The waters were rising in him, and they were angry. He was up again, pacing. Stopping at the window, he rested his forehead against the glass. It was cool against his skin. His breaths came slower, and he tried to will his heartbeat to follow suit.

"Blake killed himself?"

Seth closed his eyes and let the chill seep into his brain. "No." Something in him caved. Broke. Gave in to the inevitable. "No. He called for help." He stepped back from the windowsill, turning toward the doctor. "Only he called to demons. We blood-bound ourselves as brothers and summoned them. The night he died, though, something went wrong. What came through the portal we made, killed him. And I ran." He locked eyes with the doctor. "Some fucking friend I am, right?"

"Sounds as if you were terrified."

He snorted. "I still am."

"Of someone finding out?"

"Really?" He held his arms out and dropped them to his sides. "This isn't survivor's guilt, doc. I don't need," he made air quotes, "grief counseling." Sliding into the chair beside the laptop table, he said, "What we pulled from hell, the shit-thing that killed Blake, chased me down that night. Hunted me. It latched on and isn't going to let go until I'm rotting in my grave."

He waited for a reaction, disbelief or otherwise, but Dr. Ryan offered nothing.

"I see things." He swallowed. "I hear its voice. Constant, like a beehive in my brain. And the nightmares. . . I don't know how to deal anymore." A shiver went through him, up his spine, and his hands shook. "I need help. I don't know what to do."

"That's why you're here."

Panic rose in him, from deep within it rose into his chest, with a vengeance. "I- I think I'm going to be sick."

Dr. Ryan pointed to the bathroom and Seth ran in, collapsing onto his knees in front of the toilet. He retched and dry heaved until his ribs ached, and his mind went numb. He washed his face and returned to the chair across from the doctor.

"Better?"

Seth, pale and drained, nodded.

"Are you okay with continuing? I'd understand if you wanted to pack it in for today."

"We can go on."

The doctor took his pen from behind his ear. "Tell me, then, what do you see?"

# # #

As they rounded the bend, Hemmingway Hospital loomed ahead. The structure had been renovated and revamped over the years. A wing for outpatient visits, a wing for maternity. Pediatrics. The main entrance, announced in large blue letters, was straight ahead. Emergency and ambulance were to the right, parking lots to either side. Five stories of surgery, illness and, their reason for being there, therapy.

Elaine parked next to a red pickup truck in the visitor's lot. "We're here." She shut off the engine. "Hopefully he won't be too long. I don't want the ice cream to melt." She glanced over her shoulder.

Olivia agreed. "Big place."

Tommy unhooked his seatbelt and scooted forward between the front seats.

"Seth should come from over there." Elaine pointed at the double doors under the Main Entrance sign. There was a steady flow of people in and out.

"They do a pretty good business."

"Sure seem to. Tell me, O.," she said, shifting to face her foster daughter. "What do you want for your birthday?"

"Birthday?" Tommy lit up.

"Olivia's is next week. We're having her party on Saturday."

"Ooh."

"When's your birthday, Tommy?" Olivia asked.

"I don't know."

"You must. Think about it for a minute."

"I've got some paperwork in my purse, Olivia. At your feet."

Olivia dug in the bag, finding a thick envelope. She handed it to Elaine.

"I've been so busy, I never even thought to check. Let's see, Tommy. Your birthday is November 23rd."

Olivia's jaw dropped. "You're pulling my leg."

"See for yourself." She handed over the paperwork.

Olivia read the page. "November 23rd. How weird is that?"

"What?" Tommy asked. "When's that?"

"Wednesday. The day before Thanksgiving." Olivia said. "The same as me."

"The same? Wow."

"Wow is right," said Elaine. "Now we have to figure out when we can throw you a party. Maybe we could do it the week after Thanksgiving. How does that sound?"

Tommy thought for a moment, nodded. "We're twins." He tapped Olivia on the shoulder, then leaned close to her face. "Birthday twins."

"I guess we are," she said. "Very cool." They high fived.

With that, the back passenger door of the car opened. Tommy saw it was Seth and went back to what he was doing.

"What's all this happy hand slapping?"

Tommy faced him, balancing between the seats. "We're twins."

Seth furrowed his brow, his lips a thin line. "Really."

Olivia laughed. "We have the same birthday."

"Well, isn't that special." He shut the door with a thud.

Tommy shook his head wildly.

Seth pulled his hood down over his eyes. "Okay, okay, little dude. Mom? I've got a prescription at Pop's Pharmacy. Can we stop on the way?"

"Of course. I'll take the back way. How'd it go?" She angled the rear-view mirror to get a better view of her son, then shifted into reverse. "Seatbelt, Tommy. Can you do it yourself?"

The boy climbed into his booster seat and snapped the two ends of the belt together, giving Elaine a thumbs up.

Seth stared out the window. "It was okay."

"Did you like the therapist?"

"He seemed all right. Thinks meds may help."

"Good." Another glance. No eye contact. No connection. No knowing if she was doing all she could to help her son. She made her way to Main Street and took the left onto Broad instead of picking up the highway toward home.

As they approached the first light before Montgomery township, the Old Towne Inn, long abandoned and run down, was to their left. Crystal Brook Cemetery, equally devoid of any caretaking, was to their right.

"Hold your breath!" said Olivia, making a point to close her mouth and squeeze her nostrils shut with her right hand.

"Why is that, again?" Elaine asked. She was happy to have some sort of conversation going. It was better than the awkward "just saw a therapist and don't want to talk about it" silence from the backseat. It was almost loud enough to drown out Tommy's humming of the alphabet song.

"Supposedly, and I do mean supposedly, you'll breathe in someone's soul."

From the back seat Tommy noisily breathed in the biggest lungful of air he could muster, sending Olivia and Elaine into peals of laughter.

"You know, you shouldn't be so superstitious," Elaine said as the light turned green.

"One man's superstition is-"

"Still a superstition."

"I'll give you that," said Olivia. "But!"

Elaine made a right onto Beach Road. "There's always a 'but,' isn't there?"

"Yes. Do you knock on wood?"

"Sometimes."

"There you go. That's to call on the spirits that reside in the wood. For protection. You knock to stay safe. I just choose to keep my soul, thank you. Same same."

"I don't quite think it's 'same same,' but I'll let you have it this time."

Elaine waited for the traffic to stop and turned into the small lot beside the fluorescent Pop's sign. The pavement was potholed and broken, in sorry need of repair. Weeds grew between the cracks. "You have your prescription?"

Seth gave the door handle a tug. "He called it in."

"You did say that. Need some cash in case there's a copay?"

"Yeah." He stood outside the driver's door while she fished in her purse.

Elaine rolled down her window. "Here's twenty. I can't imagine it being anywhere near that, but just in case."

"Thanks."

She watched him trod over bits of asphalt to the door with the lottery stickers and wondered if she'd ever again see the son she used to know.

Dom strode down Main Street, past the Pop's yellow storefront, hands in the pockets of his pea coat. He didn't need Epsom salts, hemorrhoid pillows or window clings with fall leaves. He was surprised they hadn't updated their window to Christmas decorations yet. Little elves begging you to buy peppermint lip gloss and Santa pushing antacids.

He waited at the corner for the light to turn and felt the ragged edge of the business card in his pocket. Smirking, he crossed as the traffic cleared. "Grief support group, my ass." He'd done the voluntary stay at Hemmingway. Lost his shit, went down the rabbit hole and swam in that darkness. Almost drowned.

But then it clicked. Slammed. Like an iron gate locking into place, separating him from his pain. A numbness settled over his past and a calculated calm took over. The survivor's guilt could have killed him. Over Amanda's death. Brian's. He'd been there when Amanda killed the caretaker at Forest Hills, too. Not her fault. His. Putting her into that situation. Into the whole paranormal thing. He'd brought her in on the investigation at Aarondale Correctional and the one at the Barnes house. And here he was, still breathing. It could only mean one thing.

He would be the one to destroy Black.

Setting his sights on the bookstore in the next block, he moved with the flow of the other pedestrians. Ebb and flow, people crossing back and forth, commenting on shop displays. Talking on their phones. He sidestepped a street vendor selling pretzels and almost ran into an old woman in a large hat.

"Excuse me," he said.

"You might want to slow down." She turned toward a flower display. "You might want to."

"I'd say you're right, especially on a busy day like today."

The old woman, pretzel in hand, said, "It has nothing to do with the day. It has to do with your life." She adjusted her hat, stroking the peacock feather, and faded into the crowd.

His life.

Dom hesitated long enough to grab the door handle at Books and More but didn't turn. He was done with distractions, done with anything that threatened to take him off the path so clearly laid out before him. A girl, twenty-something, sat behind the cash register. He noted her tattoos, sleeves down both arms and a spider in the middle of her neck, reaching toward her left ear.

"Hey." She placed her iced coffee on the metal shelf that ran along the wall behind her.

"Afternoon." The store was decorated somewhere between New Age and Goth. There were sage sticks and charms along the side wall, figurines everywhere, and rows of bookshelves crammed tightly into the small space. "I think you have some books set aside for me."

The girl slid off her stool, pulling a binder from beside the register. Dark blue, dulled by time and use, its plastic edges cracked. "Name?" She seemed uninterested. The job was something she did in the hours between lounging and chilling.

"Dominic Russell."

She thumbed through the pages, then bent to take a small pile of books off a shelf. One by one, she placed them in front of him. "Demons and Demonology. Light and the Dark: An Exorcist's

View." She raised an eyebrow. "Energies, Entities and Psychic Attacks." Looking up from the stack, she asked, "A little light reading?"

"Time on my hands."

"Hmm." She dropped the last book on top of the stack. "Act, Don't React: Strategies for Life."

Dom took his wallet from his coat pocket while she rang up the purchase.

"$127.50."

"Not a bad price to save a soul or two."

"What?"

He shrugged it off. "Nothing." The girl ran his credit card through the machine and waited for the obligatory "approved" to appear. He noticed the hourglass on her tee shirt with Memento Mori in cursive below it. As she handed him his card and bag of books, he guessed it might be time to learn some Latin.

On the way back to his van, Dom dodged a teenager headed into the pharmacy. He'd come from the blue Camry in the side lot.

"Oh, sorry, man," the kid offered.

"No problem." Dom stepped backward, watching him enter Pop's. The recognition staggered him. The kid was steeped in something dark and wrong, and Black had his fetid hand in it somehow. Some way. And he knew the demon was playing with him. Tag. You're it.

"You're damn right, I'm it," he said, under his breath. "And I'm coming for you."

He tucked his package under his arm and strode to his vehicle. The Camry was parked between his van and a pickup, and he glanced inside as he fumbled with his keys. He assumed the woman was the kid's mother and there were two other children with her. He hoped the entire family wasn't involved. But no one was safe where demons tread.

Chapter 11

It was dark in Seth's room. It was always dark. He'd made sure of that. Duct taped the shade to the molding, sealed up any cracks that let sunlight through. What you saw in the shadows was much less scary than what you saw in broad daylight. He scoffed at the so-called ghost hunters on television who only investigated at night, trying to make things seem creepier. Get ratings. He cleared his throat. He could show them the epitome of terrifying in broad daylight.

But what if it was all in his head? His mind so bent, so wrong, that it conjured this up . . . in an effort to what? Amnesiacs hide. Protect themselves by going blank. And people with multiple personalities, their minds run interference from something horrible. Traumatic. And yet his sick brain could be trying to destroy him. How did that make any sense? Shouldn't it be sending him unicorns and glitter, rather than hounding him to tear apart a little boy? Or kill himself? If he could figure out why he would be imploding, he might be able to give in to a diagnosis. But.

He fished a lighter from the pocket of his jeans and flicked it. The flame sputtered to life and its glow lit his corner of the room. He stared into the fire, letting it absorb his focus and attention. "You're not real."

He let go of the spark wheel. After all, the doc told him to take control of his situation. Move away when he felt it was near, go to a well-lit room. Not the best advice when something can travel along with you. He'd try it, though.

Flick. "You're not real."

Flick. "You're all in my mind."

Before he could spin it again, something foul and demented rushed him.

Am I?

An odor of raw sewage emanated from its maw, and saliva dripped into Seth's lap. The wet stain grew with every drop. Drip. Drip.

Its raspy, growl of a voice spewed forth.

Am I a figment of your feeble imagination?

Seth's stomach flipped and acid licked at the back of his throat. He could taste its fetid breath and his nostrils burned as his stomach rolled. Gagging, he spat the words, "You're not real," and ran for the bathroom.

Chapter 12

Tommy watched the street through the small side windows on either side of the front door. The streetlights were on, bathing the driveway in a yellow glow and, with every passing car, he grew more impatient. It was Olivia's birthday, and the girls would be here soon. Finally, a silver car slowed to a stop next to the mailbox and they climbed out. He could hear them saying their goodbyes to the person behind the wheel.

Tommy unlocked the door for Jules and Christie, letting them close it behind him. He peeked at the presents they were carrying.

Jules slid her sleeping bag to the floor and squatted on his level. "Do you remember me?"

"Where are your sparkly eyes?"

"Those were just for Halloween, but if you'd like, I'll wear them the next time I come. How's that?"

Tommy nodded and ran off.

"No hello for me?" Christie called after him. She propped her overnight tote, sleeping bag and pillow on top of her friend's.

"You didn't have sparkly eyes." Jules looked for their friend. "Where's Olivia?"

Elaine stepped out from the kitchen, wiping her hands on a dishrag. "In her room. Go on down. She's decorating for your sleepover."

"Decorating?" Christie asked.

"Oh, yeah. Be prepared. It's Halloween again." Elaine returned to the dishes.

"Is it always about ghosts and goblins with her?"

"Where Olivia's concerned, is there anything else?" Jules picked up Iggy before he could wag his tail off. "Come on, pup. Let's go see the tomb from hell where we'll be sleeping tonight." She started down the hallway.

"Or sleeping with one eye open, one hand on a crucifix and a foot out the door," Christie said.

Jules rolled her eyes and set Iggy down when they reached Olivia's door. She knocked three times. "To dispel anything untoward. Are you there, queen of the undead and all things spooky?"

"That's me!" Olivia said through the door. "Close your eyes."

"Really? How bad is it in there?"

"Close your eyes, Christie. Nothing's going to jump out at you. I promise," Olivia said.

Olivia swung the door back in a slow arc, a long creak emerging from the speaker on her desk. The girls walked into a purple lit, cobwebby room. Flickering candles lined the windowsill. "Courtesy of Mom," she said. "Battery powered." Black bats and crows covered the far wall. She dropped the pad of construction paper and scissors into her desk drawer. "What do you think? I love the purple lightbulb."

Jules agreed, hands on her hips. "I like, I like! Very goth, very Halloweeny."

"Very you," Christie said.

Olivia curtseyed. "Thanks."

There was another knock at the door and a small voice said, "New Mommy says there are heroes in the kitchen and then we can have birthday cake. She told me to knock, and I did. Are you coming out?"

Jules opened the door and Tommy saw the glow. He peered into the room, mouth in an O. "Wow."

"Come on, kid. Let's get some food." Jules took him by the hand.

Elaine was slicing a six-foot hero into six-inch sections, arranging them on serving plates.

"How'd you get that in the car?" Olivia reached for a turkey and provolone section and dropped it onto a paper plate. A Ghostbusters paper plate.

"It wasn't easy. Girls, these are," she pointed, "turkey, roast beef, veggie, and ham. Take what you want, there's a ton here." She leaned into the hallway and yelled, "Seth! Dinner!"

Olivia tipped the plate on its side so Elaine would see that she noticed. "Ghostbusters. So cool."

"Seemed appropriate." She went back to cutting the sandwiches.

Tommy sat beside Jules, sneaking glances at her every so often.

"I think you've got a boyfriend," Christie said.

"And maybe I do." Jules wrapped an arm around Tommy's shoulders. "What kind of sandwich do you want?"

"Ham."

Iggy wove among their ankles, sniffing for any bites dropped, any morsel on a pant leg waiting to be devoured. Tommy kicked his feet back and forth, giving him an obstacle course.

"Ham it is." She pulled over a plate and set it in front of him, ripping a tiny corner of the meat off. Watching Tommy's face, she tossed it to Iggy who caught it with a snap. His tail wagged even faster.

Tommy picked up the sandwich between his two hands and squished it as best he could to take a bite. "Coke, please."

In the middle of the table were two two-liter bottles of soda. "Is it okay, Mrs. R.?

Elaine shook her head yes. "It's a party. It's fine."

Jules poured him half a cupful. "If you finish this and want more, let me know. So," she said, turning her attention to her friend. "What's the order of events on this auspicious occasion?"

"What do you mean?" Olivia tugged a piece of tomato from her hero and dangled it above her mouth before dropping it in.

"Come on," said Christie. "You know you always have every event, birthday, whatever, planned to a T."

"Well," she chewed, picking up a stray slice of onion, and

popped that into her mouth as well. "I may have a fair idea of the festivities."

"Eww, onions," Tommy said. He began deconstructing his sandwich. "Eww, tomatoes."

"First, dinner." She handed him a napkin. "We eat. Seth eats. Check. Then, cake."

"Check." Elaine said from beside the sink. She had washed the knife she had been using and rinsed off the cutting board, setting it in the dish drainer.

"Then presents. At eight o'clock we're going to play a game called 'Exquisite Corpses.'"

"A zombie game?" Christie asked.

"Nope. You'll see." Olivia took another large bite and they had to wait while she chewed. And chewed. "Sorry." She swallowed. "I'm thinking by nine o'clock we'll be ready for some spooky stories and a late-night movie. Thoughts?"

Seth entered the room in black sweats and a Metallica tee shirt, hair tossed back. Christie and Jules ate silently, staring as he grabbed a plate and filled it with two of the sandwiches.

"Ghostbusters, eh, Olive?"

"Some of us have goals, Silas."

Jules snorted, covering her face with her hand.

Seth poured himself a cup of Sprite, balanced his plate on top, and left the kitchen.

"Can't you stay and eat with us?" Elaine asked. She knew full well he wouldn't and nothing she could say would convince him.

"And deprive these giggling girls the chance to watch my ass as I walk away?"

"Seth!"

"Silas!" Olivia yelled. The girls broke into peals of laughter.

Christie took a napkin and wiped her hands. "How long has he been calling you Olive?"

"I don't know. As long as I've been calling him Silas?" She popped another slice of onion into her mouth. Giggles erupted once more.

"Call me for cake!" For a moment, just a moment, he felt normal. Natural. But he knew better. Knew it would only allow him out for just so long before it yanked his leash. That unseen tentacle noose would tighten on his neck. He touched his doorknob and felt a chill emanate from his room. Seth lowered his eyes, shoulders sagging, and entered.

It had to be twenty degrees colder than the kitchen. He sat at his desk, shoving the computer keyboard out of the way. The mouse hit the floor. Sickening darkness swirled until a face formed in front of him. He squeezed his eyes shut, holding his breath, willing his stomach to calm. A tendril slid across his food, turning it to a moldering mess. His gut lurched.

He sat stock-still, waiting. Waiting for a talon to form and rake his skin, tearing him. Waiting for the vile creature to uncoil, and flex into his brain. Sear his mind with commands. Brand him. He'd already been marked. Doomed. Like pus running through his veins, he was infiltrated the night he and Blake sliced their palms and bound their blood to the unseen.

A picture of Tommy formed in his mind. Bloody. Broken. It wanted the boy dead and gone. Destroyed. And it wanted him to do it. He shuddered. He pushed himself farther into his chair, trying to escape the odor and intent of the solidified evil in front of him. It drilled into his chest, pain exploding through his ribcage.

A sound brought him out of it.

"Seth!"

"Silas!" and laughter. The pain eased, and he realized he'd been in a fetal position on the floor. Dust and dog hair assaulted his nostrils.

"Yeah." He picked himself up and brushed off, walking through the laundry that littered his floor. "Yeah?"

"Cake!"

He could hear his mother, the girls and the little monster enjoying the evening. Waiting for him before blowing out the candles. Tommy might help. He might get too close to the flames. Seth pushed the thought to the recesses of his mind. It wasn't his thought. He couldn't let it mix with his own.

"Sy." Olivia reached through his doorway, grabbing his hand. "Come on! Mom's ready to light the candles."

Elaine had a long handled lighter suspended above the cake. Fifteen candles were set among tombstones and skeleton bones, with shredded chocolate as the cemetery dirt. The largest gravestone was icing-etched with Olivia's name and the smaller ones, the family.

"I love it!"

"I thought you would." Elaine gave Seth a forlorn look. An apologetic, pleading with her eyes, I ordered it months ago, but this is her interest and I'm not disrespecting your feelings, really. She grabbed another set of Ghostbuster plates and a box of plastic forks.

He mouthed the words, "I know."

"Look, Tommy, there's your name." Jules pointed it out and Tommy scrutinized it, taking great pride in having a stone in the little cake cemetery.

"Hey," said Christie. "There's ours, Jules! We're buried together."

"And that one must be for Seth," Tommy said. He laid eyes on the older boy from across the table, meeting his stare. "The one with no name."

Electricity ran up Seth's spine.

"Are you ready?" Elaine asked. She clicked the button on the handle of the lighter.

"Cool cake, Mrs. R." Christie said. Jules echoed her.

As she lit the candles, they sang. "Happy birthday to you. Happy birthday to you. Happy birthday, dear Olivia. Happy birthday to you."

Except Seth. His eyes were still on Tommy.

Jules and Christie clapped while Olivia bowed. "Cut the cake!"

Seth saw it first. Saw Tommy grab the knife. He lunged, pulling it from the boy's hands. "That's not for you." He handed the instrument to his mother.

Tommy's eyes narrowed. "I was gonna cut the cake."

Something echoed in Seth's mind, over and over like ripples on water. *I was gonna cut the cake. I was gonna cut the cake. I was . . . I was . . . gonna cut you. Gonna cut you. Cut you.* It had to be the thing in his mind. On his back. Wound through his brain. But when he saw the kid, he loathed him.

"Only adults can use that knife, Tommy." Elaine dished up slices of cake with scoops of vanilla ice cream. "I'll never understand your interest in the paranormal, O." She handed her foster daughter the first plate.

"I don't know," she shrugged. "Maybe I was a witch in a former life. Maybe even burned at the stake. Or, I could have been a shaman. Reborn now for some greater purpose."

"I suppose anything is possible."

"Who knows? I could have been a table-shaker fake from the 1800s, you know, like one of the Fox sisters or something, here to pay for my indiscretions." Olivia's eyes lit up as she gasped. "I could be the reincarnation of Lorraine Warren!"

Christie shook her head. "Didn't she just pass a couple of years ago?"

"Yeah, but wouldn't it be something?"

Jules laughed. "Yeah. But it doesn't work that way."

Olivia pinched the bridge of her nose. "Work with me, Jules."

Seth waited to be handed a plate, then turned on his heel and left. He had no humor to joke with the girls any longer and couldn't remain in the room with that boy. He was holding on to his sanity as tightly as he could, but something was peeling his fingers away, one by one.

"Is he coming back for presents?" Olivia asked after Seth walked away.

"I don't think so, O. You know how he is with those headaches.

It's probably best if he can lay down for a while."

Olivia agreed and licked the ice cream off her spoon. She savored the vanilla chill on her tongue mixed with the chocolate shavings from the cake.

As the girls finished, Elaine wrapped the remaining sandwiches in plastic and put them and the soda away. "You all know where the garbage is. When you're done, if you'd just drop everything in there, I'd appreciate it."

"Not a problem, Mrs. R.," Christie said, already on her feet.

Tommy jumped up. "Present time!" He ran to the living room and sat on the edge of the sofa closest to the pile of gifts. "Present time!"

"That boy is a ball of energy," Elaine said. She took the dishrag off the faucet and ran it under warm water. "Just a minute, Tom-Tom. I need to wipe down the table."

"Okay."

The girls wandered in, and Jules took the cushion beside her little friend. Christie and Olivia sat on the floor. Elaine walked in and sat in the recliner. She smoothed her skirt across her knees. "Which one do you want to start with?"

Olivia perused the gifts, large and small, in front of her. She reached for a medium-sized box, wrapped in black and orange paper.

"Sticking with your spooky theme," said Christie.

She tried to carefully undo the tape but gave in and ripped the paper. "Cool! All You Ever Wanted to Know About Ghosts but were Afraid to Ask! Thank you." She flipped through the pages. "You know, I could probably write a few chapters here, myself."

"Yeah, yeah, sure. I thought you'd like it, though." Christie set her soda cup on the end table.

"Next present!" Tommy said. He was excited for her to get to what he'd made. "The little one. The little one next."

"This one?" Olivia picked up the box beside the tiniest present.

"No, the little one." He pointed.

"This one?" She picked up one farther away.

"No! This one!" He jumped off the sofa and grabbed a tiny jar, wrapped in red construction paper and twine. "It's from me."

Olivia took the gift. She untied the twine, taking her time. He could hardly contain himself. As the paper fell from the small jar, he yelled, "It's a ghost! I made it myself."

She turned it over, examining it. There was a small cotton ball inside with two googly eyes glued to it. "Aww, thank you. I love it." She set it on the mantel above the fireplace. "I think he looks good right there."

Self-satisfied and proud, Tommy climbed up next to Jules. He rested his head on her shoulder. "Open the big one."

Olivia reached out her hand and touched it, then directed her attention to her foster mother.

"If you'd like," Elaine said.

She grabbed a smaller one to its left. "I'll leave that one for a bit."

Olivia unwrapped another book. Dream Interpretations and Symbols, from Christie, then a small crystal ball on a stand. "Perfect for my night table, thanks, Jules." The floor became a sea of crumpled paper.

Next was a mini backpack with a crow on it. "Oh, Christie. Where'd you find it? Wow." She turned it over in her hands, checking out every angle. "So cool."

"I have my ways. Glad you like it."

"Thank you."

Two presents were left, the large flat one she knew her foster mom had brought from Tommy's house, and a small box covered in flowery paper with an elegant "Happy Birthday" scrolled across it. A stray card lay on the floor beside them.

She grabbed the box.

"From me," Elaine said, as if Olivia couldn't guess from her style of gift paper. "I hope you can use it." She pressed her lips together to contain her smile.

"What?" Olivia asked. "What did you do?" She tore at the wrap and her jaw dropped. "A voice recorder? You got me a voice recorder?" She bounded to the recliner and hugged Elaine as hard as she could. "Thank you! How did you know I wanted one so much?"

"Oh, please. You practically had it tattooed across your forehead."

Jules snorted. "You so did."

"Well, thank you." She turned to her friends. "You know, we're setting this out tonight."

"There are extra batteries in the junk drawer for you."

Olivia beamed. "Wow . . . just wow." She rested it in her lap while she considered the remaining present. The card sat at her feet. She picked it up, letting it spin on its corners between her fingers. The postmark read Hartville, Wyoming. Her grandmother must've driven there, just for the postmark. Or maybe moved. She didn't know and didn't care all that much, she told herself. She slid her finger under the flap and lifted.

"Ouch. Figures," she said. She sucked at the paper cut before taking the card from the envelope.

"Who's it from?" Christie asked. She bent forward to see better.

"My grandmother. Mom's mom. Out in Wyoming."

Jules shot Christie a look that perhaps this wasn't a subject Olivia wanted to talk about.

"Neat."

"Haven't seen her since I was five. She sends a card once in a while. I don't really remember her."

"It's nice she thinks of you."

Olivia nodded. It was a Valentine's Day card, bright red with frilly hearts and lace. Happy Birthday was scrawled in messy handwriting across the top. "She still thinks I'm five."

"Young at heart, O. Fifteen's kind of grown but still young at heart," Elaine said.

While she read the inside, a gift card fell onto her lap. She eyed it a moment, as if it was going to sprout legs, then picked it up. "I suppose I could use it at a bookstore. Books and More has a sale coming up." Her shoulders relaxed and she tucked the card into her pocket. "I've been eyeing a book there on demons."

Christie slapped her thigh. "Really?"

"A how-to guide. A 'how to summon and get them to do your bidding' kind of thing." A pause. "You know, I'm kidding. Right, Christie?" She shoved her friend's leg with her foot.

"Do I? Do I really?"

They all laughed.

Olivia crinkled her eyes. "I'll send a thank you note if we have her address."

"It's on the envelope. I'll save it for you."

Olivia set the card beside her other presents. She pulled over the tall, flat one. "Yikes."

"Just be careful, there's glass."

"I can feel it."

She tore the paper down the front of the frame. It was the most gorgeous print of a crow that she'd ever seen.

"My first mommy took that picture!"

Olivia had forgotten Tommy was there, and she didn't know what to say. She felt awkward and uncomfortable, but in utter awe of the bird before her. "It's lovely, Tommy. It's amazing."

"I know!"

"We'll hang it in my bedroom, okay?"

"Oh, yes!"

"I'll help you when you're ready to hang it up." Elaine gathered the balls of paper. "Oh, and there's one more present. I nearly forgot." She reached behind the recliner for a long, tube-like pole, covered with three different, non-matching papers. At least one was Christmas, in reds and greens, while another might have been for a baby shower in pastels. Written in black sharpie up the side was, "Happy birthday, Olive."

"A pole? He gave me a pole?" She held the thing at arm's length, trying to understand what the deal was.

Elaine stepped back. "Open it."

He'd sealed the ends with duct tape, and along the seam in the back. "What a pain in my butt." She dug her fingernails into the edges of the tape, trying to get even the slightest piece to peel back. No dice. Finally, she ripped the paper down the front of the thing. It tore and she slid it off like a sock.

He'd given her a walking stick. Hand carved. Nothing fancy, just straight and strong. "He made this?" She ran her hand down the smooth piece of wood. "It must have taken him forever."

Jules walked over to admire it. "Nice job, Silas," she said.

Olivia echoed her. "Nice job, Silas." She whispered to Elaine. "But I don't hike."

The woman shrugged. "He thought you'd like it." She began scooping up the balls of paper into a garbage bag. Christie stood to help.

Olivia rested the walking stick beside the fireplace. "What a great birthday. I think it's time for some games."

"Something we all can play before you and your minions retreat to your room for the night?" Elaine asked. She tied the garbage bag shut and slung it over her shoulder.

"Why, yes, Santa," Olivia said. "Absolutely." She bowed.

"Ho, ho, ho! Happy birthday!"

The girls sat on the floor with Tommy while Elaine deposited the bag in the kitchen then joined them. "What are we playing?"

"How about Cadavre Exquis?"

"Ca- what?" Jules said.

"It's like Exquisite Corpses, but with words. We have a piece of paper, and each person writes a line down from the story we're making. You fold the edge of the paper over your line and pass it around the circle. We each add to it and in the end have a wonderful, creepy, disjointed story."

"It might be interesting. At least it's not ghost filled," Christie said.

"Yeah, it will be. Olivia's involved."

"Let's give it a go. I'll help Tommy," Elaine said. She leaned over to whisper to him. "When it's your turn, you whisper what you want me to write."

The boy nodded.

"Okay. This story is going to be about an old, empty house. I'll start." Olivia took a piece of paper from the end table by the sofa and a pen out of its drawer. She wrote.

It was a dark and stormy night and the old house up on the hill looked creepy.

She folded the paper and handed it to Christie with a satisfied smile. Christie tapped her chin with the pen. "How do I know where you left off?"

"You don't. That's the fun of it."

She giggled.

The broom swept the dust from the corners of the room as if someone was cleaning. But no one was there.

A fold, a pass. Jules took the paper and immediately started writing.

She didn't know why she still loved him after all these years. Those dark, staring eyes. Those abs. He'd left her standing on the beach alone. All because of that old house.

"You're not writing a book, Jules. Just a line," Olivia joked.

Elaine took the paper next.

No one had been in that old house for many, many years. Ever since the sea captain had passed away.

"And you, Tommy? What do you want your part of the story to be?"

Without hesitation, he cupped his hand to Elaine's ear and whispered, "And a black cat walked by."

"Good one," she said as she wrote. "I like that." She handed the paper back to Olivia. "How many times should we pass it?"

"I don't know. A few."

"Let's read it now!" Tommy sat on Elaine's lap. "I want to hear the story."

"Soon, little man. Let's make it just a little longer." She stroked his hair. "And, after we read it, it'll be time for bed."

"Noooo."

"Yup. The girls will still be here in the morning. You can see them then. But little boys need their sleep."

"Okay. After the story."

"Yes."

After a few more rounds, Olivia unraveled the finished product like a scroll, and read.

It was a dark and stormy night and the old house up on the hill looked creepy.

The broom swept the dust from the corners of the room as if someone was cleaning. But no one was there.

She didn't know why she still loved him after all these years. Those dark, staring eyes. Those abs. He'd left her standing on the beach alone. All because of that old house.

No one had been in that old house for many, many years. Ever since the sea captain had passed away.

And a black cat walked by.

The furniture was covered in old sheets and cobwebs were everywhere. Thick dust coated the floor.

The door under the sink opened. A can of cleanser and some sponges toppled out.

She rested a hand on her heart. Despair filled her bones. She knew what she had to do. Knew if she ever wanted him to return, she'd have to take matters into her own hands.

Old Grey Beard retired from the sea and had moved to the house to get away from it all.

And a black cat walked by.

The door to the basement opened with a dull creak. It was there. It was waiting.

A bucket sat in the sink, waiting to be filled with water that never came. The pipes were dry.

She brushed the dirt off her wedding dress and repositioned her tiara.

Old Grey Beard stood at the window, staring off to sea.

And a black cat walked by.

"Wow. Way to show off your cleaning skills, Christie." Jules snickered.

"Yeah? And what are you? A romance writer? Those abs! Those piercing eyes! Maybe Seth should have played."

Jules threw a pillow at her. "Maybe he should have."

"Girls, girls," said Olivia. "I do believe that Tommy's lines were the best and most appropriate to the genre. Black cats and haunted houses are the best."

His eyes shined and he snuggled into Elaine.

"You know, it's almost a poetic little ditty."

"I like it," said Olivia.

"And with that, it's bedtime." Elaine stood and stretched. "Maybe for me, too."

"Oh, Mom. It's only nine o'clock."

She held up her palm. "As much as I'd love to watch some gory horror romp through a girl's summer camp or some such movie you have planned, I will happily go to my room and lose myself in a book for a few hours. Enjoy your sleepover, girls. If there's anything you need, feel free to knock on my door. You have the run of the house, the television, refrigerator. Just please don't wake me up after midnight unless it's an emergency."

Olivia gave her foster mother a tight squeeze. "Thank you."

"Enjoy the rest of your birthday, sweetie." Elaine took Tommy by the hand and led him down the hall. "Good-night, girls."

"Night, Mrs. R.," they echoed.

"Night, girls!" Tommy said. "We're playing in the morning." He looked up into Elaine's face. "They said they'd play."

"That'll be nice. But first, pajamas, brushed teeth and a good night's sleep."

Olivia watched them walk away and said, "I, for one, think getting into pajamas sounds amazing. Who's in?"

"Me!" Jules raised her hand.

"I'm sleeping in my sweats, so I'm good."

"We might as well grab our things and set up in your room, Olivia."

"Let's do it." She picked Christie's pillow up off the pile, turning it over in her hands. "Eeyore? Really?"

"What's wrong with Eeyore? He's sadly charming and the most misunderstood." She grabbed the pillow and hit Olivia with it, surprising her.

"Nice one. But revenge is a dish." She dove for a sofa pillow, swinging it in an arc around her body. "And I'll be serving it up!" She whacked Christie on the back, sweeping the area. Jules ran behind the recliner.

"I give, I give," Christie said between laughs. "Let's get set up."

"Okay. A truce." Olivia held out her hand and let the pillow drop to the floor without removing her gaze from Christie. She two-fingered pointed from her eyes to her friend's. "For now."

Jules coughed. "You're ridiculous."

"And you think you're safe?"

"Not in this house," she smirked. "Not for a minute."

"Smart woman," Olivia said. "Let's get this party started."

# # #

As they walked into her room, a loud, long creak sounded from the speaker on Olivia's desk. She ran to hit the off switch, juggling the gifts in her arms. Jules reached behind the little black box for her, wedging her finger into the tiny hole where the button resided.

"Thanks, girl."

"You got it." She finger-gunned her friend.

"Where do you think we should put the recorder tonight?" Olivia let her presents gently topple from her arms to the bed.

"Where do you want this?" Christie held the walking stick out to her side, her sleeping bag and pillow gripped tightly in her left hand.

"Here."

Christie handed it to her. Olivia ran her hand along the smooth piece of wood, appreciating the time her brother must have put into making it. Placing its end on the floor, she twirled it, catching it before it fell. "It's cool and all, but when would I ever use it? Silas is the outdoor person in the house."

Jules pushed up a pair of nonexistent glasses by the nosepiece and said in her best English accent, "I haven't the foggiest."

Olivia climbed into her closet, positioning the walking stick beside the backpack. Working her way out, stepping over her laundry basket, she said, "Where should we put my recorder?" She took it off the bed and examined the controls. "I mean, we need to try it before we're out in the field."

Christie unrolled her sleeping bag. "Out in what field?"

"The. Paranormal. Field. Christina." Olivia enunciated every syllable.

Jules was in the corner of the room, changing. She pulled a NIN tee shirt over her head and fluffed out her hair. "I vote for Seth's room." She stared at the other two girls, her cheeks growing red. She blinked her eyes. "What?"

"Seth's it is!"

"Wait, what? We're going to ask Seth if we can put a recorder in his room tonight?" Christie asked. "What do you think you're going to hear?"

"No. We'll sneak it in without him knowing. We'll retrieve it tomorrow and have a listen." She smacked her blanket and sat. "I think it's a great test."

"And what do you think you're going to hear?"

Before Olivia could answer, Jules began moaning. Regular, rhythmic groans.

Christie shook her head and put her hand over her face.

"God, I hope not." Olivia rolled her eyes. "But I guess it could happen." She giggled. "But maybe we'll get some EVP's. Some good ole ghostly phenomenon."

"Should you be doing that in your own house? What if it stirs up some ghosts? I'd be afraid of bringing them in."

"You're afraid of your shadow, Christie." Jules ducked as Christie pretended to throw Eeyore one more time.

"I just think you should be careful in your own home."

"And I will be. But listening to see if a spirit wants to say hello won't hurt."

"I'll listen. But if anything says hello, I'll be out that front door faster than you can say boo."

"Boo!"

This time the pillow flew straight at Jules, and she fell to her sleeping bag in over-exaggerated death throes.

"Listen. Were you afraid of your grandfather when he was alive?" Olivia's tone changed. Serious, now, explaining her passion and philosophy.

"Of course not."

"Then why would you be afraid of his ghost? Still the same guy, just incorporeal."

"I don't know. It's just not my thing."

"And that's cool. But it's my thing. My super thing."

"What about evil? Demons and devils?"

"Your upbringing is showing." Jules added, sprawled across her bag. "All the hellfire and brimstone. It's weighing down your mind. You need to be receptive to new ideas."

"I, for one," Olivia continued, "don't believe in the devil. There's no horny guy-"

Jules snickered, almost unable to contain herself.

"No horned guy, I should say."

Burying her face in her pillow, Jules let Olivia continue.

"No red-skinned animal-man waiting with a pitchfork to doom souls to forever torment. I'm not buying it. As for demons and tormentor-type things, I guess they exist. But maybe they're from some other dimension. Or they're just negative aspects of other positive things. I don't know. But I'll be studying up on them as I go. Knowledge is a wonderful thing." She winked at Christie. "For now, we'll be careful and if there's anything negative, we'll keep our distance."

"Who's we?"

Jules chimed in, jumping up. She raised her arms as if directing traffic. "Step away from the demon!"

"Well, I assumed we'd all ghost hunt together. At some point." She tucked her new books between two crow bookends on her desk, next to her other paranormal tomes. "I mean, you do support me in my endeavors, yes?"

Christie sighed. "Yes. Yes, I do. Just don't get me eaten by some Bigfoot alien ghoul-thing, okay?"

"Cross my heart. If some Bigfoot alien ghoul-thing comes along, we feed him Jules."

When their laughing died down, Jules said, "I'm thinking of changing my name." She pulled the plastic container with Olivia's nail polishes off the shelf and started going through it.

"To what?" Christie shoved her bag under Olivia's bed.

"Jewels."

"That is your name."

"No. J-e-w-e-l-s. Sparkly. But one name, like Madonna or Cher."

"Isn't there already a singer by that name?"

"This has an 's' on the end. Anyway, it's been on my mind."

"You're not a singer. What will people know you for?"

"Do they need to? I can just be Jewels the cashier or Jewels the insurance rep. Make a name for myself in an industry."

"Jewels, the day-drinking hobo."

She shrugged. "Everyone needs a hobby."

Olivia flopped onto her bed and stared at her ceiling. Her eyes followed a small crack that started at the corner and ran halfway across her wall. She traced it with her toes. "I had a dream last night."

"Oh?" Christie was examining the crystals on Olivia's desk.

"What about?" Jules asked. She'd decided on a bottle of bright red polish.

"I remember being on the side of a mountain, looking out over a city. It was night. And I knew, I just knew, if I snapped my fingers," she snapped them, for effect, "all the lights would go out."

"The lights in the city?"

"In the world."

Christie spoke first. "Interesting. You should look it up in your dream book."

"I will."

"You know, not everything is paranormal. It probably means the opposite, anyway. Like, you're scared of failing Mr. Peterson's geometry test and your mind decided to enact a power outage to close school."

"I dreamed I walked into his class naked." Jules held up an old piece of bubble gum, still in the wrapper, that was at the bottom of the polish bucket. Olivia shook her head yes.

"Besides," Christie went on, "what would it mean, anyway? You're going to take over the world?" She smirked. "I'd like to see that."

"Yeah, you're probably right. But on the other hand, if it is a premonition, you'll want to stick by me."

Jules chimed in. "Use your powers for good, Olivia. There's enough bad in this world."

"No guarantees. Muahaha!" Olivia laughed so hard, she cried.

Tommy lay in bed, listening to the muffled sounds of the girls in Olivia's room. Feeling the thing in Seth's. It pulsed with fear-anger whenever he thought about it. That didn't bother him, though. It would be gone soon enough. He reached over the edge of the bed for the orange front loader on the floor. He drove it under his blanket while he waited.

A shadow formed in the mudroom and coalesced into the shape of a man. Tommy smiled. It was tall, nearly bumping its head as it moved through his doorway, shrinking to the size of a boy. By the time it was beside his bed, it was the size and shape of a cat and hopped up next to him. It curled into a ball of buzzing flies.

"Hello, Jetty," Tommy said. He cuddled his best friend and went to sleep.

The girls stood behind Olivia's door, tense with anticipation. Nervous with adrenalin. A noise. "Was that the bathroom door?" Olivia held the voice recorder, ready to move.

Jules peeked. "Yes! Code red, code red," she whispered.

"Red?" Christie bobbed behind Jules' shoulder, trying to see.

"I don't know, let's go. Hurry!"

The girls moved urgently, a rushed tiptoeing to Seth's room. Christie stood lookout while Olivia and Jules turned the doorknob together, holding their breath, and gained entry. Olivia stood, unmoving. She couldn't walk forward. It was as though an invisible shield barred her from entering. A force. Something didn't want her in that room.

"Olivia?" Jules whispered.

"I-"

"Come on, he won't catch us. Here, give it to me." Jules took the voice recorder and dashed inside. She searched for a spot where it wouldn't be obvious and hit record. "It's got a red 'on' light. Olivia, how is he not going to notice that?"

A draft circled Christie. "Why's it so cold?" She rubbed her arms.

"Must have the window a crack or something." She set the recorder under his bed. "He'll never see it there." She glanced at the corner of the room and slowly up to the ceiling. It felt dark there. A dead darkness she didn't like.

"Code red!" A shrill whisper came from the hallway. "The toilet's flushing!"

Jules shoved Olivia, tripping over her, then Christie, as Seth stepped out of the bathroom.

"What the hell is up with you three?"

"Nothing, nothing." They giggled, nervous he might suspect something. "Just getting a snack."

"Yes! A snack!"

They ran into the kitchen, erupting once more into laughter as they fell over each other. Jules spied around the corner. "The coast is clear." She collapsed into a chair at the dining room table. "What's up with his room, anyway? I expected some band posters, Axe Body Spray bottles lying about, a tee shirt I could swipe."

"Geez, Jules." Christie shook her head. "You've got it bad."

"Guilty. Got to admit, he is a hunky thing."

Olivia covered her face with her arm, holding up her palm. "Stop, stop! My brain is going to burst and run out my ears."

Jules shrugged. "What can I say?"

"That you're horny and he's a warm body?"

Jules chuckled. "Where's Eeyore when you need him?" She slid the saltshaker at Olivia, who caught it at the edge of the table and tossed a pinch over her left shoulder.

"Nobody's throwing Eeyore anymore tonight. Tell me more about this burning love you have for Olivia's brother." She bent forward, elbows on the table. "And what was his room like?"

Olivia eyed her friends, sitting back in her chair and crossing her arms. "And at what point did he become a hottie?"

"Let's talk about his room." Jules let the corners of her mouth turn upward a little, keeping her secret-not-a-secret a little longer.

"Tell me." Christie slid closer.

"You, too?" Olivia said. "Am I missing something?"

"He's your brother. You can't be into him," Jules said.

"Foster brother. But I still don't get it. Silas just ain't that hot."

Another snicker from Christie. Jules ignored it. She shook some pepper onto the table and ran her finger through it in a swirl as she changed the subject. "It was cold in there. Weird cold, and I didn't see a window ajar anywhere. It seemed like the place of someone who didn't care. A real mess. Not like a regular mess, though. I can't describe it. Cold."

"Dark. It felt very dark to me."

Jules nodded.

"You could have turned on a light," Christie added, suppressing a laugh. Something she did when the conversation was going to take a path she didn't want to consider.

Olivia side-eyed her. "Could have. Don't think it would have felt much different."

Jules, intent on the black pepper designs she was making, said, "Nope. Something's off in there. Do you think it has to do with his friend's death?"

"Maybe." Olivia thought it sounded like a reasonable explanation but didn't put any stock into it. The investigator in her couldn't wait to listen to the recorder in the morning. Her instincts were nagging at her, and not in a good way. "He's seeing a therapist. Maybe it'll all get better soon."

"I hope so." Jules wiped the pepper off the table and dumped it into the trash.

"Let's watch a movie. You pick, Olivia. I'd even watch Dr. Sleep again."

"You're on!"

Chapter 13

The girls piled into the kitchen through the sliding glass door, depositing Dunkin' Donuts bags and two cardboard cupholders onto the table. Olivia divvied up the drinks. Elaine walked in, tying the belt of her bathrobe, with Tommy not far behind. "You girls were up early."

"Yes, we were," said Olivia. "This one is for you." She handed over a tall Dunkin' cup. "Black with a splash of creamer."

"Thank you." She pried up the plastic top and breathed in the steam. "Ah, exactly how I like it."

Jules took the corner cup and sat with a satisfied smile.

"I don't know how you all like coffee so much." Christie reached for the plastic bottle of orange juice, cracking the seal. "This is cold and refreshing."

"It's an acquired taste. You just haven't acquired it yet," said Jules.

"And don't plan on it."

"What's in the bags?" Tommy poked one, listening to it rustle. "I don't like coffee."

"We got you chocolate milk."

"Oh, I like that."

"And the bags have muffins. Blueberry, chocolate chip. There might even be a banana or corn muffin. I'm not sure." She unfolded a few napkins and laid everything out. Tommy picked blueberry.

"You girls went all out this morning."

"I wanted to say thank you for my party," said Olivia. "And my babysitting money was burning a hole in my pocket."

Elaine laughed. "Well, it's much appreciated. And you're

welcome."

"The soda is for Silas."

"Really? For breakfast?"

"It's what he likes." She unfolded a napkin. Reaching for a chocolate chip muffin, she said, "He can drink it whenever. I didn't want to leave him out."

Elaine raised her cup. "You're a good kid."

"And it might soften his disposition."

Seth appeared from the hallway, stretching the drawstring of his pants. "What will?"

"The soda I picked up for you."

He grabbed the bottle and held it against his forehead. "Thanks, Olive, but it won't. Oh! Muffins."

"Have a good breakfast, son. I need you to do that yardwork today." Elaine took a swig of her coffee, relishing it. "It's going to be a beautiful day and if you're not going to school this semester, you've got to kick in a little extra time for me."

He let out a short and unconvincing moan.

"Gutters and rake the lawn. It'll be quick."

"You know it's not quick, Mom."

"It won't take that long. An hour or so? The season is getting late, and we'll be running out of time before a storm blows in. I don't want the leaves to freeze in the gutter and give us bigger issues."

"An hour? You think it'll take that long?" He threw himself at the refrigerator, arm across his forehead in a swoon.

The girls snickered.

"Just don't wait too long. You can't see to rake in the dark."

"Yes, ma'am." He saluted his mother, stuffed half a blueberry muffin into his mouth and left.

Elaine shook her head. "That boy'll be the death of me some day."

"Let's hope not."

"Not me." Tommy said between bites of muffin. There were crumbs across his chin. "He won't get me."

"What?" Elaine asked. "Oh, honey. I was joking."

"I know." Another bite, swallow. "But he won't get me."

She frowned. "Why do you think he'd want to? He wouldn't hurt a fly."

"He doesn't like me."

"Yes, he does."

Tommy shook his head, peeling back more of the cupcake wrapper on his muffin. Crumbs poured onto the table. "It's okay," he said. "I don't like him, either." He swiped the crumbs and wrapper into his hand and walked them to the trash. Picking up Iggy's squeaky toy, he said, "Come on, puppy! Let's go play." He ran into the living room. Iggy scampered after him, toenails clicking against the wood floor.

Elaine looked at Olivia. "I wonder if I should be concerned."

"I don't think so. He just hasn't gotten to know Silas yet. I mean Seth."

"That's got to be it, Mrs. R.," Christie said. "Seth can come on strong, and it may take Tommy a little while to get used to him."

Jules swallowed, setting her cup on the table. "It may be that he hasn't had a male role model, either. Not that Seth's a role model, am I right?" She raised her hand to high-five Olivia, and then embarrassment clicked in that Elaine was sitting right there. "Just kidding, Mrs. R." She lowered her hand.

"Not a problem, Jules."

"I just meant that maybe the kid isn't used to being with men. Olivia said he lived with his mom. Who knows how much contact he's had with the opposite sex?"

"It's his sex, Jules," Christie said.

"You know what I mean." She rolled her eyes. "The opposite sex of his mother."

"Bizarre."

"That could be it," Elaine said. "I just don't want to miss something. He hasn't done any grieving or even shown that he's missed his mom."

"Maybe he's in shock?"

"I don't know. Maybe. But it might be good for him to spend some time with Seth. Get to know him. Do a little male bonding. It might be good for both of them."

A rhythmic squeak, squeak, squeak got louder as it got closer, along with a giggle. "It was me. I was squeezing it." He gave it a long, hard squeeze to punctuate the point. "Can I have another muffin?"

"What do you say?" Elaine asked.

"Please?"

"Of course, you can. But when you're done, I want you to get dressed, brush your teeth and then you can go outside while Seth does a little work."

"Can I help?"

"I'm sure he'll let you do something."

"Okay!" He picked up a muffin and dug in.

The girls gathered in Olivia's room, leaving the door ajar. Olivia stood at the corner, while Jules and Christie were behind it, periodically peeking.

"Can you see anything?" Christie whispered. "All I can see is Jules' big head."

"You're lucky it's my head and not my butt you're staring at."

"Hey, what did you call me?" Olivia said, holding back laughter and any sound that could call attention to their hiding spot.

"Why's it taking him so long to get dressed? It's not like shedding a hoodie and sweats takes any time."

"Who knows? Silas moves at Silas' speed." Olivia pretended to run in slow motion to her desk and back. "A sloth is as a sloth does." She bit her tongue, falling against her friends.

Jules and Christie couldn't contain themselves any longer. Giddy with apprehension, they gripped each other's hands. As Seth stepped out of his room, he heard them tittering.

"What is wrong with you guys?"

Olivia kicked her door shut, waited, then cracked it open. She listened as her foster mother told him to wear a jacket, to take Tommy along. There was a slight complaint at that, but he acquiesced. Maybe he was learning. Doubtful.

When the patio door closed, Olivia and her crew tiptoed to his room. Christie brought up the rear. "How are we going to do this?" She glanced over her shoulder, half expecting Seth to somehow jump them from behind.

"How do you think? We're stepping inside, Olivia grabs the voice recorder and we run like madmen back to her room."

Christie nodded, agreeing with the plan before her. Another glance.

"What do you keep looking at?" Jules didn't even try to veil her annoyance.

"It feels like we're being watched."

"Why are you always the first one spooked?"

"I'm not spooked. I just feel like something's there."

Jules held her palm in the air. "Hence, spooked. All we're doing is retrieving the recorder."

"And listening to it," Olivia said. She rushed to Seth's bed and reached beneath it for the recorder. She couldn't find it.

Panic set in. She laid on her side and fished back and forth, getting grossed out by the sheer thickness of the dust. She pushed a little farther, her shoulder pressing into the metal bedframe, and touched a piece of plastic. "Almost there," she said. "Almost have it." One last shove and it was clenched in her hand. "Go, go, go!"

They scrambled back to her room, slamming the door and leaning against it, panting.

"What's wrong with us?"

"I don't know, and I don't care," Olivia said, holding up the recorder like a prize. "But we have this!"

Seth rested the rake against the side of the house and carried the ladder out of the garage. He set it up beside the front steps. Securing the base, he climbed, waving to his mother as he passed the picture window. The sun felt good on his back; the heat easing his aching muscles. Maybe it'd help his scratches heal. Not that there was any point to that. He'd just have more tonight.

At the top of the ladder, he pulled on a pair of work gloves. They were stained and stiff, but the leather felt good against his skin. He grabbed thick piles of damp leaves and dropped them onto the stones below.

Tommy stepped outside. "Why are you doing that?" He was still in pajamas but with his jacket on.

"Mom asked me to. You were there."

"But why?" He circled the bottom of the ladder to get a better view of what Seth was doing.

Seth exhaled. "If you leave the leaves up here, they block the gutter. It ices and winter snow has nowhere to go. It saves the gutter."

"It's not going to save you."

"What?"

Tommy ducked under it, humming London Bridge is Falling Down and hit the ladder with his shoulder on his last run through.

"Hey!" Seth startled and threw a handful of muck at the boy, hitting him square in the back of the head. "You don't mess with people on ladders."

Tommy squinted at Seth. "I'll tell New Mommy you did that."

"Whatever." Seth scooped another nasty gutter-clog onto the ground.

Tommy ran to get the rake and dragged it behind him down the driveway. The scratching sound bore through Seth's brain, and he pressed his face into his shoulder in an attempt to shut it out. Fingernails on a blackboard. Freddy Krueger knife-nails.

Tommy veered onto the grass before Seth could scream at him. The sound calmed to the metallic ping of the tines as they got stuck, bounced and hit the ground.

Seth worked his way to the side, stopping to move the ladder every few feet. Clumps of leaves littered the perimeter of the house. Nothing that couldn't be cleaned up later or left for spring.

"Hey, kid."

Tommy was laying in his current leaf pile, among the many he'd made. He'd been following a wooly bear. "Yeah?"

"I'm going to need that rake in a few minutes. When I go to the back of the house."

"Okay."

He picked up the ladder, carrying it around the corner and out of Tommy's sight. "When I yell, bring it to me. Okay?"

"Okay."

"Okay?" he called, louder than the first.

"Okay!"

Jules and Christie crowded onto Olivia's bed, and she clicked the silver button. Play. Olivia clutched her pillow in eager excitement.

They heard movement. Mumbling.

"What is he saying?" Christie asked.

"Shh." Olivia cut her off. "I can't hear." She rewound to the beginning, turning up the volume.

Step, step, step, step.
Step, step, step, step.

Softer footsteps, then louder. Closer. Olivia paused the recording. "Pacing."

"And rubbing his arms, I think."

"Arms. Right." Jules said. She snickered at the thought.

"Serious, Jules," Olivia said. "It's pretty cold in there." She hit play.

Just let me sleep tonight. Just let me sleep. Just let me sleep.

It became a chant. A mantra. As if he wasn't even aware that he was repeating the phrase over and over. And then they heard a guttural growl.

No

Olivia jammed down the stop button. She paled and stared at the piece of equipment in her hand. She'd known something felt off. At once, she was intrigued and concerned.

"What the hell was that?" Jules was bent over the recorder, watching it like a television. She took a hold of Olivia's arm, digging fingernails into her skin. "Did something say 'no'?"

Christie's eyes were closed, her lips moving as she silently recited the Lord's Prayer.

Olivia knew she had to diffuse the tension for her friends but needed to hear it once more. She hit rewind.

"Don't play it, Olivia." Christie was saying. "That's some next-level wrong."

"Cover your ears, my dear. I'm playing it one more time."

Christie did as her friend instructed and moved to the window. She watched Milo and another crow at the bath.

Jules and Olivia heard it again as they had the first time. Olivia clicked it off. She wanted to let it run, listen to the entire recording, but she knew better. This was personal. This was hers. "Nah. It's not a 'no,' Jules," she lied. "It's like a truck going by or some sort of glitch. A malfunction."

Jules leaned against the wall, arms folded. "Oh, yeah. I've heard that these things can pick up a piece of a radio station sometimes."

That's not how it works, thought Olivia. That's not what the deal is. It wasn't an old-time reel to reel tape machine with static and background noise. Digital was pretty accurate. It had recorded a voice in Seth's room. And it was damned clear.

Christie deposited herself on Olivia's desk chair and rolled to the bed. "I feel so silly. Can't believe I scared myself like that. If it's broken, you should ask Mrs. R. to return it and exchange it."

Olivia agreed and tucked the recorder in the corner of her headboard. "Maybe I'll do that. Come on, let's hang my print before you guys have to leave."

"I'll see if your mom has a level."

"Great idea, Christie. Would hate to have to eyeball it." She winked and Jules giggled, but Olivia's mind wasn't on hanging pictures. Her only thought was on whatever might be in Seth's room. And why.

"Okay, Tommy!" Seth yelled. "I'm ready for the rake!" He waited at the side of the house for Tommy to come running. Nothing. "Come on, kid. You said you'd bring it." His blood pressure was rising as he stood there, waiting for what he was sure wasn't coming. "What's the deal?" He tramped around the corner and saw the rake where he'd left it, with Tommy nowhere in sight. "Figures. He's going to have to learn when you say you're going to do something, you do it."

As he picked it up, a stone hit his right shoulder. He whirled. There was no one he could see. "Tommy! I know it was you. I know you're mad about the leaf pile. Sorry I threw the muck at you, but you don't throw rocks." Before he could take a step, another stone whizzed by. From a different direction. "Quit it, kid. I said I was sorry."

Another. It grazed his forehead and he ducked, shielding his face. "Stop it!" He bobbed left and right, searching for a direction that he could pinpoint as the source, then ran to the side yard. A final stone caught his temple, ripping a small piece of skin. Blood dripped along his cheekbone. "Son of a bitch!"

He threw the rake to the ground and caught sight of Tommy through Olivia's bedroom window. Inside. He was inside. Who was throwing the rocks? He spun. Anxiety gripped his chest. His breathing quickened. What the hell was after him? But that was key, wasn't it? Hell? He shut his eyes and tried to calm himself, but dread washed over him. Like a mouse waiting for a cat to strike, its heart beating like a jackhammer. Sitting statue-still, waiting for impending doom.

He bent for the rake and heard a tap, tap, tap on the window. Olivia lifted it about two inches. "Don't do too much near Milo's spot. Raking churns up all the little bugs and things that are wintering. Kills them."

"Yeah. Sure, Olive."

"Thanks. I told Mom we should. She's okay with that."

"Okay."

As she stepped away from the window, a huge crow, larger than Milo, perched in the tree nearest the bird bath. Vigilant, it kept watch as Seth worked.

Done and done. He dropped onto the sofa, satisfied that his list of chores was finished. Gutters, check. Raking, except for Milo's spot, check. Not a ton of work but he was drained. Supposedly the antidepressant would kick in within the next couple of weeks and maybe then he'd have more energy. Hah. Supposedly, lifting his mood and getting some consistent sleep might fade his hallucinations. If he actually believed they were hallucinations, maybe. If he didn't have a demon breathing down his neck night and day, following his every move. Monitoring every thought.

Unless it was all in his mind.

A chill settled over his shoulders. He wasn't alone. He'd never be alone, and no pill would ever change that. He'd take them, put in the futile effort. But he knew.

A rolled-up piece of paper on the end table caught his attention. He unraveled the scroll and read the first line.

It was a dark and stormy night and the old house up on the hill looked creepy.

One of Olivia's birthday games. Magnificent dead things or something. He smirked, seeing what story the girls came up with. But then he read the last line.

And a black cat walked by.

Every last line.

And a black cat walked by.
A black cat walked
A black cat

The paper shook in his hands, and he let it fall to his lap. Step away. Breathe and realize it was a coincidence. What could a black cat mean, anyway? Seven years bad luck? Or was that if it crossed under a ladder? His hair fell into his eyes, and he pulled down his hood. It was a coincidence. There was no cat, black or otherwise. And why should he be afraid of a cat?

Olivia buttoned her pajama top, slid her feet into her slippers and waited. She knew he'd be coming out soon. He always hit the kitchen for a glass of water and whatever concoction of medication he was taking. Antidepressants, Tylenol, cold medicine, whatever he was going for. He'd be out and she needed to confront him. Have a conversation. Alone.

She heard the familiar click-release of the lock and the soft thud of his socks along the wood floor. She power-walked and caught up with him at the sink.

"Hey."

Seth fumbled, dropping his cup. "Geez, Olive. What the hell?"

"Sorry, Sy." She rocked forward and back on her heels. Water flowed from the faucet while they waited for it to get cold.

"You want something?"

"Can I ask you a question?"

"Ask away." He flipped the handle upward and watched as the drips slowed to a stop.

"What's up with your room?"

He took a single step backward, turning to face her. "What do you mean?" His fear-walls were rising, defenses going up.

"Jules, Christie and I left my voice recorder in your room last night."

"You what?" He couldn't believe what he was hearing. Didn't want to even consider what she just said.

"I'm sorry. We should have asked, but we thought it'd be fun. A prank. I wanted to test out the recorder."

Panic. He felt like a caged lion searching for escape. Wall to wall, iron bars, no way out. "Why would you do that? Really? Why would you fucking do that?" He threw the plastic cup into the sink. It ricocheted and bounced across the floor, coming to rest by the radiator.

Olivia flinched. "I said I was sorry. I mean, it's your private space. I get that. But, man," she looked at the floor, "what we heard."

"No. There's no but. You didn't hear anything. Nothing. And I don't want you in there again."

"Jules put it in for me."

"This keeps getting better! Why'd you send her in?" He was pacing now, the lion threatening to tear its way out of his chest.

"It wouldn't let me in."

He stopped in front of her, voice lower. "What?"

"Whatever is in there stopped me. Like a wall."

"Take that as a warning and stay out."

"What is it, Seth? Tell me." She grabbed his arm and he ripped it away.

"You think you're so knowledgeable about ghosts and spirits and things, but there's stuff out there you need to leave alone. Walk away, Olivia."

"Is our house haunted?"

He glared at her in a tense silence, gauging his response.

"No," he said. "I am." He let the gravity of his words sink in. "This conversation is over."

He stormed out of the room. If things hadn't been bad enough, she was involved now, and he'd never wanted that. Never even conceived of that. He should have. Why would it be satisfied with only him? Why should it ever stop? He'd have to find a way. She'd upped the ante and now he'd have to fight.

Olivia sat on her bed, pulling her knees to her chest. She scooched until she was against the wall, clutching her blanket to her chin. Haunted. She didn't think he was haunted, that was for sure. But something was definitely in his room. Her brain started ticking on all the possibilities, knowing Seth wouldn't be a resource. No fountain of knowledge there. He'd pulled down the metal door of closedmindedness and chained it shut.

"This conversation is over," she mocked. "You just think that, Seth. I'll get my answers, I'll find out what's going on."

Chapter 14

Olivia took the remote out of the cupholder, clicked on the television and locked the recliner's footrest into position. "Come on, Tommy!" She flipped channels until she landed on the Macy's Thanksgiving Day Parade. "It's starting!"

Tommy ran in and climbed up beside her. "Squish over," he said.

"I'm as squished as I can get."

They huddled together as the bands and floats trekked through the city. "I can't believe you've never watched this."

"Nope. My first mommy didn't do Thanksgiving."

Olivia thought that was strange, but it was even weirder that Tommy had decided there was a first and second mommy. It had to be trauma related. Maybe someday she'd get a psych degree and figure it out. She pondered it until they saw the balloon of the big blue dog.

"Bluey!" Tommy sprawled onto the footrest, tipping them precariously close to the floor.

"Careful, kid."

"Oops." He settled in beside her.

Every so often Elaine would peek in from the kitchen. She had too many things to do to watch the parade with them. The turkey, stuffing, green bean casserole, pie. Mashed potatoes, gravy. She perused her jars of seasonings. Sage, rosemary. Cooking for an army of four. But wasn't the best thing about the day? Knowing there'd be leftovers for a week? She dried her hands on the red-checked apron Seth had given her last Christmas.

Seth. Now he was another whole bucket of snakes, as her mother would say. A whole bucket. But maybe therapy would help. And medicine. Help calm him. Let him grieve. Help him let go. She was trying to give him space to deal with his emotions and wondering if he'd need her again. Talk with her. Confide in her. It'd been a long time since he'd done that. Even before Blake's death he had been pulling away. At the time, she'd thought it was a teen thing, but hindsight is twenty-twenty. She should have noticed the warning signs, the red flags. At least he was getting therapy. At least he was talking to someone.

She made a face at the turkey lying on its side in the sink, and grimaced as she slid her hand inside to remove the gizzards. At least he was getting help. She wrinkled her nose, held the bag with two fingers, and gingerly dropped it into the garbage.

After she patted the bird dry with a paper towel, she hefted it into the pan. "What a back breaker," she muttered. "Why do I always buy the biggest bird for a small family?" She sprinkled salt and pepper across the skin, then added a little paprika for color. "There now. That's a happy turkey." She put her hands into bright yellow oven mitts and adjusted the oven rack to its lowest position. "Seth!"

He shuffled into the kitchen as if she'd woken him from a thirty-year coma. "Yeah?"

"Would you put the bird in the oven, please?"

"Sure." He lifted it as she stepped out of the way. "I thought you said last year you'd never buy a huge ass turkey again." Sliding it in, he shut the door with his elbow.

"I'm sure I never said 'huge ass' anything. But a big turkey just feels right."

He smiled. A slight one, but she saw it. Perhaps there was hope.

Elaine pawed through the back of her clothes closet, wishing her home had more storage. No coat closet, no real linen closet, and here she was moving boxes to find a Thanksgiving tablecloth. It happened every year and every year it annoyed her.

She shoved aside a bag with Christmas lights and moved a laundry basket filled with odds and ends, broken hangers and things that had no other place to reside. Her hand brushed a Ziploc bag stuffed with fabric printed with images of pumpkins, gourds and the like. The tablecloth! Success. She noticed Seth's old dart board, still boxed, against the side wall. It took some maneuvering, tipping the laundry basket on its side, trying hard to not let everything dump, but she got it.

She angled the closet doors closed, giving her room its neat as a pin façade, and carried her finds into the living room.

"Olivia, I thought you'd like to set this up. Might be fun later for you and Seth. Heck, I might even give it a whirl. You can hang it at the far end of the hallway." She hoped it'd keep him interacting with them for a little while. Maybe he'd feel the hominess of the holiday. Lighten up and play. Feel better for a little while, if that was possible. It was something fun from his past. She pushed her worries to the back of her mind.

"Sure, Mom," Olivia said. "After the parade?"

"Anytime is fine."

Tommy half-crawled over the side of the chair to see what she was holding. "What's that?"

"A dart board." She read the details on the box. "Metal tipped darts," she read. "You're too young for this type, Tommy. You'll have to watch. But if you like it, maybe we can buy one that's just your size."

"Okay." He plopped himself back into place.

Elaine left to check if the turkey needed basting yet. It didn't, of course, but it was better to concentrate on that than her son. She hummed a repetitive tune and began browning the sausage for the stuffing.

Seth walked into the kitchen, taking a carrot stick off the tray his mother had arranged. "I still don't know why you always make so much food."

"I don't see you minding," she smirked.

He dipped a piece of broccoli into a dish of ranch dressing. "No spinach dip this year?"

"I didn't know if Tommy would like it."

"Our dip revolves around a five-year-old's tastes? What are we having for dinner? Boxed mac and cheese? Oreos for dessert?" Seth dipped a couple of green and red pepper slices and bit the ends off of each.

"Turkey, as usual, sir. Just the dip has changed."

"Hmpf."

"Hmpf, what?"

"I don't see why he gets to dictate everything."

"Dictate?" she said. "He didn't dictate anything. I thought he should be included in case he didn't want spinach."

"You change the dip but leave the vegetables? How do you know he likes vegetables? He's five. He probably hates them."

"All the better for you, then. It was just a thought, give me a break."

"Yeah, yeah."

She wiped off the cutting board. "You're jealous."

He stared at his mother as he chewed until she became uncomfortable and turned to wash the pans that were cooling in the sink. "I can assure you, I'm not."

"Well, you're something. You're hypersensitive where he's concerned."

"I like my spinach dip is all."

Elaine shut off the water and held the edge of the sink. She then turned to her son and gave him a small shove toward the living room. "Out. Let me finish cooking."

"I thought the oven was doing that. You're just hovering."

"Out. Go." She shooed him. "I'll call everyone when it's finished."

# # #

"Hey, check it out." Seth picked up the dart board box, holding it at its corners and spinning it. "We haven't played darts in a long time."

Olivia's gaze remained on the television. "Mom said we could put it up after the parade."

"I'm setting it up now. I'm pretty good, you know."

She sat bolt upright, always ready for a little healthy competition. "But I'm better."

"You're on." Seth lit up. "You'll need some time to practice to get up to snuff. We'll play next month some time?"

Olivia scrambled out of the chair and stood toe to toe with him. "We'll play right now." Tommy scooched to the middle of their seat. "Don't cry too hard when I whoop your," she glanced toward the kitchen and lowered her voice, "ass."

"There'll be an ass whooping," he said. "But it won't be mine."

They ran to the end of the hallway, shoving each other as they went. Seth examined the back of the board. "I need a hammer," he said.

Off like lightning, Olivia ran to the cabinet under the kitchen sink and rummaged through the bucket that held Elaine's "every day" tools, picture hangers, screwdrivers, penny nails.

"What do you need?" Elaine asked.

"Hammer?"

"Junk drawer." She pointed with the turkey baster.

"Thanks!" Olivia ran back to Seth with a small hammer, handing it over as if it was a scalpel to a surgeon. "Hammer."

"No nail?"

She clenched her fists in mock exasperation and returned to the kitchen, digging through the bucket until she found a container of assorted nails and screws. Back at Seth's side, she popped the lid.

"Nail."

"I only need one, Olive. Sheesh." His eyes shined as he searched for one the right size.

"Come on, come on. I can't stand here all day, Silas."

She set the box on the floor at his feet as he tapped a nail into the wall and hung the board.

"There." He admired his work, tilting it until he felt it was level.

Olivia folded her arms. "You could do that for a living."

"Traveling Dart Board Hanger? I sure could." He took a handful of darts out of the box and separated them by color. "Meet you here at midnight? So you can work on your throwing arm."

"Let's go. Now. High noon, pardner. How far back do we have to stand?" She felt inside the box, hoping for instructions or suggestions.

"I think it's eight or nine feet. Like by the bathroom door."

Olivia scooped up the blue darts and moved into place, aiming.

"Whoa, girl." He sidestepped and squat-creeped to her. "Those things are sharp."

"Quack." Hand over her mouth, her shoulders quaked at the sight of him duck-walking. She saluted. "Yes, sir! Are we ready?"

"Ready to kick your butt? Sure am!" Seth threw the first dart, landing four points.

"Hah!"

"Let me warm up."

"Warm up the bench. Let me show you how it's done." Olivia aimed. Just as she was about to throw, Seth pretended to sneeze. She side-eyed him. "Cheater." She threw, hitting the twelve. "Sucker." She bowed and extended her arm for him to take the next shot.

Seth threw. It hit the board with a thunk.

"Twenty. Not bad, not bad."

"Look again, Olive. It's on the ring. That's triple if you please. Try sixty."

"A lucky hit."

"The skill of a marksman."

Olivia readied her dart, taking long and hard to aim. She threw. One point.

"Haha! Who's the sucker?"

She brushed him off. "I'm just warming up."

"That sixty threw you, didn't it?" He poked her side. "Admit it. Knocked your socks off."

"Nah. Just buying time so I can see your face when I hit the bullseye."

"It'll be one of shock because you'll have to pierce my dart to do it."

Seth lined up his throw as Tommy pushed between them, running toward the board.

"I want to play!"

Olivia tried to grab his arm and pull him back, but he slipped through her grasp. A cold breeze trailed him. Seth threw and the dart nicked Tommy's arm, raking his skin. The boy erupted into a crying scream. Olivia scooped him up and Elaine came running.

"What happened? What happened?"

Tommy said, "Him! Him!" through broken sobs as he let go of Olivia and clung to Elaine.

"I'm sure it was an accident. He didn't mean it."

"He did. He did! He hates me."

Elaine went into the bathroom to examine his arm. "There's not even any blood, Tommy man. Just a scratch. You're fine."

"No, no. He hates me." He sniffled as Elaine washed the red welt and put a Spiderman Band-Aid over it.

Olivia dropped her arms to her sides. "Why'd you throw? You were still aiming when he went between us."

"I didn't."

"You didn't what?"

"I didn't throw." He looked stunned, staring at Olivia, then the dart board.

"Don't be a jerk. Own up. If you didn't, who did?"

"Yeah. Who." He turned, tripping over Iggy as he slunk to his bedroom. "Stupid mutt!"

Olivia was sure she saw a faint shadow disappear after him, as a barrier went back up. A shield to her eyes, her sensitivities. A wall to keep her out.

"Yeah," she said. "Who."

He closed the door and fell against it. He hadn't thrown that dart. Knew in his bones he hadn't. When Tommy pushed between them, waves of hatred pulsed from his demon. He heard the growl and watched the dart fly. *It* scratched the boy. And it was plotting. Possessing his thoughts, controlling his actions. Damning him.

Seth slid to the floor. The only thought in his mind was that next time, he'd throw harder.

The knock on his door startled him out of a thick sleep. He woke, still on the floor, clammy and cold. His hoodie was damp. Clingy. A fever dream in the arctic.

"Yeah?" Shaking the cobwebs from his brain, he pulled the shirt off over his head and squinted in the dark for the pile of laundry he hadn't put away.

"Dinner's on the table."

His mouth was sleep-dry as his fingers found a heavy sweatshirt at the bottom of the pile. He tugged it over his head. "I'll be right out." Reaching to his nightstand, he knocked his deodorant stick to the floor. It fell at his feet and when he reached for it, the searing pain down his spine was back. More scratches. More proof this wasn't all in his head as he'd hoped. Unless he'd done it when he was asleep. Yeah, if the floor was made of splintered wood and the back of his hoodie was in tatters. He didn't want to turn on the lights to check.

"Screw deodorant," he muttered. He'd shower later, anyway, washing away the blood that had crusted across his back. He tugged the shirt over his stomach as he unlocked the door.

The smell of turkey made his mouth water and he realized he

hadn't eaten since the day before. His stomach rumbled, an aching emptiness.

"Well," Elaine said. "Someone's hungry."

"Damn, Silas." Olivia was at the table, fork in hand, waiting for him.

Elaine peered over her the top of her glasses. "O."

"Sorry," she said. "Darn, Silas."

The table was elaborately set for the four of them. Crystal water glasses, wooden bread bowl complete with warming towel, and fancy plates with fat turkeys at their centers.

"Ah, the traditional turkey plates."

Elaine stifled a smile. "They're Spode, thank you very much. And they embody the," she pointed at Seth with a spatula, "turkiness of the day." She let it clang into the sink.

Tommy giggled and kicked his feet into the leg of his chair. "Turkiness."

"I thought it would be easier to go buffet-style this year." She stood at the counter, serving fork poised over the meat platter. "White meat or dark, Tommy?"

"I don't know."

"A little of both, maybe?" She placed some on his plate, then scooped mashed potatoes, gravy and green beans beside it. "Here you go."

"Thank you!" He dove in with his spoon, digging into the potatoes first.

"You guys can get your own."

They stood in line behind Elaine, Olivia last. Seth needed to get some food into his stomach, just to calm the ache. To quiet the noise. He stuffed a piece of turkey into his mouth as he put more onto his plate.

"Hey!" Olivia said. "I'm hungry, too, you know. Move on." She elbowed him.

"Back off, O." The exhaustion in his voice surprised her.

She held up her hands. "No problem, man."

He filled his plate and sat between his mother and Olivia.

"The rolls are fresh out of the oven. I figured they were the one thing that we'd have room for on the table, and the one thing everyone goes to for seconds and thirds. And the cranberry sauce."

"I like rolls," said Tommy. "And gravy."

"Well, I'm glad. Don't forget to have some green beans."

He wrinkled his nose and poked one with his fork.

Elaine tore a roll in half and buttered it. "You don't have to eat them all if you don't like them, but I do expect you to taste one."

He pushed the next bean, letting it roll into the mashed potatoes. Once it was covered in gravy, he jammed it into his mouth and chewed with loud, smacking sounds.

Olivia laughed and covered her mouth with a napkin. "They aren't that bad, Tommy. I swear it."

"That bad?" Seth said. The food was helping his demeanor. Elaine handed him the roll and began buttering another.

"You know what I meant, Silas."

"Sure, Olive. Sure, I do." He turned toward his mother. "And you do, too, don't you?"

Olivia snickered.

"All right, you two." Elaine set down her knife. "I want to know what everyone's thankful for."

Seth rolled his eyes. With a mouthful of turkey, he moaned. "Really?"

"It's quick and easy, and there's always something to be grateful for. Tommy, you start. What are you happy about this Thanksgiving?"

"Mashed potatoes and gravy!"

Elaine took a sip of sparkling water. "Glad you like them."

"Antidepressants!"

Seth and Olivia dropped their napkins and bent to pick them up at the same time. He threw his at her and she held her breath, pressing her lips together to keep from laughing. They sat up with a flourish.

Elaine hesitated, not knowing if he was serious.

He touched her arm. "Joking," he said. "Or not. No worries, Mom. It's okay."

"Good. You know, I'm grateful that you're talking to someone and maybe feeling better?" She leaned into that question, her voice hopeful.

"Yeah, sure. Maybe. It's too soon to know. But we'll see." He put on a fake smile that seemed to convince her, wanting her to relax and move on to the next person.

"Olivia. What are you thankful for?" Forkful of turkey, scoop of sweet potatoes.

"Oh, you know, the usual. Friends, family, school. I'm really liking the books I got for my birthday."

"Very nice."

"Yeah, I've been learning a lot. And the voice recorder? Pretty cool piece of equipment."

Seth shot her a glance. A meaningful, 'don't go there' stare. Olivia shifted in her seat and scooped some cranberry sauce onto her plate.

Elaine set down her knife. "Have you gotten to try it out yet?"

"Just around the house." She averted her eyes from Seth.

"Find anything ghostly?"

Olivia wanted to spill the beans but thought better of it. "I'm not saying this house is haunted." She winked at Seth. "Nope. I'm not."

"There's no ghost in this house." Tommy held his spoon above his mouth and let the gravy drip onto his tongue. He swallowed. "That's not what's here."

Olivia sat forward. "What's here?"

Seth's eyes felt wider than he wanted them to be, and he was no longer hungry. Palpitations jump-started in his chest.

"Jetty. My cat."

Elaine motioned for Olivia to let it go. "What cat is that, Tommy?"

"My cat. From my old house."

Bright zigzags filled Seth's vision and his brain began to throb.

"There's no cat here," Elaine said.

"He's sometimes a cat. Sometimes a boy." Tommy's eyes sparkled. "Jetty is always here. He's my best friend."

Elaine nodded. An imaginary friend. She'd need to write this down for the social worker. Maybe it was his way of grieving. She was somewhat relieved, but a little concerned. "I'm sure he is, honey. I'm sure he likes to watch you play and make certain you're safe and happy."

"He does." Tommy picked up his plate. "Can I lick it?"

Olivia snorted. "Use your roll."

Tommy held his roll above the plate and shyly glanced toward Elaine for approval.

"Yes, use your roll." She sat back, hands in her lap. "It's more polite."

Seth poured some of the Pellegrino onto a napkin and wiped his forehead. "Everything's great, Mom. As usual. But I'm getting a migraine. I'm going outside for a little while." He slid his chair away from the table and stood.

"You sure? Maybe just lie down?"

"I'm sure. No worries. I'll be back in time for dessert."

"Take your jacket."

At the front door he tucked his feet into an old pair of sneakers and left.

The fresh air felt good against his face as he walked, hands shoved deep into the pockets of his sweatshirt. He crossed the street and followed the sidewalk to the vacant house, then cut catty-cornered behind its yard and into the woods. One look over his shoulder as he crossed into the tree line. One glance back at the old Harper house.

Blake had found the path years before and they'd made any

number of forts high on the hill, deep in the trees. No one had found them, but probably no one had ever tried. As long as they went home when the streetlights came on, all was good. That's how his mother grew up and she wanted him to have the same freedom. He guessed that didn't translate into blood oaths and summoning demons. She'd lose her shit if she knew what they'd done. Hell, he was losing his on a daily basis.

Seth pushed through an old blueberry bush and stepped onto a well-worn path he knew like the back of his hand. At the fork he took the left and trod onward. Roots and rocks punched up through the dirt, and a dead tree had fallen across the path during the last big storm. A small break in the trees lay ahead. He and Blake had used it as their space. Their get-away-from-it-all spot. A campfire pit was at the center and the remnants of prior visits littered the ground. Empty beer bottles, potato chip bags. A pocketknife was stabbed into the ashes at the center of the pit.

He picked up the knife and wiped the blade across his pant leg as his head throbbed. Taking note of the trees surrounding him, he found the ones that held the inverted pentagrams Blake had carved. Five of them, each forming a point of the larger star with the fire pit at the center. He walked to the first. It was head high, etched deep into the tree trunk. As the sun set, he used the edge of the blade to scrape it. Dig into the bark and try to erase what had been etched not that far in the past, but so deeply into their souls.

His mind was blank as he worked, one tree after another, scratching at the bark, trying to rid the area and himself of the evil they'd unleashed. The wind kicked up and it reminded him that winter was coming. Snow was in the air, as his grandmother would say. He wondered what she'd have to say if she could see him now.

The sun was gone by the time he reached the final tree, hands burning in the bitter air, red and raw from the rough bark and wind. It was colder here. As if he'd stepped into a walk-in freezer. A twig snapped. He turned, calling out to the night.

"Hello?"

Another snap, this time to his left. Louder. A small branch, maybe. Seth's heart beat faster. It could be a deer, he thought. A bear on a late season hunt. A bobcat. Another snap. Closer. To his right this time. Not an animal. Not boughs breaking in the breeze. Something was watching him. Something didn't like what he was doing.

He stabbed the blade into the bark, using all his strength to grind it into the pentagram. "I am taking power over my own destiny. I am taking back my life."

Another stab. Scrape.

A large branch crashed to the ground not ten feet away.

"You have no right to my life. I am in control!"

Out of nowhere, it rushed him, raking talons across his cheek. Hatred surrounded him, blacking out the moon, the stars. The trees. A scream of triumph echoed through the clearing. It vibrated in his bones. He was pulled backward and thrown, landing beside the fire pit, the air knocked from his lungs.

Powerless and stunned, he watched in horror as the trees healed themselves, reclaiming the pentagrams he'd worked so hard to destroy.

His cheek warmed with blood, rising where his flesh was torn, and he dropped the knife.

Message received.

It was time to go home. The streetlights would be on.

Chapter 15

Olivia peeked at her clock, rolled out of bed and remembered it was Black Friday. It was 8:00 am and pajama day in the Resnick house. She loved this day. Elaine would be out until late afternoon. She had the house almost to herself and a day to do nothing but enjoy it. She danced her way to the bathroom, brushed her hair and tied it up in a ponytail.

Tommy was sitting on the sofa, his green blanket across his shoulders, a box of Cheerios in his lap, watching Paw Patrol.

"You must've been up early," she said, taking her jacket off the coat rack.

He dug deep into the box for the next handful of cereal. "Where you going?"

"Outside to feed Milo. I'll be right back."

Keeping his eyes on the show, he asked. "Where's New Mommy?"

Olivia squatted to tie her sneakers. "She went Christmas shopping. She always goes on Black Friday."

"Why's it black?" Tommy looked out the window. "It's morning."

She paused, shoelaces in hand, thinking. "I don't know. It's just a thing. The day after Thanksgiving is always called Black Friday and a lot of people go to the stores. It's Mom's thing every year."

Tommy went back to the cartoon and Olivia stepped out to the patio.

Milo was waiting on a branch close to the bird bath. She sat on the edge of the stone, peanuts in her palm, and extended her hand in his direction. Stone still. Most days he'd approach with caution and wait her out, making her leave the food on the ground before he'd take it. But here and there he would hop onto her hand for a short moment to take the snack.

"Hello, Milo," she said. "Hello, little guy."

He took a peanut and flew.

"I have more when you're ready."

A flurry of toenails on glass startled her and she turned toward the house. Tommy was pressed against the door, holding Iggy in his arms. She waved.

Turning, she was shocked to see another crow about three feet from the bird bath. He was larger than Milo. "Well, now. Are you a friend of Milo's?" She spoke as softly as she could, but he didn't seem fearful of her. "I won't hurt you, big boy."

Olivia caught a glimpse over her shoulder. Tommy was still at the window, a big smile on his lips, and he pointed at the bird. She gave him a thumbs up and scooched backward until she was against the house so the bird could grab some peanuts if he wanted to. After a few minutes, she stood and went inside.

"What'd you think of that, Tommy? Another crow came to visit."

"That was Jetty." He grabbed the remote and was cycling through cartoon channels.

"I thought Jetty was a cat." She raised an eyebrow at him.

He tried to raise one of his at her, managing only to furrow his brown and cross his eyes. "He can be anything he wants to be."

"Ah, okay. Well, if this guy sticks around, I'm going to call him Crow Daddy. It's a name from one of my favorite movies."

"I like it. You can call him that."

"Glad I have your seal of approval."

"What's that mean?"

Olivia sat beside him on the sofa and reached for the Cheerios box. "It means you like it." They snuggled into his blanket and changed channels.

# # #

At 11:00 am, Seth wandered into the kitchen. He was still thick-headed from the night before, with residual sensitivities from his headache. The light hurt. The noise of cartoons hurt. Not bad enough to drill his brain or drive him to anger, but enough to be an aching annoyance. He slid a plate out of the cabinet, careful not to clang the ceramic against anything else. He was well aware what that would feel like inside his head. Propping the refrigerator door with his foot, he started stacking containers on the counter.

"Are you making a sandwich?" Olivia called from the living room. There was an over-sweet tone in her voice. He had known if she was within earshot, she'd be on it. Always was.

"Maybe."

"A *turkey* sandwich, Sy?"

"Yes, Olive. Is there anything else on Black Friday?" He popped the lid off each container. Turkey, gravy, stuffing. Everything that went into an amazing "morning after" brunch.

"No. No, there isn't."

He twisted the metal tie off the plastic bread wrapper.

"Will there be gravy on that sandwich?"

"I'm betting there could be." Seth took a knife out of the silverware drawer and stuck it into the gravy. Smearing it across a slice of bread, he said, "Why, Olive?"

"I was wondering . . ."

"Yes?"

"Just wondering, mind you . . ."

He pulled two more slices of bread from the bag and set them on the counter. "Yes?"

"Only if you have the time . . ."

"Would you like me to make you a sandwich, Olive?"

"Oh, Silas! How nice of you to offer! Yes. Yes, I would."

Before he could pick up the next slice, a little voice yelled, "Me, too!" It set his teeth on edge and his grip on the knife tightened.

Tommy appeared beside him, looking up into his face. "Can I have a sandwich, too, Silas?"

Seth took a deep breath and forced away the urge to throw the kid across the room. "That's not my name." He clenched his teeth hard enough his jaw ached.

"It's what Olivia calls you."

"That's something that's between her and me. Just us. It's our thing."

Tommy shrugged and pulled one of Iggy's toys, a stuffed beaver, from between the counter and the refrigerator. "Will you make me a sandwich?"

"Sure. If you're quiet. I have a headache." He reached into the bread bag for two more slices.

"You always have a headache."

"I don't always."

"Yeah, you do."

Seth turned, wanting to yell but trying to keep a hold on his emotions.

"What happened to your face?" Olivia had walked into the kitchen, and he'd been so intent on the boy that he hadn't noticed her.

He returned to what he was doing, slapping turkey on bread, scooping stuffing onto the mess. Not even wanting to eat anymore. Not wanting to explain something he couldn't. Not wanting to be near the little bastard. "Had a fight with a tree branch."

"Doesn't look like any tree scratch I've ever seen." She stood beside him, examining his cheek. "Looks more like a cat did it, or . . . no, it's too wide. A bird of prey. Something big."

"It was a tree." He put each sandwich on a plate. "A big goddamned tree."

Olivia gave him a slow nod and took her sandwich.

"A tree, Olivia."

"Okay, okay. A big ass tree. Whatever." She put a plate on the table in front of Tommy.

"I want to eat in the living room."

"Go for it, kid," Seth said. "It's Black Friday."

Tommy took his plate and left.

"Black Friday does not mean gravy sandwiches in the living room."

"It doesn't mean a box of Cheerios, either."

"That's not a gravy sandwich."

Seth peered around the corner at Tommy trying to hold his sandwich and take a bite without it coming apart. "Perhaps not," he said. "Good luck with that."

"Oh, no, Silas. He who dealt the gravy deals with the gravy."

"Not it," he said, touching his nose. He shoved the bread bag away from the edge of the counter and picked up his plate to leave.

"Oh, no. No, no, no. You can't walk away from this mess," she pointed at the containers, their covers, and cutlery, "and the potential for that one. No way, brother." She grabbed his shoulder.

"You're taking part in the spoils of that mess. Step up, Olive." He took a big bite of his sandwich, the gravy dripping down his chin, and stuck his face in hers. "Hmm?"

Olivia burst out laughing.

Seth searched for a napkin, came up empty and wiped his face on his sleeve.

"Sy!" She covered her face with her hand.

"Yes?"

"Are you going to join us in the living room?"

He sighed, not wanting to be alone in his room. Not wanting to be exposed to the boy any longer than he had to.

"Come on."

"For a little bit."

"You know you'll like it."

"Anyone ever tell you you're a pest?"

Seth took the recliner, putting the footrest up and balancing his plate on his knees. Olivia sat beside Tommy, who still had the remote.

"What are we watching?"

Before Tommy could answer, a phone rang. Olivia's hand automatically went to her back pocket, forgetting she was in pajamas. No cell phone.

"Hey, kid. Could you run to my room and get my phone? It's plugged in on my desk."

Olivia held his plate as Tommy ran down the hallway, sliding past her doorway in his pajama feet. Returning just as fast, he handed her the phone.

"Hello? Hey, Jules. What's doing?" She stood and strolled down the hallway. Iggy followed.

Tommy walked over to the recliner. "Your room looks like a tomb."

Seth scowled. "How do you know what a tomb looks like?"

"How do you know what a mausoleum looks like?"

"What?" He had to have misheard. Had to have. Could the kid know? Could Tommy somehow know what transpired between he and Blake? And the demon? There was no way. But what five-year-old knows that word? "What did you say?"

Tommy took his plate into the kitchen, putting it on the counter. He walked to the sofa, picking up his truck from the floor.

Seth stared at him. "What did you just say to me?"

"I don't know. What?"

Seth shook his head. He rubbed his eyes and wished life would go back to normal. Wished it hard.

"So, where do I find it?" Olivia asked. "Is it a Facebook quiz or what? From where? And what do you do?" She thumbed through her timeline, not seeing what her friend was talking about. She let her door swing shut behind her and deposited her sandwich on the desk.

Jules explained. "I sent you a link. Just take it. Tells you what your future career will be, and some are pretty funny."

"Okay, okay. Let me see." Olivia clicked the link, making her way past advertisements and nonsense. "Your Future Awaits, is that it?"

"Yes! Call me after you take it, and we'll compare notes. I won't tell you what I got till you have yours."

"Okay, cool. Did you try Christie?"

"Not yet. I'm going to now."

"K, Jules. I'll call soon."

"Bye."

Olivia sat on her bed and clicked "Take the Quiz." The questions popped up over a winter scene background. A hillside covered in snow with skiers, a lodge, and trees decorated for Christmas. "So, let's see. What's my favorite color? Not sure how revealing that could be, but here we go." She typed "purple" and hit the button to continue.

It took about three minutes, if that, and she had her career path. She would be the CEO of a major corporation by the time she was thirty, with aspirations to rule the world. Olivia snorted. That was far from what she felt in her soul. She wanted to be a medium. Take her sensitivities, roll them up into a ball, cultivate her abilities and run with them. Not only speak with the dead but work with them. Solve crimes. Give readings. She could do a little of that now, but she wanted to take it farther. Every touch of the paranormal fueled her desire.

She sat back, phone in hand. She guessed she aspired to more than the mundane. Perhaps she'd head a ghost corporation someday. Given fifteen or twenty years, who knows what could be possible?

She moved to her window, positioned her hands and shoved upward. It didn't budge. Once more. "Come on," she said, running her hand along its edge, trying to see if something was wedged in its way. "I can take over the world but not get this unstuck?" Another try. The window didn't move.

"Sy?" she called. No response. Cracking her door about two inches, she tried again. "Sy!"

"What?" It was a muffled reply.

She waited. "Sy!"

Louder now. "What?!"

Olivia stuck her face into the hallway as Seth did the same. He plodded toward her.

"Need something?"

"Help me open my window? I can't."

"You weak or what?"

"No, I'm strong as the Hulk." She raised her arm in the air, making a fist. "Muscle, am I right?"

He scoffed. "And you can't lift your window, why?"

"Something's blocking it."

Seth felt along its top edge and flipped a small handle from left to right. "Can't open a locked window, Olive." He heaved it upward, letting in a blast of chilled air.

"I didn't know there was a lock up there."

"Apparently. You're welcome."

"Thanks."

Olivia went to measure how much of a ledge Milo would need for a perch. Seth gave her chair a spin and walked out.

Seth was shocked to see Tommy standing at his door. He'd left it ajar when Olivia had called him, and the boy was poised as if his next step was inside.

"Hey. That's one room you don't go into." Seth crossed in front of him, blocking the way.

"Why not?"

"It's mine and it's private." Seth reached in, feeling for the Nerf gun that was always propped against his wall. His hand struck paydirt and he grabbed it. "Now, back to the living room with you." He pointed the way with his RapidStrike CS-18. It was blue and orange, had a shot distance of over seventy-five feet, with eighteen darts at the ready. They walked together, Tommy with his head down. Seth like a man with a prisoner.

Tommy picked up a toy plane from the sofa while Seth eased into the recliner. The little boy flew the airplane up and down, closer and closer to Seth. Closer to the chair. Zooming past his head.

"Don't come near me."

"I'm not near you."

Dip, soar. Past Seth's feet, above his arm.

"Look, kid. I'm going to play 'Keep Away' with you. Every time you get too close, I'm going to shoot you with a dart. Got it?"

The sound of Elaine's car parking in the driveway caught Tommy's attention for a split second. "No, you won't."

They locked eyes.

"Try me."

Tommy used the arm of the sofa as a runway and crashed his plane into Seth's leg. Seth fired, hitting him in the arm. The boy stopped dead in his tracks.

"Do it again."

Seth aimed. He fired a shot, hitting Tommy square in the forehead. The boy's eyes welled up and, with a calculated smile, he ran to the door screaming for Elaine. Seth sighed. He'd be getting the brunt of it, again. For nothing. As he steeled himself to deal with the fallout, a large shadow crossed the picture window, moving toward the patio side of the house. He went to the sliding glass door. A large mass solidified into the body of a crow. Seth followed outside, adrenalin pumping. He peered around the perimeter.

Olivia was at her window. He listened as she called Milo, then this other thing. She didn't see that it wasn't a crow. Didn't understand it was evil. The weight of the Nerf gun in his hand brought him back to reality. His reality. He aimed, firing at the birds. In a flapping of wings, he disbanded the murder. They took to the trees.

"Hey! Leave them alone!"

"It's not what it seems! It's not a bird!"

He sighted the gun to fire at the tree where the largest crow landed.

Olivia slammed her window shut, but he could hear her yelling for their mother. He exhaled and went inside, knowing he'd be a real target now. He pulled the sliding door closed.

"Mom!"

Olivia was yelling; Tommy was crying. Elaine, arms full of packages, was nothing less than exasperated as Seth stepped into the living room.

"What's going on?" She dropped her bags beside the coat rack, drawing Tommy into her arms and wiping his tears. "You first, O."

"He shot at my birds. The smoking gun is right there in his hand."

"Nerf, Olive. It's a Nerf. No smoke."

She sneered at him. "Is that your defense?"

Elaine, still in her coat, tucked her keys into her purse. "You shot a dart at her crows?"

"Darts," Olivia corrected.

"Darts. You shot darts at her birds?" She took off her gloves and began unbuttoning her coat.

Seth left his arms at his sides, shaking his head. "Yeah, but it's-" His voice trailed off. Better to let it go. His mother wouldn't get it. He wasn't sure he did.

"And Tommy? What happened to you?"

He turned toward her with a face of innocence. A mask of manipulation. "Seth shot me. In the face." His chin quivered.

Elaine threw up her hands. "What's your issue?"

"Forehead," he corrected. "He kept flying his plane in my face. I warned him first. Told him to quit."

"Seth, really. You're the bigger guy here. You could have handled it differently."

"And he could have stopped."

Elaine pursed her lips, annoyed. "I go out and you can't handle a few hours alone together? Come on. And to shoot at Olivia's birds? Was that necessary? She's been working with them for so long and you may have ended it. Why?"

He stared at his mother as the seconds ticked by, feeling as if he was on trial. No explanation he gave would sound rational. Reasonable. He didn't live in that kind of world anymore. "Forget it, Mom. Forget it. I'm the disturbed one, I guess. I'm a delinquent." Tossing the Nerf gun onto the sofa, he walked from the room taking slow, deliberate steps. "I'll just stay in my room from here on. No worries."

"Oh, Seth, come on."

Once again, he was alone and under siege.

Hours ticked by. Seth sat in the corner of his room, his back to the wall. He had pulled the blanket from his bed and cocooned himself. Safe. If there was a safe anymore. At least nothing could sneak up on him. Come from behind. He let himself nod off in the darkness, shifting now and then as a butt cheek went numb or a foot went pins and needles. He was tired. So tired of dealing with this shit. Tired of being beaten down, constantly pushed. The growling voice in his mind was getting louder. More insistent. More violent.

Kill him
Kill him
Kill him

It mixed with his own thoughts until he almost couldn't separate them. Hatred and anger were boiling up in him, first at the entity slowly stealing his soul and now at Tommy. All of this was the boy's fault. Everything came down to him. The root of everything wrong in his life. If he could get rid of Tommy, he could get his life back.

Kill him

A knock on the door stabbed through his obsessive thoughts, piercing his brain like an ice pick.

"Seth?"

His mother. Somewhere in the recesses of his being he knew she was trying to help. Be understanding. But she was harboring the little fugitive from hell and if she got in his way, he didn't know what would happen. The thought rolled his stomach and filled him with a newfound terror.

"There's spaghetti and meatballs on the table. And we're going to set up the tree in a bit. I'd like it if you joined us."

There was a concerned sadness in her voice that tugged at him. He didn't want her upset. Didn't want to hurt his mother. He needed to fight harder, with what he had left between himself and insanity, before he lost his soul.

"Seth?"

"Yeah, Mom. I'll be out."

He listened to her footsteps fade and tried to muster some energy. Stand. When he wasn't focused on Tommy, his entire being felt drained. Sick. Used and discarded, an empty husk. Leaving his blanket in a heap on the floor, he unlocked the door and shuffled out.

Christmas carols greeted him. His mother had already pulled boxes of decorations into the living room and had the bottom tier of the tree into place.

"Olivia, show Tommy how to spread out the branches so they look nice." She bent over the box to find the next section and saw her son. "I was hoping you wouldn't miss anything. Grab some spaghetti and come sit on the sofa. We'll get this part done and you can help decorate." She hesitated, a hopeful gleam in her eye. "If you're up for it?"

He nodded. "I'll stay a while." Maybe a little light therapy, some time away from the darkness, would help his disposition. Maybe it'd help his mental stability. And maybe the demon thing would dig its talons deeper into his flesh as he tried.

# # #

"Any bare spots?" Elaine stepped back, admiring and scrutinizing the tree. She'd trimmed it with a silver garland once the branches had been fluffed up.

"One near the top on the left."

"I see it!" She bent a few to cover the hole. "Now?"

Seth swallowed his last mouthful of spaghetti. "Seems fine."

"Good." She put her hands on her hips. "Who's ready to do the ornaments?"

"Me! Me!" Tommy bounced, waving his hand.

Seth cringed with every "me." It was like galvanic shock, but chewing tin foil was far less disturbing. Olivia pried the top off the first tub, oohing and ahhing over the sparkling balls, angels, Santas, and everything festive her fingers touched. Tommy reached into the middle of the box.

"What's this?" He held up a silver ball, etched with gold stars.

"That's one of Seth's ornaments," Elaine said. "See?" She took it from the boy and held it up so the light could catch the name written on the back. "S-E-T-H. That spells Seth."

"Oh."

She handed him the ornament so he could hang it on the tree. "I get everyone an ornament every year, so they have a special remembrance. Look, there's one of Olivia's." She pointed out a bright red bow suspended from a wire. "O-L-I-V-I-A spells . . ."

"Olive," Seth said, settling deeper into the sofa.

Olivia threw a handful of tinsel at him.

"Olivia," Tommy said. "It spells Olivia."

"I swear, one day I'm going to get you one that says Silas."

Seth smiled a tired smile. "You say that every year."

"Oh, it's going to happen."

Tommy reached for the next decoration, then turned toward Elaine. "Is there one with my name on it?"

"Well, when I was out today, I bumped into one of Santa's helpers at the mall."

"And?" Tommy circled her.

"He gave me a little something for you. Look in that brown paper bag on the arm of the sofa."

Tommy ran over, taking the bag in his hands. Careful not to disrupt whatever might be inside, he reached in.

"A snowman!"

Elaine bent down on one knee. "See? Your name is right there."

Tommy read off the letters. "T-O-M-M-Y. Tommy."

"Great job!" Olivia said from behind the tree. She was trying to get a blue snowflake to hang straight.

"I know my letters. I learned them at my first mommy's house."

Olivia glanced at Elaine for her reaction, but there was none. Just a glossing-over of the elephant in the room. Paint it quick, make it blend in. Redirect.

"That's great, Tommy. Where do you want to hang it on the tree?"

Seth watched as his mother, Olivia and Tommy hung every one of his childhood ornaments. At least his mother let him be an observer and didn't force him to participate. He wouldn't have been able to take Tommy at his feet, pushing in front of him to grab decorations, shoving past him for a better spot on the tree. He could hardly contain himself when his mother brought out hot chocolate with marshmallows and the kid spilled it on the carpet. But no one saw him narrow his eyes or turn away. His annoyance was palpable, but everyone focused on the kid.

The tree was finally finished, the noise in the house dying down. Tommy was in bed; Olivia was in her room, probably chatting with Jules and Christie. Elaine shut off the lamp on the end table, leaving the tree glowing.

"Good night, hon," she said. "I'm so happy you stayed out with us tonight."

"Night, Mom."

"Hanging out here a little longer?"

"Yeah, I think so. The lights are cozy."

"They are." She hesitated. She wanted to ask if he wanted company but decided not to. "'Night."

"'Night."

He wrapped himself in the afghan from the back of the sofa and closed his eyes.

Sleep came quickly, as did the dream. Hard and fast. *He was in the middle of a war. Shells exploding on either side. A shockwave burst through where he stood. His demon tormentor emerged as a spinning ball of talons, gripping him like a ragdoll and dragging him off his feet. A hyena with its kill, fighting to keep its meat. His soul. It hunched over him, hot drool dripping from its mouth, its breath a cross between diarrhea and week-old vomit. The demon roared, its gaping maw revealing rows of razor-like, rotting teeth.*

An enormous mass of buzzing murder-hornets materialized on the next hill, coalescing into a fearsome abomination. It stared down the lesser demon, sending it cowering, retreating to the shadows. Far enough away to show deference, yet still circling and fiercely guarding its soon to be kill. Unwilling to give up its trophy.

This was a war not his own. It was a showdown, and he was the prize. As the world darkened, he searched for a place to flee. Somewhere that would remove him from the clutches of evil while it thundered around him.

High above, overlooking the scene, he saw her.

Olivia.

He tried to scream, get her attention, but hell was baring down on him. Fire formed in the sky, raining flames. His body blistered in the heat.

"Olivia!" It came out as a raspy screech, his lungs filling with burning smoke.

Olivia.

The black mass formed into a tall man-like thing, faceless, except for two red eyes. Hatred filled. Evil. It gazed at his sister until she signaled. And then it ripped him apart.

#

He woke, sweat-drenched and sick. Until now, his nightmares had been dark and wrong, but his own. His death. His demise. Never at his sister's hands. Her command. He wiped the blanket across his face, drying it, and tried to shake off the panic. Maybe a drink would help. A pill. A walk through the living room. Get rid of the shakes, take a deep breath and try to get a little sleep before morning. The sun wasn't up yet. He deserved a few hours of rest, if that was possible.

Pausing at the Christmas tree, he found his favorite ornament, the one with the little gold stars. He'd had it for years and for him, it was the embodiment of the holidays. The sense of Christmas wonderment. He turned it over in his hand, remembering every inch, and saw scratches through his name. As if someone had scored the thin metal, most of the way around the ornament. As he held it closer to his face to examine it, the ball shattered. He fixated on the shiny shards in his palm, then turned his hand over and let them fall to the floor.

Forgetting about the water, he walked to the sofa, folded the afghan and went to bed.

Chapter 16

Dom stood in the archway to his kitchen, waiting for the tea kettle to whistle. He stared at the demonology books sprawled across the coffee table and couch cushions. A Frankincense cone of incense burned in a small metal bowl, and he watched the tendrils of smoke rise. All of this was new to him, yet not. Knowing his direction, his purpose, had ramped everything up a notch. Fifty notches. He'd always had a knack for the paranormal. Had always been jazzed about ghost hunting. He shouldn't have been so naive to believe when they left the Forest View Apartment investigation that they'd leave behind the demon that attacked them. That killed Amanda's brother. That left him maimed. How did he not think it would follow them? That it wouldn't be a permanent force in their lives until something broke?

He broke. And rebuilt. The straw that cracked the camel's back had snapped his mind, for a little while anyway. And then it clicked. It all made sense. Why it hadn't left them. Why Amanda died. Her brother. Joe Paine. Jack Barnes. The list probably went on and on through generations, but the one constant, at this time and place, was him. It kept coming back to him. In nightmares, in life. He was still here because he would be the one to get rid of Black.

The tea kettle began its high-pitched shriek, sending steam into the air. Dom reached for his cane, still hooked on the back of a dining room chair. Shutting off the stove, he moved the yellow kettle to another burner. Its whistle fell to a sputter. He opened the cabinet to the right of the stove and ran a finger down the boxes of teas until it landed on Chamomile and Lavendar. For calm.

Since he'd found his mission, though, he'd been calm. Devoid of emotion. Hyper-focused. He knew what he had to do, and he'd find a way to do it. Strategize. Calculate. And wait. The time for a strike was coming. He didn't know when, but he would be ready.

He pulled a tea bag from the box and dropped it into his mug. It floated as he poured the boiling water, finally sinking below the surface.

Doctor Ryan had been concerned that he'd canceled his appointments. Took himself off the calendar. He closed the cabinet door and smirked. But he was fine. Everything was behind him with a single mission ahead. Doctors didn't know everything.

He made his way to the couch, setting the mug on the coffee table. He cupped his left hand and ran it along the edge of the table as he brushed off salt crystals and bits of sage, then wiped his palms over the trash basket next to the couch. He'd made little protection bags the night before and needed to straighten up before getting to the real work.

"Salt, sage and black tourmaline," he said. "Every little bit helps." He didn't have any leather pouches, so he used Ziploc baggies. He didn't need to be fancy. Bending forward to turn on his laptop, his lower back ached. It was time to add more stretching into his regimen. Body, mind and spirit, he'd be a force to be reckoned with when the time came.

Dom took a sip of tea, closing his eyes and inhaling the fragrant steam. With a clear mind, he rested his fingers over the keyboard and, in the search bar, typed *knives*.

Chapter 17

Seth sat, arms folded, on the floor beside the fireplace, its stone edge digging into his spine. He was a part of the festivities but separate. Very separate. Mounds of wadded up birthday wrap swooshed and crinkled as Iggy bounced at their feet. Tommy opened his last present.

"A truck!"

"It's a front loader," Olivia said, showing him how to move the scoop.

Tommy ran it past Olivia's legs and into Seth's foot. He grinned. To Seth, it was a gruesome, twisted grimace.

"Who wants birthday cake?" Elaine asked. She stood, smoothing her skirt. "I think it's time."

"Me!" Tommy followed her, setting the truck on the arm of the sofa. "With ice cream!"

They all filed out of the room while Seth soaked up the warmth of the fire, letting its comfort fill him. It'd been a long time since he'd felt anything but ice running through his veins and he knew when he stood, that heat would dissipate in a heartbeat. He reached out to bat Tommy's truck to the floor but as his hand hovered above it, the toy rolled. On its own. A slow, steady movement as if someone, something, was guiding it along. It got to the edge and shot off, crashing to the center of the floor, breaking a wheel as it hit.

His hand was still in the air when Tommy rounded the corner, a bowl of ice cream in one hand and a small paper plate with cake in the other.

He glared at Seth. "You broke my truck."

"I didn't."

"Well, it didn't land in the middle of the room without some help." Elaine stood with her hands on her hips. "Really, Seth. It's just a little boy's toy. Go get it, Tommy, and I'll see if I can glue the wheel."

"Okay, New Mommy." Tommy let the name roll off his tongue like butter. Picking up the wheel, he turned it over in his hand, examining it.

Seth bent close to Tommy. "I didn't do it," Seth said just above a whisper. "And you know it." His chest was tight, and his mind kept replaying the scene. He locked eyes with the boy.

Tommy drove it through the air. "Jetty did it. He doesn't want you to touch my things."

"Jetty. Your old cat."

"Um, hmm. He doesn't like you."

"Well, tell your invisible cat to stay the hell away from me."

Tommy shrugged. "Jetty does what he wants."

"So do I. So, you both better watch out." He kept his eye on Tommy as the boy flew his toy around the room once more and then ran into the kitchen. A tremor went through Seth's body. He scanned the room for any sign of movement, any type of motion. Nothing. Whatever had been there, whatever force threw the truck, was gone. He could feel the drops of blood forming where his oppressor had dug into his skin when the toy was thrown. As if it feared for its life.

He reached to his left and tugged the metal pull to turn on the lamp. Light therapy, Dr. Ryan had said. When something's weighing on you. When you're seeing things that shouldn't be there. Go to another room, another area. Turn on every light you can find. Let it blast the shadows out of existence. Ease your mind. He wasn't buying it, but with the happy noises coming from the kitchen, at least he didn't feel as isolated.

Clicking the power button on the remote, he flipped through channel after channel on the television. Tons of movies to stream, sitcoms, concerts. Nothing appealed. Nothing caught his attention for more than a few seconds. It was all mindless garbage.

"Don't start watching anything," Olivia called. "We're going to put on a movie in a few minutes."

"Yeah, okay." He dropped the remote onto the side table and waited. That's all he ever did anymore. Wait. For the next nightmare, the next attack. The next command. He was losing his will to fight. It'd be so much easier to give in, curl into a ball and let the world implode.

Seth listened to the singing in the kitchen, followed by a cheer and cake-cutting chatter. They didn't invite him to participate but that was okay. Better, in fact. He didn't have to make up an excuse or be dragged into anything. He could sink into the sofa, let it pull him down deep into himself, and disappear. Be a set of eyes with no mind, no thought of his own. It was hard to be so tired when sleep was the enemy. Waking was the enemy. Tommy was the enemy.

When his family filed into the room, they carried a big plastic bowl of popcorn. Elaine set a plate with a slice of chocolate cake and scoop of vanilla ice cream on the end table beside him. "In case you'd like some."

He nodded. It'd rot before he'd eat that kid's cake.

"What are we watching, Tommy?" Olivia asked. "Birthday boy picks."

"ParaNorman!" He settled next to her on the floor. "The ghost one!"

"You got it." She found the DVD in the rack and slid it into the player. "Have you seen it before? I think you're going to like it."

"My first mommy let me watch it."

Seth wanted to scream that his first mommy was dead, and he didn't have a new mommy, but knew that would be wrong. Knew he'd be vilified. And wouldn't that give Dr. Ryan fodder to discuss at their next session. There are no demons, son. Just the ones in your head. He'd tried, for a little while, to go along with the idea it was a concoction of his sick mind. Or maybe his effort was half-hearted. He'd hoped, though.

The movie played. Seth reached past Olivia and took a handful of popcorn from the bowl in her lap. Tommy glanced over his shoulder at him and then returned his gaze to the television.

The popcorn was still hot and smelled wonderful. His hand was slick with the butter Olivia had drizzled into the bowl and he shoveled the handful into his mouth, wiping his hand off on his pant leg. It tasted like a memory. Summer nights, when life was good. Campfires, friends. As soon as he swallowed, he reached for more.

He spit a kernel into his hand and dropped it onto the cake plate. Glad he noticed it before he bit down. He'd done that before. Nearly broke a tooth and his gums were sore for days. As he took the last bite of what was in his hand, Olivia turned and flicked a flake at him. He dodged, laughed, and inhaled, sucking popcorn into the back of his throat. He bent forward, coughing hard. Covering his mouth with his hand, tears filled his eyes as his body rejected the dry piece of popcorn that tried to lodge in his windpipe.

"Are you okay?" Elaine asked.

Olivia grabbed the remote and paused the movie.

"Hey!" Tommy yelled.

Seth continued his gut-wrenching, lung-spewing hacking until it eased to an occasional throat-clearing. He swiped at his eyes with the sleeve of his sweatshirt. "Oh, man," he said. "That was rough."

Olivia had a sheepish look on her face. "Sorry, Sy. Didn't mean to do it to you."

"Wasn't your fault." He rested against the edge of the sofa and exhaled. "You didn't do it."

Tommy held out the bowl to him. "Want some more?"

Seth stared.

"I don't think he wants any right now, Tommy. Thank you, though," Elaine said.

The little boy smiled. To Seth it was confirmation. Their battle was escalating to a war.

"Well, this should serve as a lesson to everyone not to play when there's food. Seth could have choked instead of just swallowing the wrong way."

"Just?" he said.

She patted his leg. "You know what I mean. O., you can hit play."

The movie continued. When it ended, Elaine steered Tommy down the hallway to get ready for bed. Olivia tossed Seth the remote.

"Thanks," he said. "You going to bed this early?"

"Homework. Jules said she'd call around 9:00 pm so we could do some studying together." Her phone rang and she shrugged. "That's got to be her." Iggy chased her down the hallway, his tail knocking an ornament off the tree.

Seth was alone once more. He listened to his mother in the bathroom with the kid, urging him to brush his teeth.

"Just jam it in his mouth," he said under his breath. "That'll shut him up." He stood and stretched, then picked up the ornament to rehang it. As he held it in the air, reaching to hook its metal wire over a branch, a shadow behind him reflected in the silver ball. He whipped around. Nothing. But the air seemed colder. It was probably nerves. Lately, his anxiety had been off the charts.

His hands shook as he held the ornament up to the tree, hoping not to see it happen again, to let it be a misinterpretation on his part. The fire casting shadows. Something. There was nothing. Of course, there wasn't anything. He saw nothing when the truck was thrown across the room. He saw nothing when the claws dug into his flesh. But he knew there were forces at work here and they were against him.

Seth reached the corner and flipped on the overhead light in the kitchen, then the lamps at either end of the sofa. He sat down, more trying to push out the dark than to let in the light. He hoped the brighter the light, the demons that haunted him would have to hide. Back off. Darkness always made it worse, right? Didn't all ghost hunters work in the dark?

He sat, resting his forearms on his knees, hands clasped, head down.

"You all right?" Elaine noted that all the lights were on and inclined her head toward the kitchen.

"Yeah, it's good, Mom." He didn't want to talk. Didn't want to expand on his mental illness or his evil attachment. Neither seemed appropriate and both were draining. "Just something Dr. Ryan suggested."

"Ahh, I see."

He knew she didn't. There was no understanding. She was a concerned mother whose only son was going off the deep end. A soul sold and the buyer ready to take possession.

"Do you want company?"

"No, thanks. I just need some peace. Light therapy."

"Peace is good. Could use some myself. I'm going to read in my room for a while. If you change your mind, let me know. I'd be happy to sit with you."

"Sure, Mom."

"Night, honey."

"Night."

He reached for the remote and lowered the volume on the television.

Chapter 18

Seth sat beside a plastic ficus and waited for the secretary to call his name. A scratching noise, like digging, caught his attention. In the corner of the room near the ceiling, a piece of wallpaper had peeled away. Something was clawing at the edge of the drywall, tugging and ripping it, dropping bits of dried plaster to the floor.

He peered over his shoulder to see if the receptionist was watching, but she was away from the desk. The waiting room was empty except for him, and this animal was trying to get inside. It was getting faster, harder. More persistent. He could see the pointed claws, tearing, working at a feverish pace. Louder, harsher.

A rat. It had to be a rat. Nine feet up and fighting to climb through. It was pulling at the wood now, the beams, and he could see bloody scythe-shaped appendages sticking through the wall, attempting to yank the hole wide enough to fit through. Hysteria rose in him.

"Seth?"

He nervously turned to see the receptionist, then pivoted to point out the animal. It was gone. The hole, the blood. The noise.

"Seth?"

"Yeah." He followed her into Dr. Ryan's office without a backward glance. He knew what was after him and it wasn't a rat.

"Seth, glad to see you. How has everything been going since we last spoke?" Dr. Ryan asked. He sat in one of the "therapy" chairs and Seth took the burgundy sofa. Again. "How was your

Thanksgiving?"

He slouched. "Okay, I guess."

"Just okay? Any better than before? The same?" He crossed his legs.

"It could be better." Seth watched Dr. Ryan's worn loafer bounce. A nervous habit? Had he also seen the thing in the waiting room?

"Well, that's why you're here. So we can get it better."

"Yeah." Seth made sure to face away from the window. He didn't want to see any shadows, didn't want to know about cats that disappeared.

"What's going on at home? How's the family?"

"Okay. We had a birthday party for Olivia. And one for the kid."

"How'd that go?"

"Olivia's? Fine. Mom gave her a cemetery cake, topped with little tombstones with our names on them." He cleared his throat. "A little insensitive, but Olivia likes that stuff. Ghosts, the paranormal. Can't fault Mom for getting it."

"Sounds a little rough on you. It hasn't been that long since your friend passed away."

"Yeah. But Olive's a good kid. Olivia, I mean. Olive's my nickname for her."

"Seems like you've got a good relationship with her. What's she call you?"

Seth half-smiled. "Silas."

"You two must get along pretty well."

"We do. Mostly. Brother-sister stuff, you know, but mostly okay."

"That's great. Helps to give you a foundation. A support system."

His mind immediately went to the night in the kitchen. Olivia had his back, he knew it. But he couldn't allow her to get close enough for that. He'd protect her if he had to set himself aflame. "Yeah. She's all right. Mom's going to adopt her. She's already put in the paperwork."

"Very nice."

Seth sat a little more erect. "She believes the house is haunted. Or my room at least."

"Olivia?"

"Yeah." He tapped his right foot against his left, then stopped, too aware of how awkward he felt.

"You've shared what you're seeing with her?" He held up his hand. "It's fine if you did. You should be comfortable enough to discuss what's going on with whomever you'd like."

"No. I didn't tell her anything." Seth suddenly felt warm. It was hard, dealing with a psychiatrist. Someone trained to listen and pretending not to judge.

"What makes her think it's haunted?"

"She's kind of a journalist. Very analytical. And ghosts are her thing."

"Yeah, you mentioned."

"She sneaked a voice recorder into my bedroom one night."

"How'd you feel about that?"

"Invaded. I was pretty upset when she told me."

"A prank gone wrong?"

"More of an experiment than a prank."

"And what did she hear that made her think it was haunted?"

"A growl. A voice . . ." He began jiggling his leg. He didn't want to but it helped channel some of the anxiety out of his chest.

"Any pets in your house?"

"What? Oh, yeah. A dog. Iggy."

"Does anyone in the family listen to the radio? Could the television have been on?"

"Well, I guess so? I mean, I didn't think so, but it could be possible."

"You see what I'm getting at, yes? There could be any number of natural, normal explanations for what she thinks she heard. And yet her belief in the paranormal could easily feed into your issues right now."

Seth sat quietly, taking in all of what Dr. Ryan was saying. He wanted to rock, close off from the world, but what the man said made sense. Maybe. If he didn't feel his flesh being pierced and torn. If he didn't smell the odor of rotting corpses when he walked into his room. But even those things could be a mechanism of a faltering mind. Maybe.

"I guess."

"Mix this in with Blake's dabbling in the occult, and boom! Your mind took it and ran with it."

He wanted to believe the doctor's easy answer to all that plagued him. Craved it. Medicate and take the easy way out. Let his brain relax, flatline his emotions and sleep again. He just didn't know if he could trust it. And then there was Tommy. He was another story.

"And you had a party for your foster brother?"

"Yeah. There's something wrong with that kid." He blurted it out of nowhere. Or somewhere. The brain his demon was mangling. Shredding him into a padded room.

"Tommy?"

"It's like he's out to get me."

"How so? Isn't he only . . ." the doctor checked his notes, "five?"

Seth swallowed. "Just turned five. Yeah. But every time I turn, he's in my face. Doing everything I tell him not to. And Mom," Seth rubbed his chin, "takes his side. I know it sounds childish. Petty. But I swear he's like Chucky."

"The evil doll from the movies?"

Another nod. Unease. "I know how it sounds, Doc. I do. But I'm telling you, something is twisted in him. And all they do is take his side. Everything I touch is wrong. Everything I do, I'm wrong. It's like he does it on purpose."

"Let me see if I can put another perspective on the situation, okay?"

"Sure."

"You're already anxious, depressed and to some degree feeling guilty over Blake's death, yes?"

"Okay."

"Even a little insecure, on shaky ground. Here comes this boy who is threatening your place in the family. Not in actuality, but it feels that way. Right when you need your mother the most, she's giving her time and attention to a stranger. In your own home. And, seemingly, she's going to bat for him against you. Of course, you're going to feel some resentment. Even if on a rational level you know he's just a little boy and that he's had major trauma himself."

"Yeah."

"But feelings aren't rational. Emotions don't follow logic. You're hurting and it's making you feel alone."

"That's for sure." He slumped into the cushions and shoved his hands into his pockets.

"But she's only doing what she knows how to do, and that's to mother him. She's either not aware of how deeply you're hurting, or she doesn't know how to approach you with all this."

"Or I've shut her out. Pushed her away."

"Have you?"

"I don't know." He did know. All of his time was spent in his room, shut away from interaction. Hiding since he ran away from Blake's body. Since the thing chased him down like a lion hunting a gazelle. Like a devil after a soul.

"It's pretty normal for guys your age to do that. Want their own space, put up walls between themselves and their parents . . . even when they need the love and support the most."

"That doesn't explain the kid, though. He's in my face all the time."

"Typical five-year-old wanting attention?"

"It's not only that," he scooched to the edge of the sofa. "He knows things he shouldn't. Like the word mausoleum. What kid knows that word?"

"Maybe a kid whose mother was well-read and used that type of language? Maybe he's been to burials and heard the word? Do you know anything about his parents?"

"His mom was a little weird. She was an artist. Painted some dark subjects, had a collection of grim reaper figurines."

"Well, there you have it."

"What?"

"Don't you think that the word mausoleum might have come up in their day-to-day dealings? Not necessarily through her to him, but if she was on the phone and he overheard? Or visiting a cemetery? It's possible. And even if he used the word, that doesn't mean that he knew the meaning."

Seth recalled the way Tommy glowered at him when he asked about the mausoleum. He knew. There was no question that the boy knew what he was talking about. No question at all.

"You don't seem convinced." The doctor set his notes on the side table.

"He ran under the ladder while I was on it."

"Sounds like an energetic little boy. Maybe one who didn't have a lot of attention when his mother was alive. He's probably wanting your interaction and not knowing how to get it, especially if he's not had a male role model in his life until now."

"So, you're thinking this is normal? He's happy when things go wrong for me."

"Misplaced emotions on his part. Not knowing how to react when things are serious. You're both dealing with a lot right now. Tragedy on both sides. Both at a breaking point, but you're at a point in your life where you're seeking help. He doesn't know how and isn't even aware there is help. He's flying by the seat of his pants in a world he's not ready for."

"He's not alone."

"Definitely not. But you're here and we're going to work together until you're where you need to be. Maybe you'll be the one to help change things for him. It could be good for both of you."

"You're saying befriend Chucky."

Doctor Ryan laughed. "Maybe befriend is too strong a word. Tolerate him. For a little while each day. Maybe fifteen minutes to start. A half hour, if you can do it. Just a small amount of positive attention might adjust his behavior."

He knew he'd have to keep quiet about what the monster in his room was telling him to do to the kid. They'd tie him into a white jacket and throw away the key. And the talons were sunk deep in his flesh as a reminder he wasn't alone. Like those guys who do body suspension from ceiling hooks. His life was dangling, soul exposed. And his flesh was tearing.

Elaine dropped her purse onto the counter and dumped the bag with Seth's new prescription. She unfolded the information sheet as she handed him the bottle. "Common side-effects," she read. "May make you not sleepy . . . or very drowsy. Can cause . . . headaches, anxiety, loss of appetite . . ."

"So, it may give me symptoms of what I'm already feeling? Isn't it supposed to do the opposite? Why do people take this shit?"

"Oh, honey. You know they're temporary."

"Then how do you know if it's working?"

"I guess you have to take it long enough that if you get the side effects, they go away and you feel better overall? Isn't that what Dr. Ryan said?"

"Hmm. Yeah, sure." He spun the bottle on the counter, letting it ricochet off the wall and spin into the sink. "Another month of nothing."

Elaine pulled him by his arm to face her so she could look directly into his eyes. "You've got to give it time. This is a process. It's not like they can see inside your brain to know what's going to help you the best and fastest. We'll get through this together. I love you and we'll get through it." She took his hand in hers and squeezed.

Seth gave her a half-hearted smile. "Together."

"Good." She patted his hands and shoved them away. "Now let me get this place picked up and I'll make us some lunch."

He backed off to let her play Betty Crocker while he braced himself to walk into the room where his demon had taken over.

Chapter 19

Olivia rushed in, kicking her backpack, and tearing off her coat and scarf. As she hung them on the coat rack, Iggy greeted her. Frosty the Snowman was on the television; Tommy was sitting on the floor coloring. Construction paper was strewn in front of him, and a box of markers had been dumped across the carpet.

"Half-day at school and it's Christmas break! Booyah!" She took Iggy's front paws and danced in a circle with the pup.

"You're home for days? New Mommy says you're home for days." He had red and green ink across his fingers and a smear on the carpet along the paper edge. Picking up the cap for the purple marker, he popped it onto the red and started capping the rest.

"Yes! A whole week. And it's Christmas, a bunch of days to relax, then New Year's. It's great! My favorite time of year." She paused, letting Iggy down and scuffing off her sneakers. "Do I smell gingerbread?"

"Cookies!"

"Oh, my God, can this day get any better?" She took Tommy by the hand and scooted into the kitchen. Elaine had hung sparkling lights across the top of the cabinets. Vinyl clings of Rudolph and the Bumble decorated the windows.

"Wow, this looks amazing."

"Thanks, O." Elaine dried her hands on her apron. It had a Christmas tree patchwork sewn down the front, with shiny packages on the pockets. "I thought it might be festive." She winked.

"Sure is. Are the cookies ready?"

Elaine checked the oven timer. "Soon. But they'll need to cool first so we can decorate them. I told Tommy he was in charge of the frosting."

Tommy held his forefinger in the air. "Decorate first. Then I get to lick the spoon."

Olivia laughed. "Please. Not the other way around." She took a glass from the cabinet and filled it with water. "Tommy and I have a couple of things to do in my room but if you call us when you're ready to decorate, that'd be cool."

"We do?"

Olivia nodded and put a finger to her lips, her eyes wide.

"Oh!" He shook his head. "We do." He gathered his artwork into a pile, scooping the markers onto the top.

Elaine raised an eyebrow. "That sounds secretive and Christmassy. Do what you need to do, and I'll yell when it's time."

Olivia and Tommy ran down the hall and Olivia stopped to knock on Seth's door.

A raspy voice responded. "Yeah?"

"Open the door, Sy."

"What do you want?"

"I want you to open the door."

"Not now. Get me later."

She knocked again. "Come on, Seth. Now."

She heard him shuffling, a muffled clicking of the lock. He cracked the door, grasping its edge, and leaned his forehead against it.

"What?"

His hair was greasy and hung in strands across his face, his chin stubbled. He looked like he'd been buried alive and dug his way out. On meth. Or had the flu for a month and let his hygiene go to hell. Or was on day five of some kick-ass bender.

"I need the," she glanced toward the kitchen, ". . . you know, for Mom."

He lifted his face to her, uncomprehending.

"For Christmas. Come on, Seth. Wake up." She tapped her foot while Tommy stood behind her. "Do I have to come in and get it myself?"

"What? No. No, I'll get it." He closed the door in her face.

She heard him stumble and curse, knock something over, and a box was shoved into her arms.

"Thanks," she began, but the door swung shut and latched. She motioned for Tommy to follow and carried it into her room. "He must've been in a deep, deep sleep."

"He never sleeps." Tommy climbed onto her bed.

"Maybe his new medicine will help." Olivia placed the box down gently.

Tommy opened one flap and peered inside. "It won't."

She tilted her head at him as she pulled wrapping paper from under her bed. "No?"

"He's not crazy."

Olivia took scissors and scotch tape out of her desk drawer. "No one said he's crazy. He just needs a little help."

Tommy paused. "It's not his brain."

"No?"

"Jetty's there."

"What?" She sat on the floor, carefully sliding the box down to her lap. She rested her arms across it. "What about Jetty?"

"He's in Seth's head."

"Your cat."

"Yeah," he giggled. "And that other thing's there, too. The one from his room."

Olivia's stomach tightened. "What thing?"

"You know." He met her eyes and jumped to the floor. "What are we giving New Mommy?" Bending back the cardboard flaps, he tried reading the word. "C-R-O-C-K . . ." They could hear the mixer whirring as Elaine whipped the frosting for the cookies.

"It says crockpot." She closed the box. "What were you saying about Seth's room? What's in there?"

"What's a crockpot?"

"Tom-my." She was dead serious, if not a little stern, and wanted to know what he knew. Needed to know what was going on behind the wall of her brother's self-imposed crypt.

"O-li-vi-a." He mimicked her tone.

She knew he was done with the conversation. They'd danced this dance before, and he'd won.

Tommy unrolled the Christmas paper. "Can we put a bow on top of New Mommy's present? She likes bows."

"Of course." She hesitated, twirling the scissors on her index finger. "Tommy?"

"Yeah?"

"Do you see ghosts?" She tried to sound as natural and matter of fact as she could. Maybe he'd finally talk to her. Tell her that he saw Mrs. Harper. Stop playing cat and mouse when she mentioned the paranormal.

"Maybe."

"I like ghosts." She handed him a bag of bows as she angled the crockpot box on top of the green paper with the gold calligraphy. Merry Christmas was scrawled in various languages across the wrap.

"I know." He pawed through the bag and picked a red bow.

Positioning the scissors, she ran them through the paper, snipping the last bit at the edge.

"Do you?"

He held the tape for her, then tossed it into her waiting hands. "They don't bother me."

"Will you ever tell me what you know about Seth's room?" An uneasiness grew in her as the seconds went by. Whatever was in his room didn't want her there, and Seth was declining. It's not like she hadn't seen spirits before, but this was unlike anything she'd sensed or felt. This was a block. And it felt wrong.

"No. Not me."

"Not you?" She folded the paper along the end of the present, creasing it with her fingernail.

"Nope."

"Who then?"

"Jetty."

"Jetty? Your cat will tell me."

"Yes."

Olivia finished taping the ends of the package and pushed it out of her way. "Your cat." She reached for a small box under her bed and placed it over a piece of the gift wrap, sizing it up.

Tommy sat back on his heels. "I want cookies."

"Me, too. Why don't you go see if Mom's ready for some help?"

She wrapped the last few presents, little somethings she'd picked up for Seth and Tommy, and pondered every word he'd said.

Olivia walked into the kitchen, book in hand, in time to see Tommy, his Scooby Doo shirt covered in icing, and gingerbread men looking more like blobby marshmallow people. Elaine clipped the corner off a bag of candies and set it in front of him.

"Have at it, little man. Decorate them any way you'd like."

He reached an icing-hand into the bag.

"What have you got there, O.?"

"A book of superstitions for all occasions. Any time of year, all kinds of countries. It's pretty cool."

"What's it got for Christmas?" Elaine put the last cookie sheet in the sink and filled the mixing bowls with water to soak.

Olivia thumbed through the table of contents. "Here we go. Let's see . . . Children born on Christmas Eve or Christmas Day are able to see spirits. How cool is that?"

"Seems to me since Christmas is the day that Jesus was born, people were apt to believe that anyone born then would also have special gifts."

Olivia mulled it over for a moment. "I thought he was born in October."

"It was April," Tommy said, still sticky-fingered and trying to glue a red and white mint to the belly of a gingerbread blob.

"Well, I'm not sure if anyone will ever know the true date. April is as good a time as any," said Elaine. "Almost done there, Tommy?"

"Nope." Picking up the shaker of chocolate sprinkles, he doused the cookies in front of him. "These taste good."

"Do you think November is close enough to ride the psychic wave from Christmas? I mean, after all, the 23rd of November is pretty darned close. Maybe, if not seeing spirits, I could at least hear them?" Olivia picked up a cookie and bit, smearing white buttercream across her cheeks. "Nice job, Tom Tom. Very tasty."

"Thanks!" He wiped his hands on his shirt and licked his lips. "I'm done, New Mommy."

Elaine pushed his chair to the sink and turned on the water to wash his hands. "Hold up your arms." She pulled off his shirt and wadded it into a ball, leaving it on the counter. "Now run and get a clean shirt."

Tommy leaped off the chair, sending it across the floor.

"Careful!"

"Okay!"

As she picked a fresh dishtowel from under the sink, she asked, "What else have you got for Christmas superstitions?"

"If you eat an apple on Christmas Eve, you'll have good luck."

Tommy flew into the room like hell on wheels with a monster truck tee shirt in his hands. "Here." He tossed it to Elaine and climbed onto a chair at the table. "Eeny meeny miny moe." He scooped up the most sprinkle encrusted snow-ginger-thing he could and bit it.

"If you light a candle on Christmas Eve, it must remain lit until Christmas Day, undisturbed. Or your luck runs out."

"Well, that's pretty bleak." Elaine folded Tommy's shirt and hung it across the back of his chair.

"I don't know. Sounds pretty straightforward to me. Just have a safe spot, where nothing can catch fire. Seems like it'd work pretty nicely. Candles have been a part of life, spell work, so many things, throughout history."

"You're not doing it. It's not safe to sleep with candles lit."

"Well, you wouldn't have to sleep, right? Just be awake when the clock strikes midnight. Technically, you're at Christmas Day then. Or do you think you have to be a certain number of hours into the day for it to count?"

"I don't think you'll have to worry about that since you won't be participating in that superstition. I'm sure you have a rabbit's foot in your room somewhere that you could rub instead."

Olivia smiled. "Like five or six."

"Good. You're covered, luck-wise. Next."

"Don't give shoes as a gift or the person will walk out of your life."

"Really."

"That's what it says. Right here in black and white." Olivia held up the book.

"What about sneakers?"

"Mom." Her palm kept her place as she let the pages close around it.

"Heels? Slingbacks? Slippers?"

"Semantics!"

"Well, inquiring minds want to know. What do I need to do to send the unwanted out of my life? Just hand out slipper socks?"

Olivia snorted. "Next."

Elaine waved her hand in the air motioning her to continue.

"Leaving a Christmas tree undecorated brings negative energy and evil spirits."

"I'd say we're set, wouldn't you?"

They surveyed the room, the lights, window clings, tiny red bows with gold bells adorning the archway and Santa figurines scattered throughout. Olivia could see the largest branches of the tree from where she sat, heavy with balls and garland, and she nodded. "I think we're set for the next five years."

Elaine playfully snapped the dishtowel at her. "What else have you got?"

"Those were the best." She turned the page. "But wait. New

Year's Eve is only a week away. Let's check out those."

Tommy licked his fingers and Elaine wet a paper towel to clean his face. "Come on, let's get that shirt on." She helped him with the sleeves and tugged it over his head. "Go play, little man. I need to clean up this kitchen. What've you got for New Year's, O.?"

"Here's an easy one. Eating circle shaped foods for good luck in the new year. Grapes, pizza, doughnuts. I guess I know what we're planning for dinner that night!"

"We can, if you'd like. It'd be fun to make a 'round food night.' Invite Jules and Christie, if you'd like."

Olivia shook her head. "They're both busy for the weekend. I think Christie's going to be at her cousin's and Jules' family has something going on. We might get together one night during the week, though."

"Okay. Then we'll plan a menu and have some fun with that ourselves."

"Okay." She ran her finger along the page. "No doing laundry on New Year's Day. I kind of like that one."

"Why would that be?"

"It says if you do, you're washing for the dead."

"That's morbid."

Olivia grinned. "Yeah."

"I bet it's more likely that it's an old wives tale passed down by people who didn't want to do any chores the day after they were up all night," she made air quotes, "celebrating."

"You're probably right." Olivia took a fingerful of icing and licked it.

Elaine picked up the bowl. "Finished?"

While her foster mother held it, she swiped her finger along the inside of the bowl, wiping it clean. "Yeah." She turned the page with her other hand. "On New Year's Day, the luckiest is if a tall, dark, handsome man appears on your doorstep with a gift."

"That's pretty specific. I'm not sure I know any of those and none are bringing presents."

"Well, the first guest in your home determines the type of luck for the house in the coming year. Got to make sure it's a good one."

"I'll lock the door to anyone who isn't drop dead gorgeous with their arms laden with packages."

"Now you're talking." She flipped pages, searching other holidays for anything interesting. Like when she was little and had a book of world records. She'd leaf through, hit something neat, scan the next few. Her gaze caught an entry that called to her. "Here's an interesting one."

Elaine was scrubbing the baking sheets, getting all the utensils into the dishwasher. "For which holiday?"

"It's its own thing, I guess. Not till April. The twenty-fourth. St. Mark's Eve."

Elaine thought. "I've never heard of it."

"On that date, you go to a church between the hours of 11:00 pm and 1:00 am and wait. It says there will be a procession of the dead, but not those who've already died."

"What?" Elaine closed the dishwasher and set the dial. "How's that?"

"It's a procession of the future dead. You'll see those who'll die in the coming year."

"That's creepy."

"It's so cool. It also says that some families take the ashes from their fireplaces and spread them across their hearths. In the morning, they find footprints of the doomed ones." Olivia's eyes lit up. "Can you imagine?"

"Olivia Miranda Mulvey, I cannot." Elaine stood, feigning annoyance.

"You three-named me." Olivia held back a laugh.

"I know what you're thinking."

"Who me?" She held her hands together in a circle over her head. "I'm innocent."

"Put your fake halo away. I know you better than you think I do. Don't get any ideas about smearing ashes to see who's going to die in this house. No one's checking out this year, and I don't think you need to make a mess in my living room to prove it."

Olivia got up from the table, taking long, exaggerated steps toward the living room. "I think I remember you having a dust buster somewhere?" She bolted.

"Oh, no, you don't!" Elaine ran after her.

They landed on the sofa, Elaine holding Olivia's ankles as she fake-struggled crawling to the fireplace.

"Hey, what's so funny?" Tommy ran to Olivia.

"Ghost jokes." She poked his nose with her finger.

"I know one." He picked up his truck and ran it over Olivia's foot, driving it up her calf.

"Tell me."

"How do you know Dracula has a cold?"

Elaine leaned in. "How?"

"He starts coffin!"

Olivia groaned.

Elaine smiled, shaking her head. "Good one, Tommy."

"Technically," Olivia said, sitting up, "Dracula isn't a ghost, you know. He's a vampire."

Tommy shrugged. "So?" He continued driving his car along the sofa. "How does a ghost sneeze?"

"How?"

"Ah, ah, ah, boo!"

Seth sat on his bed, the stench coming in waves from the corner of his room. Bloody diarrhea and rotting flesh assaulted his nostrils. He pressed his blanket over his nose and gagged. Nothing blocked the odor anymore and the demon rarely slept. It was in a constant alarm state, fight or flight, whenever Tommy got close.

Seth's ceiling was shredded from its pacing. And there was one thought that permeated his days.

Kill him

It was the driving need of the thing. It fueled his nightmares and invaded his waking hours, pushing, commanding. Superimposing its will over his own.

Kill him

He hated Blake for bringing this in. Hated himself. And hated Tommy for whatever he was that this hell-beast abhorred.

Light footsteps in the hallway stopped outside his door. The beast bared its fangs and hissed, crawling on all fours to settle onto Seth's back. The talons didn't have to break skin anymore. His punctures were deep, and the wounds didn't heal. Black venom dripped freely into his veins. His mind clouded.

"Go away!"

He didn't know if he had screamed or if any sound had escaped his lips. Didn't know if he'd shouted at the demon, the pain or the boy. Pulling his knees to his chest, he tucked himself into a ball of terror and anxiety.

The footsteps left.

Chapter 20

The sky was a dull, steel grey. One of those overcast, snow on the horizon, afternoons. Dom stood at his balcony doors and checked his phone for an update. Out for delivery. He kept an eye on the parking lot, watching the entrance. No mail truck. He tucked his feet into his sneakers. If the package wasn't there, maybe he could get a walk in before the non-existent sun went down. He despised the early setting of the sun in winter. He tied his laces and peered out the window once more.

"Success!"

Grabbing his keys, he made his way down the stairs to the first floor and waited beside the wall of mailboxes for his building.

"Afternoon, Dominic." The tall man in the grey-blue uniform had a large bag slung over one shoulder. He dropped it onto the floor and began sorting letters.

"How's it going, Pete?"

"Another day, another dollar."

"I hear that. Do you have a package for me?"

"You know, I believe I do. Just a moment." He shoved an electric bill into 3B and bent to toss back the flap on his bag. "Yes. Here it is." Handing the package over, he said, "Present for someone special?"

"For myself, actually."

Pete laughed. "All the better! Merry Christmas to you."

"Merry Christmas."

Dom went up the stairs to the second floor and into his apartment. "It's about time," he said. Using his key to cut the edge of the box, he slid a second box wrapped in bubble wrap out of the package. He slit the scotch tape and dropped the packing to the floor. The second box held his prize. A Raven's Claw tactical combat knife in a leather sheath, along with a sharpening stone. He unsheathed the blade and examined it. The hilt fit squarely in his hand, and he sliced the air at different angles to watch it shine.

He kicked off his shoes. On the far end of the coffee table was an abalone shell with a sage stick laying across it. He lit the bundle, holding the burning end low so it could catch deeply, and let the smoke flow over the blade. From tip to handle, over and over until he felt it was clear of any energy not his own.

"If this were a movie, I'd dub you Devil Slayer," he said. "But I'll settle for you sending a demon back to the deepest pit of hell." He picked up the stone and began to sharpen the blade.

Chapter 21

Christmas Eve. Finally. Olivia waited until she heard Elaine leave the bathroom and go to bed. Her foster mother would be in for the night. She clutched the candle she'd taken from the closet in the mudroom. Household emergency candles. Unscented. She was glad of that. Elaine would have noticed a lavender and vanilla or tropical coconut scent, for sure.

The area was prepared on her desk, a large piece of aluminum foil folded into a square and set on a plate. She'd bent up the edges on each side to catch any melted wax. This would work. She'd light it before she went to sleep and set her alarm for midnight. 12:03 am, to be exact, just in case it needed a little more time for the luck to commence. Not that she believed in luck, but who knew? There was no such thing as coincidence. Maybe luck had to do with energy and intent as most things did in the paranormal realm. If so, she had the intent. It was going to be a great year.

From her desk drawer she took out the lighter she'd gotten from the little convenience store two streets over. It had a red devil on its side, winking. She winked back, spun the spark wheel and watched the flame come to life. The acrid heat made her wrinkle her nose as she held the candle on its side to light the wick. She let the fire melt some of the wax at the tip, dripping translucent puddles that cooled to opaque on the foil. Securing the base of the candle, she waited, making sure it was tight.

Curling up in her chair, she thumbed through her phone, checking Facebook and Instagram posts and letting the candle do its thing. Safety first, she'd told herself. She watched the flame. One minute, two. Everything seemed good. Time for superstition, part two.

Olivia held her breath. She stepped quietly into the hallway and listened. The house didn't stir. Even Iggy was sound asleep, the ever-vigilant watchdog. She tiptoed to the living room.

When she got to the fireplace, she hesitated. A reach to the jacket rack. She dug in her pockets for a glove and slipped it onto her right hand. No sense having the evidence on her fingers if Elaine woke. They'd arranged the presents under the tree when Tommy went to sleep, oohing and ahhing over ribbons and bows, and speculating about the contents of every box. Now, the glow of the tree lights was perfect for what she needed to do. She stretched and flexed her fingers as she squatted at the fireplace.

She slid the glass out of her way, gripped the cast iron ball of the mesh gate and gently tugged it open. The ashes of the last fire lay under the grate, and she scooped up a small handful.

"Not too much," she whispered. "Not too much." She sprinkled it across a foot-long section of the hearth. Her alarm was set for this, too. Hours before Elaine would even consider climbing out of bed but with plenty of time that if something was going to walk through, she'd be the one to find it. She'd test every superstition and paranormal theory she could. It called her. She'd be the queen of all things ghostly if she had anything to say about it. This was only the beginning.

The sun was coming up and the house had that empty feeling. The "get things done before anyone else rises" kind of morning. He walked to the living room, thoroughly enjoying having the house to himself and anticipating a slow cup of coffee while he watched it snow.

As he stepped into the living room, the red, green and yellow Christmas lights flickered on, illuminating the single present under the tree. The tag read "Seth." He grinned. It didn't seem odd that it was the only gift. Today just felt right.

Seth pulled on his socks and took his new sneakers out of the Under Armour box. His mother always picked perfect presents. His old running shoes were worn through on the edges. Threadbare at the toes. Not that he was much of a runner, but they worked for a jog or a light hike. And these were navy blue, his favorite color, and ready to go. He tied the laces and stood, pulling on his grey hoodie. New sneakers always had that light, comfortable, almost bouncy feeling.

He felt good. Better than he had in a long time. Maybe because Christmas was in the air. Maybe the antidepressants were kicking in. Maybe everything had been all in his head. He stretched and pushed open the front door, letting the screen bang as he stepped through. He called to his mother. "I'll be home later. I-"

He was in a cemetery. The cemetery. Again. He hadn't been back since Blake died. His heart pounded. He was beside the mausoleum. But before him was a boulder and he could see Blake's broken body draped over the stone. That wasn't right. It wasn't where he'd left him.

Thunder growled and the skies darkened. Black clouds spit rain, pelting him with cold, wet drops. The leaves smelled dank, and the path was slippery.

"Why, man?" Blake shifted on the stone, following Seth with his eyes. "Why'd you leave me? I wasn't dead, man. You could have saved me."

Seth spun in a circle, a fear-panic ripping through his mind and chest. "You were dead. There was nothing I could do. I would have stayed. I would have."

"Liar!"

The sky opened, the deluge soaking him. He held his arms out from his body, terrified, longing for an out.

Blake shoved himself up on his bloody arms, then dropped, unmoving. A siren wailed in the distance, and Seth knew he had to run. Get out of there. Leave his friend. Again.

The storm rolled in with ferocity and he took off, searching left and right for a place to hide. His chest threatening to cave in and crush his heart with every breath. His legs churned, feet sliding in the mud. As he passed the boulder, he stopped.

It wasn't Blake.

Tommy's body lay splayed on top of the rock. His head was cocked to one side, neck snapped. A cold spike went through Seth's heart, chilling his guts. He looked at his palms and they were blood red.

The siren was closer now, and he could see the red and blue police lights in the distance. He ran, but his shoes came off in the thick mud. Thunder shook the ground like an earthquake beneath his feet. He clutched the shoes to his chest and climbed through a large bramble bush, then yanked off his soggy, dirty socks. Seth stuck his finger behind his heel and tried working his bare foot into the shoe. It wouldn't slide on. Lightning lit the sky and he saw the shoes, navy and white, dripping red droplets into a puddle on the ground. They were stained. He couldn't wear them. The police would hang him.

He screamed at the sky. "Why are you doing this to me?!"

Laughter boomed from everywhere and nowhere, knocking him to his knees. He dropped the shoes and ran into the night, demons on his heels.

He woke and rolled over. It took a moment to register that his sheets weren't just sweat-wet. They were wetter. His ass was in a puddle of pee. Groaning, he rolled onto the floor and pulled the sheets off the bed. The mattress already had a deepening stain.

Olivia heard a noise. Body tense and senses on high alert, she tiptoed to her room. There, silhouetted by the candle, was Tommy. Before she comprehended what was happening, she heard him take a breath and blow. A wisp of smoke floated upward, dissipating into the air. 11:59 pm.

"Tommy!" she said. Her voice was stern but quiet. "Why'd you do that?"

"New Mommy told you not to. It's not safe."

He had her. She couldn't argue with that. "Well, that's between me and Mom, right? I'll put this away if you don't tell her."

He nodded.

"What are you doing up anyway?"

"I have to go potty." He yawned.

"Go potty. Then back to bed, okay? Santa can't come if you're awake."

Another shake of his head, another yawn, and he was on his way toward the bathroom. Olivia sighed and rolled the tin foil into a ball, dropping it into her top drawer. She placed the candle on the windowsill. "So much for candle luck." Another sound caught her attention, this time from the living room. A metal on glass tink-tink. She bolted and peered into the hallway to see who was awake. Or who might be discovering the ashes she spread. The only illumination was from the Christmas tree, and she didn't see anyone. She quickly made her way to the hearth.

The metal ball on the other side of the fireplace glass was swinging. And the ashes were disturbed. Her heart fluttered with anticipation, skipping a beat. There, in the ashes, were two definite footprints. Shoe prints. With a design she didn't recognize.

"Damn it." She hadn't brought her phone.

She didn't think she could stand it if she didn't get a picture. Wouldn't have any proof that it happened. But she was pushing it tonight going back and forth. She didn't want to wake Elaine. A door swung open in the hallway, and she dove for the kitchen. Seth walked into the bathroom, shut the door and turned on the water.

"A shower? Now?" It struck her as weird but most of the things Seth was doing now were off the beaten path. But maybe she could get her phone, take a pic and not wake anyone.

She didn't see Tommy in the shadows behind the Christmas tree, a smear of ashes on his index finger. A breeze moved through the room, traveling across the hearth. It left the ashes in a pile at the front door. The boy snickered and went back to bed.

Olivia returned and, when she saw the ashes had been moved, was intrigued but disappointed. She turned off the sound on her phone and snapped a few pictures of the pile and the hearth at different angles. Maybe she'd catch the form of a spirit or a spectral hand, something that would have gotten rid of the prints. What the hell? At least she knew it wasn't just superstition, but who would believe her? Her mother would say it was a dream and Seth would tell her to leave it alone.

But she knew. Something. She wasn't sure what, yet. She knew someone was going to die this year. In their house? She shuddered. Maybe on their block? Maybe it was picking up on old Mrs. Harper. Did support shoes have that kind of tread? She supposed it was possible. But Mrs. Harper wasn't the future dead. She passed away years ago. The journalist in her was awake and battling for top billing with her paranormal investigator self. She pulled the afghan off the back of the sofa, covered up and settled in. Maybe whatever had been there would be back. And she'd be waiting.

She woke to pots and pans rattling in the kitchen and her foster mother humming and realized she'd fallen asleep on the sofa. 6:30 am. Elaine peeked into the living room.

"Morning, sleepyhead. You must've been excited for the day! What time did you get up?"

Olivia stretched the blanket to her chin. "I didn't."

"Well, get a few more minutes while I make some breakfast. I have a feeling that Tommy will be coming down that hallway soon." She spun on her heel and went back to stirring pancake batter.

Olivia sat up. The small pile of ashes was still in front of the door. She'd need to clean that up before Elaine noticed. Or not. She scooched deeper into the sofa cushions and closed her eyes, easing into a warm, comfortable half-sleep until Tommy jumped on her.

"Presents!"

Olivia pulled herself out from under him.

"Presents, Olivia!"

"I guess Santa came, didn't he?"

"Santa's not real."

"No?"

Tommy slid to the floor and crawled closer to the tree. "But presents are."

"Merry Christmas, Tommy." Elaine peeked in, spatula in hand.

He paused mid-reach for a square box wrapped in red and green paper. "Merry Christmas."

"No touching anything under the tree until everyone is up and ready. Pancakes first."

Olivia moaned. "Oh, Mom. Seth'll be in bed half the day."

"Oh, Mom," Tommy echoed. He sat on his heels, frowning.

"I'll make you a deal," Elaine said. "If he's not out by eleven, you can drag him out."

Olivia checked the clock. "That's over four hours from now."

"10:30?"

"Okay."

"You and Tommy can always open your stockings, you know. Did you forget you had them?"

Elaine stepped back into the kitchen while Olivia helped Tommy unhook his stocking from the mantel. They were arm deep into silver and gold wrapped chocolates when Seth walked in.

"Speak of the devil. Merry Christmas, Sy."

"Olive."

"Sy," said Tommy.

He glared at the little boy with chocolate-smeared lips, dressed in bright red pajamas, and leaned toward him. "My name is Seth." He tugged the ties on his hood, so it tightened, framing his face.

"Merry Christmas, honey!" Elaine came from the kitchen with a plate of pancakes, a stack of paper plates under her arm and a jar of maple syrup looped over her thumb. She deposited everything on the side table nearest the sofa. "Just let me get the forks and breakfast is on."

"I do love Christmas picnic breakfast," said Olivia. "Grab a plate, Tommy, and let's dig in."

As they cozied up to the small table, plates on their laps, Seth wandered into the kitchen. He returned a minute later with a steaming mug of coffee. Olivia wrinkled her nose.

"Coffee?"

"Caffeine is my only friend." He raised his cup. "Cheers."

"Who's the fourth stocking for?" Tommy stood in front of it, holding the toe and looking for a clue to its ownership.

"Iggy. Mom gets him a puppy stocking every year. Iggs! Where are you, pup?"

Iggy scrambled from the kitchen and bounced up onto the hearth. Olivia scratched the top of his head and lowered the stocking so he could sniff it. His tail wagged hard enough he knocked himself onto the floor. Olivia ripped apart a mesh bag and fished out a chew toy. She held it above her head.

"Here, boy! Get it!"

Iggy jumped, then climbed onto her lap with his front paws on her shoulders and barked.

"Okay, you little fiend. It's yours." She held it out and laughed as Iggy tossed it over his head. Taking a bite of her pancake, she asked, "How's the coffee, Sy?"

"Stimulating." He sat cross-legged, against the sofa, warming his hands on the mug. He was trying to absorb as much of its heat as he could, hoping it would somehow seep into his bones. His heart. Soul. Sip after sip, lukewarm mouthfuls. It all fell short. He finished the coffee and walked into the kitchen.

"Pancake, Seth?" Elaine was hopeful he'd eat something. She could tell he was losing weight, and his lack of sleep was palpable.

"Later maybe."

"You can't just have caffeine running through your veins," Olivia called after him. "It's not healthy."

Seth muttered as he poured another cup. "Caffeine, antifreeze. Not much difference."

"Antifreeze is much less healthy," Olivia said as he sat down again.

"Hence the coffee." He settled in beside her. "Seems like all we do is open presents in this house."

Olivia chewed her last bite of pancake. "Is that a bad thing? I'm thinking it's not."

"Of course not, Miss Sagittarius."

"Can't help it if you have to wait until July. Should've told Mom to hurry up."

"Hey," Elaine said. "No preemie here. In fact, he was past his due date and didn't want to come out."

"Mom." Seth stared into the coffee swirling in his cup. It made him the slightest bit dizzy.

"I tried everything. Long walks, jumping up and down," she glanced at him. "Ate a vindaloo."

Seth rolled his eyes and set his mug on the floor. "Mom. Stop. That's ridiculous."

Elaine's eyes crinkled at the corners. "Ate every last spicy drop." She winked at Olivia. "Nothing. This boy was setting up shop in there." She picked up the remote, clicked the television on, and selected Christmas Old and New. She turned the volume to low and let carols fill the room. "I think it's present time."

"I agree," Seth said. "Let's get to the task at hand."

"Changed your tune pretty fast, eh, Sy?"

"We don't need any birth stories on Christmas morning."

"You just insulted baby Jesus."

He face-palmed. "Grab a present, Olive."

"Is everybody ready?" she asked, snickering.

"I am!" Tommy yelled. He dropped his plate onto the floor and stood in front of the Christmas tree.

Olivia inclined her head toward Elaine.

"Yes, go ahead." She gathered up the pancake plate and the garbage. "I'll be right back. Give Tommy one."

The little boy leaned into the tree, not caring that the branches were poking him.

"Here, Tommy. Open this one. It's from Mom."

He took the box, eyes bright. "What is it?"

"Open it and find out." Elaine sat in the recliner.

He tore at the paper. "A dump truck!"

"There's a scissors in the drawer of the end table. O., would you hand it to Seth?"

"Why me?"

"Man hands. You've got the brute strength we need when it comes to breaking those little plastic ties they use."

"Olive could do it."

"Hey!" she said. "Don't call me 'Man Hands.'"

She tossed Seth the scissors and he caught them with his knees. "Careful, sis. Don't want to damage anything important." He reached to take the truck box from Tommy and as his hand brushed the boy's, a shiver went through his bones. As if he'd touched the dead. The thing in his brain screamed. He snapped the ties, yanked the toy from its packaging and set it at Tommy's feet. Every time the boy ran by, giving a present to whoever was on deck, his mind roared with a thunderous wind-growl of hatred.

"Who's next?" Elaine was on the edge of her seat, eyes bright.

"You, Mom. Tommy, grab that one." Olivia pointed. "Yeah, the one with the calligraphy paper."

"Oh! You guys shouldn't have," Elaine said, admiring the present from all sides. "It's much too big."

"I know what it is! I know!" Tommy did a little dance in front of her. "It's a secret, but I know."

"Should I?" She tucked a finger under the flap on the side and lifted the tape.

"Open it! Open it!"

What little excitement Seth had for the day fizzled. He sat in awkward obligation while his mother acted as if they had given her the crown jewels.

"It's just a crockpot, for God's sake."

Elaine smiled. "It's my crockpot. From my kids." She set the present down. "You're next, O. Santa-Tommy, this one is for Olivia." Elaine handed him a small, sparkling green bag with bright red tissue paper fanned at the top.

"Santa-Tommy," he chuckled. He peeked inside as he handed it over.

Olivia rummaged through the bottom of the bag, drawing out Tommy's anticipation. "I don't know, maybe there's nothing in here."

"There is! I saw it!"

She took out a small, velvet storage case.

"It's from Books and More, I hope you like it."

Olivia gently pressed the lid of the box to reveal an amethyst on an elaborate chain. "A pendulum?"

"I thought it was a necklace." Elaine winked.

"You got me a pendulum?"

"Is that good or bad?"

"Good, Mom! Thank you." She hugged her foster mother and examined the stone more closely. "You know, it could almost be a necklace. But I like this better." She placed it in its case and set it beside her. "Seth's next." She steadied herself on all fours, trying to spy the present she had for her brother. "Here, Sy. From me." She placed it on his leg.

"I'm not up for-"

"You'll open it and like it, Sy."

"Yes, ma'am." He shredded the paper, including the tissue inside. A bracelet dropped into his lap.

"Careful, man."

"Cool, Olive." He ran the beads through his fingers, the smooth dark circles were somehow comforting.

"Obsidian, hematite and blue tiger eye." She met his eyes. "For protection." She drew out the syllables of the last word.

"Cool." He set it down.

Olivia touched his forearm. "Put it on."

A bit of warmth returned to his skin where the gemstones rested. But only there.

"Thanks."

"Me next! Me."

"Let me see." Olivia tugged the next present from under the tree. "It's for . . . Tommy."

"Yay!"

Seth closed his eyes and listened to the Christmas commotion.

His mother unwrapped a monogramed mug and there was talk of winter clothes and little boy snow boots. But he was in a tunnel. Mind and soul. Deep underground with the roar of the approaching train almost drowning out the chaos of the living room. The dark abyss drawing him deeper, farther away from the light.

"Sy, wake up." Olivia shook his leg and tossed a small package at him. He caught it against his stomach.

"I'm awake."

"You could've fooled me."

"All right, you two, no bickering," Elaine said. "That one's from me, Seth."

He nodded. "Thanks, Mom."

"I hope you like it. I thought you and Olivia might get your competitive juices flowing on this instead of each other. At the very least you'll have some fun with it. I might even play a little."

He tore at the paper and a game fell into his lap. The black and orange dragon logo caught his eye immediately. "Mortal Kombat, cool. We will."

"I'll kick your ass," Olivia said.

"Language, O.," Elaine chimed in.

"I'll kick your ever-loving butt."

"You and what army?"

"Olivia, aren't you playing Santa Claus?" Elaine asked, looking under the tree. "I see there are a few more left."

"Olive."

"Yes?"

"The little yellow paper bag with the three presents in it. There's one for each of you. That's next." He sat back, closing his eyes once more.

Olivia picked up the bag by its string handles. Inside were three small presents, each wrapped in loose leaf paper and stuck heavily closed with scotch tape. The names were scrawled in pencil. "This one says Mom." She handed it over. "And this one 'Tommy,' and . . . Olive." She rolled her eyes.

They dug in and unwrapped his presents at once. Elaine was the first done.

"Hand sanitizer. Thank you, Seth. It'll come in handy, I'm sure."

His lips curled slightly at his mother's joke.

"I'll keep it in the car so we can all use it after those sketchy gas station stops."

"A Pop's Pharmacy back scratcher?" Olivia asked. "Really."

"Brand name, that." He didn't open his eyes. "You know you like your back scratched."

"Rubbed, man. Rubbed."

"Tomato, to-mah-to."

"No, Sy. It's totally different."

Elaine held up her hand, not that Seth could see it. "It's the thought that counts."

"And I'm really poor at the moment."

Olivia snorted. "But you shop at the best places."

"You bet."

"Can I have mine?" Tommy said. He turned over the ball of paper that seemed to be nothing more than pages crumpled. He poked the edge of it and it rolled to a stop at Olivia's feet. She picked it up and examined it. Tommy had already turned his attention to the presents remaining under the tree.

Olivia ripped the paper and tossed him a small bag of "coal." "Here, kid. It's candy."

Tommy caught the red mesh bag and sniffed the black licorice rocks. Nothing that smelled like that could taste good. He stepped over to where Seth sat.

Seth startled out of his tunnel as Tommy shoved the bag into his palm.

"Open this for me?"

They locked eyes. The voice was wrong, and the coal burned in his hand. He tried pulling away but could only sit, staring into the evil-faced child scowling at him with eyes as red as the flesh that was boiling off the bones of his hand.

"Coal is for bad boys, Seth. Am I a bad boy?"

He wanted to scream, send the kid straight to hell, beat the shit out of him and run, but was paralyzed.

"Am I a bad boy?"

With every word, Tommy squeezed the coal a little harder, pressed it deeper, into his palm. His tissues were sizzling like steaks on a hot grill. How could his mother sit there and watch him be tortured?

"Am I a . . ."

"Well, Seth, are you going to open it for him or what?" Elaine asked.

He snapped to reality. "What?"

"Tommy asked you to open the candy. You okay? You must've dozed off."

"I, yeah. I must have." He stuck a finger into the mesh and tugged, pouring candy into his hand. His intact hand. No burn. He handed it all to Tommy.

The little boy scrunched up his nose. "Eww. Only bad boys would like that." He then whispered, "Am I a bad boy?"

Seth recoiled.

Tommy clapped his hands. "There's three presents left!"

"So, it seems! There's one for Olivia," Elaine paused, pretending to have trouble reading the tags. Tommy ran the present over.

"This one is for Seth." Another pause.

"And? Is it for me?" Tommy climbed into her lap, between her and the final present. "I see my name! I see Tommy."

Elaine hugged him. "Yes. It's for you!"

He scrambled off and threw himself into unwrapping. Olivia waited, holding hers.

"What did you get?"

Tommy held up the box.

"Trouble! It's a game, Tommy. We'll all play later. Very cool." Olivia said. "What do you think's in here?" She shook her box. Nothing moved.

"Oh, I know!" He rested a hand on the present. "I know exactly what this is."

"You do?" Olivia said. "Tell me!"

Tommy shook his head. "No. You've got to do it. But I know what it is."

"Okay." Olivia ran a fingernail down one of the creases in the gift wrap and slit "Merry Christmas" down the middle. "Hmm. Just a generic box. Are you sure you know what this is?"

"Yes! Yes, I do."

Olivia turned the present on its side and pulled a Ouija board out onto the carpet. She squealed. "A real one?!"

"It came from my old house." Tommy danced, wiggling his butt. "I knew it. I knew it."

"I hope it's okay. I saw it at the other house and thought of you."

"I love it! Not just a cardboard one from the toy section of Walmart. Wow. And the grain of the wood is so nice. Thank you." Olivia admired the board in her hands. Maybe now she could take things to the next level. She shivered as a gust of cool air blew across her back and she took quick note of the fireplace. The logs were still burning, toasty as ever.

"You're very welcome." Elaine sighed. "And the last present goes to Seth." She kicked a medium sized box over to him.

He let it sit on the floor and worked it one-handed. Even though his hand was intact, he still favored it. At least the box opened easily. Black Adidas Falcon running shoes. Something to get him out of the house. "Thanks, Mom."

"What is it?" Olivia looked up from her board. "What'd you get?"

Seth stuck his hand under the tongues of both shoes and held them up. "Running shoes."

She didn't hear him. Didn't register "running shoes." All she saw were the bottoms of his sneakers, the lines of tread that matched the footprints from the night before. Inside, a part of her was dancing and high fiving that the experiment with the ashes had worked and she'd glimpsed the future. But then it registered. The future dead.

Olivia paled.

Chapter 22

She said her goodnights and, Ouija board clutched to her chest, secluded herself in her room. She thought about getting cozy on her bed, but this board deserved a prestigious spot. She set it on her chair while she cleared her desk. Textbooks went to the floor. She peeled back the pages of a memo pad she used for school assignments until she had a fresh one, and placed it to the side, took a pen from the plastic movie monster cup, and laid it across the page. Her gaze fell on the candle, still on the windowsill from the night before.

"Perfect." Grabbing her lighter, she spun the spark wheel and touched the flame to the wick. It sizzled, then whisper-roared to life. She was excited to try this new board to see what it could do. Her old one never produced much if you didn't count the night with Christie and Jules. The glass they were using as a planchette slid across the board and shattered. It'd scared them all but, in hindsight, the glass could have been flawed. Maybe they'd pressed too hard. Or maybe the universe was telling her it wasn't the right time, and her friends just weren't into it. Maybe a serious, solitary user was what the spirits desired.

But she needed a planchette, and not a glass one. Digging through her desk drawer, she pulled out a checkers chip. She tossed it aside. "Doesn't seem right." Reaching deeper, her hand knocked into the small jar where she kept the change from school lunches and the occasional trip to the bookstore in Montgomery. She lifted it up, gently shaking it. "A penny for your thoughts? A nickel for the ferryman?" She fished to the bottom of the jar.

"A quarter might just do it." She slid it across the wood. "Hope the spirits are okay with that." She laid the coin in the center of the board. "Let's do this." Resting two fingers on the top of it, she closed her eyes and exhaled, relaxing and clearing her mind.

"Is there anyone here tonight who would like to communicate?" Olivia immediately sensed a presence. That feeling of not being alone when you know the room is empty. When the atmosphere shifts. Someone had joined her.

"I know you're here. I can be pretty sensitive. I invite you to communicate with me through the board. It's easy." Goosebumps traveled up her arms. It was hard to contain herself, but she needed to. She didn't want to scare whoever it was away.

"What's your name? You can spell it through the letters on this board." She heard a faint whistling outside. Odd. Perhaps her neighbor was having a smoke on his porch. Did people whistle when they smoked? She shook off the thought and focused.

A cold breeze enveloped her, sending a shiver up her spine.

"Getting a closer look? Good. Just shove the coin I'm touching to the letters you need."

On the inside she was jumping for joy. Communication with someone from beyond the grave. This was different from when she talked with Mrs. Harper. She'd always felt that it was the old woman's strength that allowed her to see and hear their visits together. Not in her control. But this! This was on her terms. This was personal. She was in charge.

A small vibration went through the quarter. It slid.

"J." Letter one. She was on this.

"E. So far, so good."

"T. T. Y." She paused to write the name. "J. E. T. T. Y. Jetty?" She hesitated. "Tommy's cat?"

The makeshift planchette slid to YES.

Olivia sat back in her chair, repositioning her hands on the coin. "Are you messing with me?" The quarter turned cold beneath her fingertips, and it slid again.

I am Jet

"Okay. Nice to meet you, Jet. My name is -"
Her fingers followed the quarter to the O. It spelled out her name.
"So, you know who I am."

Yes

"I guess that levels the playing field. Kind of sets us on even ground." She hadn't thought it might have knowledge of her, but anything was possible. Spirits were always around; it was just bringing them out. Knowing how to get them to show themselves.
"What year were you born?" Not a twitch from the coin. "Where were you born?" She paused. "Not interested in the mundane, Jet?" she said to herself. She ran through a short list of questions in her mind that she figured all ghost hunters would ask, trying to think of something that might continue their conversation. Give her a little something more about this spirit called Jet. "Why are you here?"

For you

"Me? You're here because of me? Out of all the spirits wanting to chat, what made you get to the front of the line tonight? What about me?"
The quarter slid to GOODBYE.
A knock. "I need a glass of water."
Tommy. She pushed her chair away from the desk, disappointed the session had to end. There were so many things she wanted to ask. To know. Seth. The future dead. She shivered.
"Sure, kid."
Maybe Jet would know what the deal was. Maybe he could help.
As they walked to the kitchen, Olivia wondered what Jet meant.

#

A snarling beast, saliva flowing in long threads from its jowls, held Seth by the neck over a ravine of lava. It squeezed his airway closed, talon-like nails cutting into his neck. Seth flailed, fighting for a final breath.

A sinister cawing cut through the darkness. The beast swung its head in the direction of the maniacal sound, dropping Seth into the red-hot river below him. His skin boiled off his bones.

As he woke, the sleeves of his hoodie were smoking.

He ripped off the shirt, scrambling for the light to check his arms. Red, raw. He ran his hands up his forearms, checking and rechecking. Sweating. The pain was there but no blisters. Thankful tears welled in his eyes, and he fell against the wall.

Wiping his face, he stared into the darkest corner of his room. His words came as a cry-choked plea. "Kill me." He swallowed. "Kill me. Please."

A laugh erupted. Closer. Shriller. He tucked himself into the fetal position, shoulders shaking, and wept until exhaustion took him.

Olivia checked her phone for the time. The light from her window was dull grey and large snowflakes were falling. She stretched, peering out at the side yard. Milo would need a little extra food today and she'd have to make sure he had water. She could hear that her foster mom had on the television news. Stuffing her feet into an old pair of slippers, she shuffled to the living room and curled up on the sofa.

"Morning, O." Elaine said, putting up the collar of her robe. "Weatherman says we could get up to a foot."

"Well, that's not fair."

"What?"

"To get a foot of snow when school's closed for winter break.

I'm missing out on a snow day."

"Spoiled brat." Seth's voice came from the kitchen.

"Like you can talk. You're not even going to school. What do you care about snow days?"

"I wasn't the one complaining." He walked into the living room, cup in one hand, bagel in the other. His white tank top was yellowed, with coffee stains down the front.

"Aren't you cold? It's twenty-five degrees outside." Elaine sat in the recliner with the afghan across her lap.

"Nope, I'm good."

"At least change that shirt today."

"And shave," Olivia said. "You're looking ratty."

He rubbed his chin with the back of his hand as he chewed. "Takes one to know one."

Olivia stuck out her tongue, then went to the coat rack. She pulled on a boot, taking care to tuck in her pajama pant leg.

"Where are you going?"

"Milo and Crow Daddy need food. You know how it is." She winked at Elaine as she gestured with her thumb at Seth. "Gotta keep them fed. Am I right?"

"In your pajamas?"

"Crows wait for no man," she held her forefinger in the air, "to get dressed."

Elaine rested her forehead in her palms. "I don't know what it is with you two. Cold as heck and snowing and you think you're at the beach."

"At the beach? In pajamas? Mom. What are you thinking?"

"Yeah, yeah. Don't catch a chill."

"I'll only be a minute." Olivia threw a scarf around her neck, zipped her jacket and followed Seth into the kitchen. She mixed a handful of Iggy's food with some peanuts.

Seth went straight to the counter. A half-full jar of Folger's instant was beside the sink, and he positioned it beside his mug. He spooned two heaping scoops into his cup.

"Oh, my God, I'm going to puke."

"Turn the other way."

"You do know you already had coffee in your cup, right? You just put coffee in coffee, Sy."

He stirred, grinding the spoon against the sides of the cup to get the crystals to dissolve. "Yeah."

She leaned closer, connecting with his eyes. "You going Nightmare on Elm Street on me or what? Your bags have bags."

"I think your crow screams in my dreams." He placed the spoon at the edge of the sink in case he needed more.

"What? Milo does wh-"

"Not him. The other one."

"Crow Dad-"

He held up his hand, squeezing his eyes shut so hard he saw light flashes. "Don't call it that."

"Him."

"What?" He shook his head. "Stop. Just stop. I need some space, my coffee. Just . . . back off, Olivia. I can't think right now."

"Fine, fine." She flipped the latch, stepping outside.

A fine mist of snow hit Seth and he flinched. It was like that now. Cold meant pain. Twisted nightmares. Poison dripping through his veins, gnawing at his mind. He shuddered and shut the door. The lock snapped into place, and he stared at it. Had he done that? He glanced at the bird bath. Olivia had her eyes shielded, searching the trees for her pets. Reaching forward, he tentatively popped the lock up and waited.

Olivia bounded inside, shaking the snow off her hair and draping her scarf on the back of a chair. Iggy licked at the wet flakes. "Whoa, it's cold today!"

"Not so much if you had dressed for it," Elaine called from the living room.

"For sure! I will later. It's packing snow. Great for a snowman." She squinted at Seth. "Maybe you'll come out, too. Get some fresh air on your sorry face." She only half-joked. His skin had a pallor that was nowhere near healthy and those bags . . . she didn't think he was sleeping at all.

"Yeah, yeah. I'll be out. Going to have to shovel for Mom anyway." He set his half-drunk coffee on the table and watched the snow fall.

He trudged to the end of the driveway, shovel in hand. The zipper on his jacket had long since broken and the wind whipped up under its flaps, into his sweatshirt. It triggered a nerve at his core, and he trembled, waiting for the next attack. When none came, he dug the shovel in deep beside the mailbox and began working his way up the driveway. A steady rhythm of scoop, toss. Scoop. Toss. Hypnotic in its simplicity. Mind numbing. The snow had muffled all the usual outdoor sounds, except for the occasional banging and scraping as one of the town plows passed on a side street.

"Olivia's bringing you gloves!"

The voice broke his concentration and he nodded. He didn't know how much they'd help now, with half the driveway finished. His solitude was destroyed as Tommy did a stiff-legged Michelin Man run into the snow with Olivia right behind him.

"Here," she said, tossing the gloves at him.

They fell at his feet. "Really, Olive?"

"Learn to catch, Sy."

"Learn to throw." He picked them up, slapping them together to knock off the snow.

"Come on, Tommy. Do you want to make a snowman or snow angels?"

"Snowman!"

Olivia showed him how to pack the snow into a ball, and roll it along the ground, getting it bigger and bigger. They concentrated on their work, letting Seth get back to his. Only Iggy was wild, bouncing at the window, whining to join them. Elaine let him out. "There you go, pooch."

The dog ran past Tommy and buried his face deep in the snow, bobbed up and continued in long loops around the front yard, only to pause by Seth and bark at the shovel.

"Go on," Seth complained. He poked the tool in Iggy's face, causing him to hop backward and bark louder.

"Iggy, come here!" Olivia said. The dog cocked his head to the side and ran to her. "Geez, Sy. Lighten up. He just wants to play."

"I have a headache and he's on my last nerve."

"You only have one nerve. Calm down." Olivia pet Iggy, helping him shake snow off his muzzle. "Okay, Tommy. Next snowball. Smaller than the first. This one's for his belly."

They rolled while Iggy pranced in the path they made.

Seth finished the driveway and cleaned the steps to the front door. He rested the shovel against the house.

"You going in?"

"Yeah. I'm done."

"Come help us."

Seth squinted at the sky. The flakes were smaller now and the storm was moving out. "Nah, I don't think so."

"Please? Come on, Sy. Just for a few minutes."

He wanted to leave. Retreat. Get into a ball and try to get warm. From the inside out, not that that was possible anymore.

"Come on." She teased. "I'll let you put the carrot on."

"Okay. For the carrot."

Stepping toward his sister, his foot landed square on the rake under the bed of snow. He dodged the handle but lost his footing, twisting, and landed on his chest in the wet mess. But it wasn't snow. It was water. He had fallen into a pool of water and floated under the ice. He felt above him and only found a frozen ceiling. Panic. It was dark and bone searing cold, the water soaking his clothes and sinking him deeper. He held his breath, arms flailing, fighting to find a break in the ice.

Olivia pulled on the back of his jacket, yanking him from the snowbank. "What the hell, Sy?"

He sucked in the cold air, wheezing like an asthmatic as he scrambled to grasp land, and get his bearings. The water was gone.

"Seth!"

He held up his hand and waved her off. "I'm okay."

"You are?"

"I am. Must've hit my head or something."

"Yeah," she said. "Must've." Not that she believed it. What she'd witnessed had nothing to do with a bump on the head. Or a non-existent one.

"Just give me a second."

Out of nowhere, a snowball hit Seth between the eyes. He recoiled, heard Tommy laughing, and lunged, rushing the boy.

Olivia jumped between them, grabbing Seth. "What are you doing?"

"That little punk!"

"It was a snowball!" She was six inches shorter than him, but she'd never been one to back down. "Get a handle on things!"

Tommy hid behind Olivia, gripping her pants.

She lowered her voice, unblinking. "He didn't mean it."

"Now you're defending him?" Seth said in utter shock. "I thought better of you." He turned on his heel, went up the steps into the house and slammed the door.

"I didn't mean it. I'm sorry."

Olivia knelt beside him. "That's okay, kid. I know you didn't. Seth just needs some time alone." Or with his therapist. With stronger meds. This was getting too weird. Too wrong. Maybe whatever was in his room was pushing him over the edge. Maybe Jet could give her some insight. She'd talk with him later tonight.

Right now, she had a snowman to finish.

Seth hung his jacket on the coat rack and left his sneakers under it. He dropped into the recliner. He was angry and they were all against him. The people who should have his back were drawn in by the little maggot. He was warm now. Hot. His blood was on fire, and he could feel his pulse beating in his temple. A migraine in the making, but he didn't care. He was alone. An island. And he'd have to take care of things on his own. Without them.

The television was on, and he grabbed the remote. Cycling through the channels, he found *The Twilight Zone*. He smirked. That figured. That's where he'd been living since Blake died. With the monster in his room and now the devil child who ruled the rest of the house. He seethed in hatred. He could almost, almost understand his mother. She had to care for the kid. But Olivia!

At least he knew where he stood.

"It's a Good Life" began. The boy on the screen could have been Tommy with everyone afraid to cross him. Afraid to say boo to the obvious problem in the house. Someone should have murdered the bastard. Taken him out so they could live a normal life. Gotten rid of the issue.

The front door flew open with Olivia and Tommy behind it, laughing and talking. Seth heard zippers and the swooshing of jackets being taken off, a flurry of activity. He focused on the television.

"Oh, Twilight Zone," Olivia said. "After I get changed, I'll watch it with you." She ran off.

Tommy walked closer to the set, taking in the show. Little Anthony Fremont had just wished an animal into the cornfield. Tommy watched a little longer, then touched the edge of the screen. It changed to static. He backed up and it cleared. A step forward, static.

"How are you doing that?" Seth said, leaning to the side to see. "Stop it."

The boy pressed his fingers into the screen. *Into* it. He swirled his hand through the black and white noise and flicked it at Seth.

Seth flinched.

Tommy laughed and took off toward the mudroom.

Shaking, Seth pulled the afghan up to his chin. The show was back on. Everyone was afraid of Anthony's powers. Tommy's powers. He covered his face with the blanket. He had to be losing his mind. None of this could be real. He'd fallen off the cliff of sanity and was clutching at the edge, with Tommy's foot hovering above him ready to strike.

A banging on the front door and Iggy barking brought him to consciousness. He threw the sofa pillow he'd been using at the dog. "Shut up!" Iggy ran about three feet and started to howl. "What the hell?"

"I'm coming. I'm coming." Elaine shushed Iggy, holding him to the side. "Tommy! What are you doing outside like that?" She swung the screen door out of his way. "Without even a coat! And alone!" She brushed him off. "What were you thinking? You can't go out like that."

"He did it." Tommy stood stoically, staring at Seth, while Elaine rubbed his hands.

"What?" Elaine spun.

An even louder, "What?!" echoed from Seth. He sat bolt upright. "I did not!"

Elaine looked over her shoulder at her son. "Did you?"

"What? No! I've been in this chair since I came in from shoveling."

"He did it. He put me outside."

"Liar." The veins on Seth's neck stood out as rage engulfed him.

"Seth! He's just a little boy."

"And he's a liar. I don't know why you hate me, kid, but the feeling is mutual."

"All right, Seth, enough. I don't know what happened here. I don't know who else could have put Tommy outside. Olivia's in her room and I certainly didn't do it. Why would you be so mean?"

"Maybe he did it to pin it on me, did you ever think of that?"

"Really? I don't know what possesses you sometimes." She took Tommy's hand and led him into the kitchen. "Let's get you some cocoa, little man, and warm you up."

"Yeah," Seth muttered, watching them leave the room. "What does it matter what I say?" He dropped the afghan onto the floor. Taking a deep breath, he went to his room. He paced, almost ignoring the foul stench growing thicker around him. That was the least of his worries.

"He's got it out for me. That kid just has it out for me and he's going to throw me under the bus every lying chance he gets." His eyes were wide, thoughts jumbled. "I have to stop him. Get him. I have to get him before he can get me."

The creature on his ceiling nodded.

Olivia lit the candle on her desk. The quarter was already resting on *Hello*. Maybe Tommy had been in her room. She'd have to talk with him. Her things were her things and he needed to respect that.

The quarter was cool to her fingertips as she moved it to the middle of the board and, before she could ask anything, the air chilled. "Eager to chat, are we?"

The coin moved.

Yes

"So am I. Is this Jet?"

The metal vibrated under her touch and then circled the word *Yes*.

"I've got some questions I hope you can answer." A pause. Olivia waited to see if there was any comment, any response. She exhaled. "Do you see, I mean, are you aware of the things that go on in the house?" The journalist inside her was scrambling, she knew what she wanted to ask but it all seemed too vague. "Are you with me? Do you watch everything? Aargh! Are you here more than just through the board?"

I am

A whistling began, faint and far away. Outside somewhere and coming closer. Olivia turned her head to peer out the window, into the darkness, when the temperature dipped even more. The sound muted. She refocused her attention on the board.

"Do you know what's going on with Seth? Do you know why he's so messed up lately?"

Yes

"Is he really sick? Mentally ill?"

No

Relief. She hadn't known how worried she'd been until Jet told her Seth was fine. A weight lifted from her shoulders. "So, he'll be okay."

No

"Is there something more to this? Does it have to do with whatever's in his room?"

Yes

"What is it?"

A nuisance

"Why am I not able to sense it? I can pick up on a lot of things."

You were blocked

"It blocked me?"

I did

"You did? Why?"

Safety

"Safety? My safety?"

Yes

Here he was, barely a friend, and keeping her safe. Watching over her. Tommy's cat friend, supposedly. But what was he protecting her from? There was only one thing she could imagine. Her voice came out as a near whisper.

"Is it a demon?"

It seemed to take forever for the makeshift planchette to move, sliding directly to *Yes*. She swallowed. "I knew it." But from all that she'd read, evil could be dealt with. Most of the time some elbow grease, a little telling it who's boss, salt, holy water. It was doable. "But why him? What does it want?"

Possession
Destruction

"Well, it's not going to get it, if I have anything to say about it." She let out a slow breath. "All right. How does Seth get rid of it?" No response. Not a twitch. The seconds ticked by. A minute. Her inner journalist took over. If your subject avoids answering, reword the question. "Can Seth get rid of it?"

No

The answer took the wind out of her sails. There must be a way. There was always a way. "Can I?"

No

Her hands shook as a vibration went through the planchette once more. She held her breath as it spelled the next words.

Not alone

"We can? Let's do it!"

Patience
When the time is right

Elaine shook the dog food bag over the metal bowl and listened. "Iggs?" She shook it again. "Iggy?" There was no churning of toenails along the wood floor, no scrappy pup bouncing at her feet. She called a little louder. "Iggy!" No response. "O., go knock on Seth's door and see if Iggy's in there with him, please."

"Why would he have Iggy?"

"I don't know. Just check, would you? He never misses breakfast."

Olivia went down the hall, peeking into Elaine's bedroom and the bathroom before knocking on Seth's door. "Hey, Sy!"

A complaining moan, a shuffling. The door opened. "What?" He rubbed an arm across his eyes and yawned.

"Mom sent me. Is Iggy with you?"

"What?"

"Iggy. Catch up, Sy. Is he in there?"

"Why would he be?"

Olivia stepped backward on her left foot and crossed her arms. "I don't know. Why's the sky blue? Just trying to find the dog, Sy."

Seth ducked past Olivia and called to his mother. "I don't have the dog."

Tommy stood beside Elaine. "He did it. He let Iggy out. I saw him."

Elaine shoved the bag under the counter and shut the cabinet door. "What, Tommy?"

"I saw him let Iggy outside."

"Iggy can't go out alone."

"He was mad. Iggy was scratching at his door."

Elaine strode into the living room and stopped at the coat rack, Tommy at her heels.

Seth stood in the archway, hands against the frame. "What?"

With one hand zipping her boot, she said, "Really, Seth? Really? What's happening with you lately? You know he can't just be tossed outside when you get frustrated."

"I didn't do it."

"I saw him," Tommy said, hiding behind Elaine's legs. "I saw you."

"You did not. That's a lie."

Tommy shook his head furiously. "You did it."

"You probably did it, you little freak. Probably wished it into the cornfield."

"Seth, stop it." Elaine bent to zip her other boot.

Tommy's lips curved into a fiendish grin then melted into the face he showed everyone else.

"Well, we know the pup's not in the house, don't we." Elaine continued, taking her jacket off the rack. "Now I've got to go out and see if I can find him. Olivia, watch Tommy. Take him to your room or . . . something." She glanced at Seth. "You and I will talk later."

"No need."

Elaine's lips tensed to a tight line, her voice low and controlled. "Look. We all know you've been going through a lot, but I've about had it with this thing between you and Tommy. Maybe you did let Iggy out and didn't realize it. Maybe the meds have clouded your thinking. People have been known to sleepwalk, have whole conversations and not remember them."

"It's not the meds! God damn it, Mom. It's him. He hates me and he lies to you. And you believe him! Whose mother are you anyway?" He was at the end of his rope, and it was unraveling.

"I'm the mother of every child in this house." Elaine gave a curt nod to Olivia, who directed Tommy to her room.

Seth took a step toward his mother, his voice desperate but quiet. "Can't he just be moved to another foster home?"

"It doesn't work that way. You can't just shuffle a child around like that. He needs stability. Understanding."

"So do I."

She touched his arm. "I know. And I love you, but-"

He cut her off, his words drenched in hurt and anger. "There should never be a 'but' after those words, Mother." He saw where her loyalties ran. "Go find the dog. Take care of your children. I'll be in my room."

With her hand on the doorknob, Elaine watched helplessly as Seth left the room. Her heart sank lower with each of his footsteps away from her. She wished everything could go back to normal, wanted him to be okay, that whatever was gripping his mind would clear. She felt empty. A failure.

She unlocked the front door and looked out across the yard, thinking how odd it was there were no paw prints in the fresh snow.

Chapter 23

Olivia waved goodbye to Elaine and rang the doorbell at 57 Peachtree. Jules' house. It was red brick with a bright porch light that made her think of the old black and white crime shows. The "where were you on the night of" type of interrogations. She peeked over her shoulder at the cemetery across the street. It was small, little more than a family plot, and some of the stones were worn to illegibility. She'd investigate there someday. It had a vibe. She swung her backpack off and let it hang by her ankles.

"Olivia, come in!" Jules' mother held the door open wide so she could walk in with her things. "Christie and Julia are in the basement setting up."

"Great, thank you!"

She crossed through the kitchen as she had a hundred times before and went to the basement door. It creaked and she said to Jules' father, who was sitting at the kitchen table, "A little WD-40, am I right?"

"And some duct tape." He chuckled.

Olivia walked down the stairs with a spring in her step. It'd been a running joke with them for years. Whenever something broke, Mr. Denton always said, "I can fix that. Just a little WD-40, Elmer's Glue and some duct tape."

At the bottom of the stairs, she turned left into a huge rec room and called out, "Happy New Year!"

Christie and Jules looked up from the crepe paper streamers they were taping to the support beam in the center of the room. "Happy New Year!"

"Not bad for December 29th, eh?" Jules asked.

"Well, we could've gotten together on the actual New Year's Eve if you guys were going to be home. But no. You dirty gadabouts."

"Talk to our parents about that. They made their plans, we just follow along," Christie said. "Now come help us get these things strung from the ceiling. There's a step ladder in the corner."

Olivia dropped her sleeping bag and backpack on the sofa, and her jacket on the back of a chair. Snacks were in the middle of the room on a card table. "Seems like your mom went all out on our party."

"Don't be eyeing those," Jules said. She stood on the second rung of the ladder. "Get your ass over here and decorate."

"Yes, ma'am!"

Olivia took the long end of the strand and spun it before handing the end to Jules.

"Hey," Jules said, more subdued, "Have they found Iggy yet?" She took the streamer, cut a piece of scotch tape, and stuck the paper to the ceiling.

Olivia sighed. "Nothing yet. I think he's gone."

"Sorry. That sucks."

"Yeah, it does."

"Do you know how he got out?" Christie came up from behind, a gold and purple Happy New Year sign in her hands. She was digging at the edges of a sticky price tag.

"Nope. Tommy says he saw Seth let Iggy out. Seth swears he didn't do it."

"And what do you think?" Jules asked.

"I don't know. I mean, Tommy seems like a good kid. And I know Sy. But I think they're both messed up. Tommy hasn't shown it yet, but it's in there. And Seth is a big ball of crazy. He'll be okay, though. Just wish I knew what actually happened."

"Maybe he'll come home on his own. They do, you know. Get running sometimes, get a little lost. Having too much fun romping to listen."

Olivia gave a half-hearted smile. "He does love to romp."

"Maybe when he gets hungry, he'll be back." Christie offered.

"Maybe."

"There's always hope."

Olivia nodded. But she knew in her heart Iggy wasn't coming back. Something deep inside her knew that if Tommy and Seth were involved, it wasn't going to happen. They worked for a few minutes twisting streamers, tossing sparkling confetti and tacking up the sign in the corner of the room.

"What's the itinerary for tonight?" Olivia asked, dropping onto the sofa beside her things.

A low rumble began in the small room adjacent to the rec room and they waited while the boiler roared to life. The house was old, and you could feel the shaking in the floor, hear the trickle as hot water moved through the pipes.

"The usual. A movie, constant access to food, girl talk. You've probably got a Ouija board tucked into your backpack or some sort of ghost hunting gear you want to mess with." Jules eyed Olivia over the rim of her Happy New Year glittery glasses. They were round with a spray of plastic fireworks off each eyepiece that made her look like an owl.

"I might have." Olivia tapped her chin and tried to appear innocent.

Christie dropped her hands to her sides. "Seems like that's what we're about."

"Glad we finally won you over."

"I'll take one for the team."

Olivia laughed. "We are the team."

Jules put her hands on her hips and surveyed the area. "I think we're set. Movie and snacks first, ghost stuff late when it's spookier. Dad has something planned for midnight, but he won't tell me what."

"Probably something with WD-40."

A man's voice called from the top of the stairs. "Hey, what's going on down there?"

"Just talking about you, Dad."

"Carry on then."

They heard him close the basement door and walk away.

"You dad is so cool," Christie said.

"Yeah, he's okay." Jules spread a handful of DVDs in front of them. "I've got fresh popcorn made and we can sit back, relax and enjoy. What do you want to watch?"

Olivia rummaged through the disks, handing them one by one to Christie. "Red Riding Hood, The Hunger Games, Ferris Bueller's Day off." She paused. "What'd you do, Jules, raid your parents DVD cabinet?"

Christie snickered. "Twilight? Please, no sparkling vampires!"

"It's not that bad," Jules said.

"Not that good, either." Olivia continued to rummage through the titles. "Brave. Now that's cool. Bride of Frankenstein, always a classic."

"If you're searching for Doctor Sleep, we don't have a copy."

"Tell your dad he's falling behind in his collection." Olivia held up a DVD. "Saw?"

Jules stared at Christie.

"What?" She dropped the remaining roll of crepe paper into a plastic bag and shoved it under their snack table.

"Saw?"

She went back to what she was doing, picking up bits of tape and empty packaging, bagging them up. "If you want. I can always cover my face at the bad parts."

Jules hugged her. "You're the best. I don't know why you love us like you do."

"God knows."

"Here, take the popcorn, get comfortable and I'll start the movie."

Olivia took a handful. "You know, eating round foods on New

Year's Eve is supposed to be good luck."

"Why?" Christie held up an unpopped kernel, then crunched it between her teeth.

"Something to do with luck coming full circle from one year to the next, I think. Not sure."

Jules stood in front of the DVD player, waiting for the movie to come to life. "Speaking of luck, did you guys see the spill Janice Parsons nearly took down the second-floor stairs after third period last week?"

"I was right behind her," Christie said. "She almost went down face first. It was like something snagged her backpack at the last second, or she would've been hurt."

Olivia held popcorn over her head and leaned back, dropping pieces one by one into her mouth. "Stranger things have happened. People get saved all the time. Ghosts, guardian angels, whatever's out there watching over us."

"Or, it could have been luck. Just plain luck," Jules added. "Coincidence."

At the same time, Jules and Christie said, "I don't believe in coincidence," mimicking Olivia.

"Well, I don't."

"But you've got to at least entertain the thought that some things might be."

"No, I don't."

"And there you have it, folks. The world according to Olivia Mulvey," Jules said.

"You've got that right." Olivia snickered. "But enough about me. Let's get to that nightmare wielding maniac already."

Jules hit play.

The credits rolled and Christie sat back. "Whoa," she said. "That was sick."

"Sick bad or . . .?" Jules asked.

"Sick good." She pulled over the stack of DVDs. "Do you have the second one?"

"Oh, my God, we've created a monster." Olivia gave her a playful shove.

"Perhaps, perhaps. But I need to find out what happens next."

"You do know there's like eight or nine movies, right?"

"Then we need to get started. The sooner, the better."

Olivia got up and walked over to the table, picking up a red Solo cup.

"Soda's in the fridge."

In the far corner of the room sat a large, old refrigerator. It had the Frigidaire name and crown logo at the top, with a large, long pull-down handle. Olivia tugged it. It opened with a bright light illuminating a two-liter bottle of Coke and one of orange soda.

"Is this thing cool or what? A vintage refrigerator."

"Whatever floats your boat. It's my grandma's. We brought it from her house when she passed away."

"Kind of a conversation piece. You know, like when you bring a boy down here. 'Come, I want to show you my Frigidaire. It's," she drew out the last word, "vintage."

Jules threw an empty cup at her.

"Maybe," Christie added, "it'd be for her victims. Some sort of torture device."

"Damn, girl. What did that film awaken in you?"

Christie shrugged. "I don't know, but when you take over the world, you might want to stay on my good side."

"I'd second that!" Jules said.

Olivia took the Coke from the fridge and stood at the table to pour. "You guys want?" She held up the bottle. "Get it now or you're on your own."

Christie raised her hand and Olivia grabbed a second cup.

"I vote for some hot snacks. Mom picked up mini pizzas to throw in the oven. Then, some ghostly goings on?"

"Let's do it," Christie said.

Olivia and Jules locked eyes, then turned and stared at their friend, heads cocked to the side.

"What?" She glanced from one to the other. "What?" A smile played about her lips. "I don't know what you're talking about." Giving her hair a flip, she started up the stairs. "Are you two coming or not?"

Olivia slipped the Ouija board from her bag and set it on the floor in front of them. "I'm telling you; this is real. I've been talking with a spirit the last few days."

"More real than your last board? You know that glass broke on its own."

"Yes, more real. I've been communicating with the spirit that Tommy sees. Or knows about. The one he calls his cat, Jet."

"We're talking with a ghost cat now?" Jules joked. "Boo kitty kitty kitty."

Christie put her hand over her mouth, shoulders shaking.

"Be respectful, girls. This is important to me."

"Okay, okay," said Jules. "Meow will."

Christie and Jules were bent over holding onto each other, Christie's laugh becoming a squeal the longer it went on. Olivia cracked a smile but wished they would settle down. She wanted to share this with them.

"My ribs!"

"All right, you two."

Jules wiped tears from her eyes. "Sorry."

"Yeah, sorry," Christie said.

"It's real. I told you both about the ashes."

Christie took a sip of her coke and put the cup on the floor. "Now that was creepy."

"Was it?" Jules looked at Olivia. "That's tougher to accept. Running shoe tread? Showing who's going to die? That's straight out of Ripley's, if you ask me. Too far-fetched."

"I hope you're right."

Olivia placed a shot glass in the center of the board. She borrowed it from her foster mom for the night. Far better than a quarter and they'd all be able to get their fingers on it. She relaxed her shoulders and calmed her mind.

"Is there anyone with us tonight?"

"Rap once for yes, twice for no," Jules added.

Christie snorted. "How can they rap twice if they're not here?"

The temperature in the room had fallen and the low hum of the boiler began.

"You know what I mean. When we start asking questions."

"Geez, Jules." Olivia rolled her eyes. "And why do we need raps when they can talk through the board?"

Jules coughed into her elbow. "My bad. Is there anyone with us tonight?"

A loud knock came from the wall behind them.

"Quit it, Olivia," said Christie.

"I didn't do it. My hands are right in front of you."

"You must've set it up somehow."

"I got here after you. And since when have I ever tried to fake activity?"

Jules shook her head. "It was the house settling. Get it together, Christie. Where's that balls-to-the-wall attitude of earlier?"

"It was there till something banged on it."

A vibration in the shot glass caught their attention. It circled the board three times, their touch unwavering, and landed on *Hello.*

"Now, we're getting somewhere. Is that you, Jet?"

The small planchette glided to *Yes.*

Christie glanced over her shoulder. "Do you guys hear whistling?"

Jules shook her head. "Water in the pipes."

Christie hesitated, listening intently. "Yeah, you're right. Funny, I thought it was a person for a second."

Sitting back, Olivia cracked her knuckles. "Go on, girls. Ask away. Jet'll tell you whatever you want to know."

Jules scooched forward, speaking directly to the planchette. "What will I be when I'm thirty? What career will I have?"

"Trying to get a better connection? You know the spirit is around us, right? It's not like the board is a microphone."

"I thought it was kind of like a ghost telephone."

The girls laughed. The glass moved again, stopping on the letters L, A, W, Y, E and R.

"Lawyer. Well, it's got me pegged. That's exactly what I'm going to be."

"Oh, come on," said Christie. "We all know that the only thing you've ever wanted to be was a lawyer. I've read about these things and it's the subconscious sending little electric pulses to the glass. We're probably influencing it with what we already know."

"Ah, so that's why your fears were gone. You think you've debunked it!" Olivia understood now. "There's one way to test your theory. You ask the next question and make sure it's something only you know."

Christie uncrossed her legs. She shifted to one side, the other.

"I smell wood burning."

"Let her be, Jules. Let her come up with something good," Olivia said quietly.

"You don't have to whisper. I'm right here. And I've got it." Christie squared her shoulders and asked, "What's the name of my dead grandfather?"

There was immediate action on the board and the glass moved with determination. P, A, U, L.

"Paul." Olivia read the word, almost triumphantly, and faced her friend. "Well?"

"It is."

Olivia let out a whoop and did a little dance at her spot, keeping her fingers on the glass. "Believe now?"

"Nope. You must know his name. I probably mentioned it sometime and your brain filed it away."

Before they could protest, the glass moved again. M, A, S, O, N.

"Mason. What's Mason?" Jules asked.

The color drained from Christie's face and she slowly pulled her hands away from the shot glass, tucking a strand of hair behind her ear. "We didn't ask a question."

"What is it? What?"

"We were still talking. It was moving while we were talking. How could we influence it if we weren't even thinking of a question?"

"Who is Mason?" Jules pressed.

"His brother."

"Whose?"

"My grandpa had a brother named Mason who died when he was like fourteen. Drowned. He was rarely mentioned."

The boiler quit, leaving them in a silence that reverberated in their ears. They absorbed the information, letting the moment sink in. Jules' eyes were wide.

Olivia spoke first. "Well, I think that pretty much establishes that Jet is with us. What an amazing validation!" She was thrilled. Jet had shown himself to be the real deal in front of her friends. This was momentous. "What do you want to know next?"

"Does Richard Jameson like Christie?"

"Jules!" Christie went from white as a sheet to red cheeked. Shock and fear transformed into embarrassment at its utmost.

"Really?" Olivia said. "We have access to the knowledge of the universe, and you ask about Richard Jameson?"

"Okay, okay. Something bigger." Jules thought for a minute. "Like if you'll rule the world?"

Olivia rolled her eyes.

"Hey, it's no worse than the cootie catchers we used to make in fourth grade, except this is more accurate, am I right? Magic 8 Ball and all that?" Jules winked at Christie.

"It's more than that, Jules. So much more. He's going to teach me. Expand my sensitivities. And you know I'm all in. I've wanted that for a long time. I'll be like an apprentice. A protégé."

"A protégé."

"Yep. Maybe I'll even learn to move objects with my mind," she leaned in close to her friends, then howled.

Christie jumped and the girls laughed. "You've got to stop that."

"Jump scares are the best scares."

"Maybe. I just wish you wouldn't get so chatty with something you can't see."

"Afraid I'll take over the world?"

"No. I just don't want you to get mixed up with something dark. Evil." Christie tucked the same piece of hair behind her ear.

"What do you think I'm talking to, Christie?"

"The problem is, I don't know. And you don't. The Bible says demons are the ultimate tricksters."

"I defy you to find the word trickster in the Bible," Jules chimed in.

Christie took her fingers off the shot glass and stretched them. "It's all fun and games until someone gets possessed," she deadpanned.

Jules and Olivia stared at Christie until the three of them couldn't hold it in any longer. "Oh, my God, there's the Christie we know and love! Balls back to the wall, ay, sister?"

"Just be smart. You, especially, should understand there's a lot of darkness out there."

"And what is darkness, really?" Olivia asked. She picked up the shot glass, holding it like a monocle.

"Here we go."

"An absence of light, is it not?"

"Little Miss Philosophical has showed up."

Christie clasped her hands over her stomach, closed her eyes and pretended to snore.

Olivia winked at Jules. "The moon doesn't hate the night. It shines in spite of the darkness."

"Its light comes from the sun, Olivia. Argument invalid."

"And yet it's there every single night and day. Unwavering. Unafraid."

"The darkness isn't a demon and it's not desiring to devour the moon's soul. You can't personify them."

"And I am unwavering and unafraid. I am, as the moon, a beacon."

"Good Lord." Jules was the first to say it.

"Good Lord is right." Christie tossed a paper cup at Olivia. "You need some religion."

She deflected it and set the shot glass beside her. "Oh, I'll get some, all right. Maybe I'll start my own. Come minions!" She motioned to the girls. "Come! Worship me!"

Jules dropped at Olivia's feet, rolling onto her back. She batted her eyes. "Oh, my beacon! Don't smite me!"

"You're blasphemous." Christie stood, smirking and nudging Jules with her foot. "And you're not helping."

"Well, I am in league with the devil, yes?" Olivia stretched. "I promise I'll be careful, Christie. Seriously. Okay?"

"Okay."

Jules' father's voice boomed from the hallway. "Pre-New Year begins in five! Four! Three! Two! One!" He ran in with four sparklers, spraying sparks around the room. He handed one to each of the girls and kept one for himself. "Happy Pre-New Year!" Grabbing a noise maker from the table, he spun it, the noise overshadowed by his and the girls' shouts and woo-hooing. Jules' mother stood at the doorway, taking video of the shenanigans on her cellphone. As soon as his sparkler fizzled, he said, "Goodnight, ladies. We'll send you each a copy of the video so you can keep it for posterity." He bowed low and exited with his wife.

"I love your parents, Jules," said Christie.

"Me, too."

"Yeah," Jules nodded. "They're kind of cool." She glanced at the floor and said, "One last question for the board, guys." They settled onto the floor, returning the shot glass to its center.

In her best imitation of a medium, Jules dramatically closed her eyes and said, "Oh, Jet, tell me. Will Olivia rule the world?"

They watched, eager for an answer to the question.

Nothing.

"Or at least her part of it?" Christie added.

The glass darted to *Yes*.

Jules squealed. "I knew it!" She danced, hands in the air. Olivia kept her gaze on the planchette.

"Nice power move, Olivia, but next time let the all-seeing answer. We all know you thirst for power." Christie held up a DVD. "Who's up for part two?"

Jules rubbed her eyes. "Let's do it." She moved to the DVD player, hand outstretched.

"Let's." Olivia scooped up the shot glass and slid it and the board into her bag. She didn't tell her friends that she hadn't moved the planchette. That she hadn't even been looking at the board when it moved.

Jet had made the prophecy, and she didn't know how she'd ever deliver on it.

Chapter 24

Olivia rolled her desk chair into position, letting her fingers hover over the quarter in the middle of the board. The temperature immediately fell and the hairs on her arms bristled.

"No," she said. She tucked her hands under her thighs. "Nope. I know you're here and you know I know. I've seen spirits and even heard a few. I think it's time we skip the board, and you show yourself. As cool as it is, I don't think we need it. Do you?"

The chill in the air dipped enough that she could see her breath. "You say you're going to help me. Tweak my sensitivities. Get my ghostly motor running. At the very least I want to hear your voice, but I think it's only fair if I see you first. Kind of meet the person I'm speaking to, you know? Especially if you're making predictions about my future."

She turned her head to the left and slowly spun her chair to face the door. Folding her hands in her lap, she waited. It was a gamble. She hoped he'd appear, give her an idea, a picture of his former self. Let her see who he was when he was still alive. Maybe he'd tell her his real name and she could research his history.

The air by the door shifted, like heat waves in summer sun. An almost imperceptible motion that could be passed off as a trick of the light. Almost. Her heart beat a little faster as the ripple greyed like storm clouds rolling into a confined space, the shape of a boy in shadow form, then darkening. Growing. Coalescing into a seven-foot-tall specter. It stood before her, a faceless solid black mist.

Olivia stared into what should have been its face, yet it remained shapeless. Void. It was mesmerizing. She let a sound escape her lips.

"Jet."

That name is for children
You are not a child

The voice came from everywhere yet was for she alone. Inside her mind. A thought not her own, yet it resonated through her like electricity in a rainstorm. Her jaw worked. She didn't know what to say, or how to address the being before her.

Call me
BLACK

She sensed the name more than heard it. Tasted it on her lips and silently repeated it. Felt the darkness that encompassed it. In her mind's eye, she knew he was hiding a multitude of secrets, like writhing snakes behind a wall, controlling what he was allowing her to see.

Olivia closed her eyes, opening herself to the thought of him. Of Black. He was more than human, more than anything that had walked the earth. There was a power in his name. A strength she hadn't met before. He was a commander. A ruler.

A knock on her bedroom door brought her out of the revelation.

"Olivia, come on. New Mommy said you'd be watching me. When does the ball drop? Is it soon? I want to watch it."

The doorknob rattled and she heard Tommy's muted voice. Muffled. As if it had to fight its way through a thick sea to reach her.

"Olivia!"

Her door locked.

Are you ready to learn?

There were a thousand answers she could have given, reasons

why she should turn and run, burn the board, break it and sit in church for the rest of her life to try to rid herself of what Black could be. But gifts were gifts. And power was enticing. It was all in how you used it, right? She knew in her heart, being, and soul, that this could turn so bad but all she could feel was the right of it all. Finally learning what she'd wanted to know for so long.

Are you?

She whisper-answered, "Yes."
The thing without a face grinned.

Tommy snatched his hand from the doorknob. The metal had turned searing cold and wrong. It was different. He wiped his hand down the front of his pajama shirt. Jetty was different.

And he was alone.

He wandered to the living room and sat in a ball on the sofa, knees tucked to his chin. The television was on. Crowds danced and shouted, counting down, while a sparkling ball hung suspended above them. He wondered if it would squash them like bugs.

Tommy was asleep when Olivia entered the living room. She turned off the television, now on some band, the streets of the city long since emptied, and picked up the little boy. He snuggled into her neck as she carried him to his room, gently bending to tuck him into bed.

Pulling the covers up to his chin, she checked her phone with the other hand. It was weird she hadn't heard from her friends all night. Yeah, they were away, but even out with their families you'd think they could find two minutes to text a Happy New Year message. Something. She hadn't heard from them since their party and her messages to them sat unread.

She shrugged.

A little blue dot caught her eye. A message from Jules' mom. She'd sent the video from the other night. It said it was delivered on the thirtieth, but she didn't remember it coming in. She clicked on the triangular play button and smiled, lost in the memory as she watched it unfold. Jules' dad running in with sparklers, she and the girls laughing and yelling.

But there. Looming in the corner, unnoticed, unwavering in the lights, was a tall darkness. A massive shadow cast by nothing. She ran the video three, four more times, stopping and restarting, then going frame by frame. It wasn't there, then it was. No forming, taking shape. Just one second not there and the next . . . boom.

Black.

She recognized her mentor. He was distinct in his indistinctness. She could almost feel him through the screen.

She couldn't wait to show Jules. Christie would watch, reluctantly, while reciting to Olivia all the reasons she'd be going to hell and saying the Lord's Prayer as she watched the little movie over and over. She snapped a screenshot. Her proof. Her validation.

Olivia tucked the phone into her pocket and went to bed.

The light in the hallway cut his vision like a serrated knife. Seth covered his eyes and ducked when the light bulb above him popped and shattered.

"What was that, Sy, some new dance move?" Olivia pushed past him on her way to the living room.

"Yeah. Dance." He glanced cautiously over his shoulder, grimacing as he searched for any remnant of the broken bulb, but it was intact. Lit. A log snapped in the fireplace, and he startled. Jittery. Unnerved.

Olivia tossed her phone onto the sofa cushion and picked up the PS3 controller. Still no word from the girls. "You want to play?" She motioned toward the Mortal Kombat game he'd gotten for Christmas.

"Head hurts, Olive. I don't think so."

"Come on, push through it. We haven't had a good head-to-head in a long time and school starts tomorrow."

He hesitated, lips tight in mock annoyance.

Olivia put her hands up, turned her face. "Fine, fine. Go nurse your head. I'd just have beaten you anyway. Like the last time."

"What?" He slid in beside her, taking the second controller and game box off the end table. "You know that never happened." Reaching across her, he turned off the lamp.

"I know what I know, loser." A satisfied smile crossed her lips as Seth pressed the start button. The game roared to life.

He cycled through the character screen, trying to decide which to pick. Tommy bounded into the room and stood in front of the television, intent on the screen.

"What show is this?"

"Mortal Kombat." Seth craned to see, and Tommy moved in front of him. "It's a game." He leaned to the right.

Tommy shifted from side to side, getting close to the screen and examining the avatar.

"Come on, kid. I'm trying to do something here."

"Sit by me, little man. So Sy can see."

Tommy jumped onto the sofa beside Olivia. "Can I play?"

She shook her head. "Sorry. This one's only for bigger kids."

"I'm bigger."

"You need to be older. This one's kind of violent."

"I don't mind."

Olivia hugged him. "Maybe not. But Mom would." She returned her attention to the game. "Who are you picking?"

Before he could answer, Tommy was on his feet. He pointed. "Who's that?"

"Bakara."

"What does he do?"

Seth rolled his eyes and continued to cycle.

"Different things," said Olivia. "They all have different strengths and use different weapons. How about Freddy Krueger, Sy?"

"Too commercial. Not realistic."

"Yeah?"

He half-smiled. "Yeah."

"What does he do?" Tommy asked again, sliding to the edge of the sofa and pointing at another character. "Olivia, what does he do?"

"I don't know them all. Just bits. How about Nightwolf, Sy? Reptile?"

"Don't rush me. I want to see them all."

"Ugh." She fell backward onto the sofa cushion. "It's going to take you half an hour just to choose your guy."

He raised an eyebrow. "And? You got somewhere to be?"

"Who's that?" Tommy dropped onto his butt and moved a few inches closer to the television.

"Sub-Zero." Seth read the character's stats.

"He looks cool. You should be him."

Seth clicked back to the beginning of the list. "Scorpion." He'd wanted Sub-Zero but couldn't. There'd be no way he'd give that kid the satisfaction.

"I knew it!" Olivia picked up her controller. "I knew you'd end up back at the beginning."

"You'll take just as long."

"Sindel." A few clicks on the controller and she raised her hand to high-five him, satisfied. "Sindel." Seth stared at her, arms resting on his knees. "Well, they don't have Rose the Hat."

"Write the company."

"Maybe I will."

"Who's Sindel?" Tommy sat, legs stretched out in front of him, running his toes along the edge of the wall under the television.

"An old woman," said Seth.

"A queen. An old soul, just like me."

"What's her superpower?"

Seth could feel the tension growing in his shoulders, a heaviness settling over his body. A poison tendril injected into his brain, intent on destroying his will. The boy. "There's not a superpower." He rubbed his eyes. "It's not like that."

"Her weapon is her scream."

"Just what my head needs. A screamer."

"We'll keep the volume low. Why don't you take something?"

Seth massaged his temples. "Just keep him quiet and I'll be okay."

Olivia hesitated but started the game.

"I hope Olivia wins."

"Of course, you do, twerp." He held up his middle finger.

Tommy stuck out his tongue.

Before Seth could react, the game announced, "Round one! FIGHT!" and Olivia got in the first hit. Tommy jumped up, clapping.

"Yay!"

Seth mashed his buttons, fiercely going after Olivia's character. They flew across the screen trading blows, grunts and injuries. With every connection Sindel made on Scorpion, Tommy cheered.

"Shut the hell up." Seth worked the controller, fiercely focused on the screen.

Olivia landed a blow that knocked Seth's character to the ground.

"Go Olivia!" Tommy blew a raspberry at Seth, loud and long.

"I'm telling you, Olive. Shut him up."

"Yeah, Tommy. Let Seth concentrate," Olivia said. "It'll be more satisfying when I win."

"Yeah, yeah." Seth's character appeared from behind Sindel for another attack.

Sindel levitated, landing a blow. Olivia took the first round amid Tommy's yells.

"Round two. FIGHT!"

Olivia came on strong, but Seth had to bob back and forth,

trying to see around Tommy. The demon in his brain was pouring venom through his body, screaming for him to put an end to the noise. The mockery. The child. This was the true battle, not what was on the screen. Not even his personal fight for sanity. His sight blurred and he fought it back.

Stop him fight him kill him stop him kill him kill him kill him

It had grown into a chant, a mantra that competed with the game, growing louder, faster. His concentration faltered, he missed a blow, and Olivia's character slammed his to the ground. The game's narrator commanded "FINISH HIM!" as Olivia delivered the final blow.

Tommy erupted into a dance, wiggling his butt in Seth's direction, sing-songing nah-na-nah-na-nah-na, directly in front of the game.

And then he heard the boy's voice in his head, vying for his focus.

I dare you

He couldn't take it anymore, the sound of the game etching into his brain, the chanting of the demon in his mind, and the taunting of the child in front of him. A jagged electricity pierced his vision. He bolted at the boy, grabbing his arm.

"Get the fuck out of my way!" he yelled, yanking hard to the left.

Tommy stumbled toward the fireplace, tripping over his feet, arms extended to catch himself. His hands slammed through the mesh screen, and he caught himself on the andiron. He screamed.

Olivia shot into action, shoving Seth out of the way and pulling Tommy into her arms. She rocked him as he cried, cradling his head with one arm, trying to examine his hands. "You're okay. You're okay." She glared at Seth. "What the hell is wrong with you?"

Elaine ran into the room. "What happened?" She scooped

Tommy up. "What happened?" She looked from Olivia to Seth. Tommy's face was slick with snot and tears. He buried his face in her chest. "Seth. Tell me." Her voice was quivering between anger and fear.

"It was them. Him." He answered quietly. "Inside my head." His hands were balled into fists, and he held them against his temples. Pressure. Pressure would help release the vise closing on his mind.

"You're not making sense. Someone tell me what went on here before I lose it."

Tommy's sobs were calming to sniffles, his cheeks red and wet. Olivia gently uncurled his fists, checking his palms and every finger. Miraculously, they were fine. Unbelievably. She looked into his face, searching for an answer to an unspoken question.

"Seth pushed him into the fireplace."

Elaine's face went white.

"I moved him out of my way."

Olivia turned to face her brother. "You shoved him into the fireplace." She enunciated every word.

"My God, Seth." Elaine sat Tommy down, scrutinizing every bit of skin on his hands. "My God."

The small boy sniffled.

"Why can't he just leave me alone?" Seth paced.

Elaine positioned herself between him and Tommy. "You need help, Seth. This isn't normal. He's a little boy."

"That's what he lets you think."

She shook her head, trying to understand why her son was acting this way. Losing his mind. He'd been falling apart since Blake's death, but she thought it was depression. Anxiety. Not whatever this was. She grasped at the straws of what could explain it. Held onto them like a life preserver in the turbulent sea of his mental health. "Maybe it's this med. It could be wrong for you. Screwing with your brain chemistry."

"Again with that? It's not the fucking medicine! It's him! Everything's been worse since he showed up. Why can't you see?"

Elaine turned. "He doesn't mean that, honey."

Seth stopped pacing. "Yes, I do." He pointed at his mother. "And don't speak for me." He scrutinized each person, one by one. His eyes were wide and his breathing ragged. Shaking, he said, "I can't do this anymore. I can't. Call Dr. Ryan. If you can't send the kid away, send me. Send me. If I'm a danger, throw away the key." He staggered into his room. The lock clicked into place.

Elaine and Olivia stood in shocked silence while Tommy found a couple of his trucks and started driving them along the floor. Olivia was the first to speak.

"What are you going to do?"

Her foster mother took a deep breath and let it out slowly. "What I have to." She took her phone out of her purse and thumbed through the contacts until she found Dr. Ryan's emergency number. Her thumb hovered over the button until she garnered the strength to make the call.

As it rang, she motioned for Olivia to watch Tommy and she stepped outside.

Olivia moved near the door, hoping to keep an ear on the conversation. Tommy didn't seem to notice anything more than his toys.

"You fell into the fireplace. I saw that."

"Yup." He drove one truck past her foot and under the sofa.

"I saw your hands. They went right into the grate. That metal thing that holds the logs."

"Yup." Up and over the end table.

"But you didn't get burned."

He crossed his legs. "Let's play in my room."

"I'm waiting for Mom."

She watched him. The upset was gone, the tears. The concern.

"How were you not burned, Tommy? Your hands should have been blistered."

He met her gaze. "Don't you know? You say you know things, but you don't."

"Then tell me. How did you not get burned?"

He considered what she said and answered, "Jetty."

Elaine stepped through the front door, bringing a blast of arctic air. She stomped her feet, still holding the phone to her ear, then walked to Seth's door. "I have Dr. Ryan on the phone."

A pause.

When Seth's voice came, it was raspy and broken. "Slide it under the door."

# # #

Olivia pulled her knees to her chest, the only illumination in her room the pale glow from the moon through her window. Her emotions had been stretched to their limit. She was exhausted but couldn't sleep. It seemed wrong to relax when her brother was in Hemingway. Whatever he was going through, he was alone. More alone than she was, and in a foreign place. A cold, sterile hospital. She thought it had to be better than what she'd seen in movies, but all she could picture were long, empty corridors. Cement walled rooms. Loneliness. Desperation. Fear.

When he walked past her to leave, he was a shell of himself. Withdrawn. His hands were deep in the kangaroo pocket of his sweatshirt, the hood covering his face. They didn't make eye contact. He didn't say goodbye.

She waited up for Elaine to come home, listening from her room, the lights off. The front door shut quietly, and she heard the shuffling of her foster mother taking off her boots, hanging her coat. Elaine had gone directly to bed.

The chill that had become familiar filled her room. She laid down, turning to the wall. "Can you just keep me company tonight? I don't feel like talking." Closing her eyes, she let the comfort of the presence lull her to sleep.

Chapter 25

Elaine sat at the kitchen table, stirring her coffee.

"Morning, Mom."

"Morning, O." The presence of another person jarred her into the reality of the morning. "School?"

"Yeah."

"You don't have to go, you know. I'm sure neither of us got much sleep last night. You could probably use a mental health day." Her voice caught on the irony of her statement.

Olivia swallowed. "I know. It'd be weird, though. Empty. No Seth. No Iggy." She glanced down at the water bowl, still beside the sliding glass door. "I think I'd feel better in school. More distractions."

Elaine agreed. "They only took him in for a few days. They'll make sure he's stable, adjust his meds. It's not as if he's a danger."

"I know."

"It was just an outburst. A boiling over of his anger, frustration. Anxiety. It wasn't even meant at Tommy. It could've been any of us."

"Yeah, sure. I know."

"He's struggling right now, O. Really struggling. But he'll be okay."

Olivia leaned over, resting her chin on her foster mother's head. "He will be."

Elaine pulled away and wiped her eyes. "Yes."

Turning on her heel, Olivia grabbed a paper towel and held it under the faucet. She let the water run cold. When it was saturated, she squeezed out the excess and handed it to her foster mother, along with the bottle of Tylenol from the cabinet.

"For your headache and those puffy eyes," she said. "Before Tommy gets up."

Elaine smiled. "Thanks, kid."

"I'll be home right after school. We'll get through this." A quick hug. She grabbed her backpack and went for the door. She couldn't wait to see her friends and breathe.

Slinging her bookbag onto her back, she traversed the busy hallway. It was good to be in the hustle and bustle of the day. She checked the clock. Ten minutes till the first homeroom bell. Great. She made her way to her locker and spun the combination dial.

"Hey."

The voice came from behind her. Jules. She yanked her first period textbook from under the stack of books and turned. Her friend stood a few feet away looking like less than her usual put-together self. Her hair was tied into a messy ponytail and there were bags under her eyes.

"What's wrong? Are you okay? I messaged. And called." She wanted to wait for an answer, but her news pushed its way through. "Seth got committed last night."

"Here. You left this at my house." Jules shoved a wooden board into her arms.

Olivia flailed to grab whatever it was without dropping her books.

"What? No, I didn't." It wasn't possible, but somehow the spirit board was in her hands.

"Obviously, you did." Jules pushed a stray strand of hair out of her face. "Take it. Close it. Do whatever you need to and burn it. I'm done. With all of it. And you."

Stunned, Olivia rested the board against the lockers. "I don't understand. What's going on?"

Jules ran her hand up her right arm, shoving the sleeve to the elbow. Her forearm was a mass of bruises and, in the middle, three deep scratches. "Since that night there've been footsteps. Knocking. Something tried to push me down the stairs. Some*thing*. But nothing was there, Olivia." Jules frowned. "Nothing. We're done with all your paranormal shit."

"We?"

"Christie is terrified. Whatever it is followed her, too."

Olivia's mind spun as she took it all in. There had to be some mistake. Some misunderstanding. "Maybe it wasn't the board. You live across from a cemetery. It's probably something from there. We can figure this out."

"I've always lived by the cemetery. Nothing like this has ever happened before. You're on your own. We're out." She turned to leave. Over her shoulder, she said, "Sorry about Seth. Maybe this thing got him, too. You might want to consult those ashes again."

Olivia stood with her mouth open in disbelief and watched Jules take the side corridor to get to her homeroom. The bell rang and the hallway emptied, like rats deserting a sinking ship. Olivia felt like that ship. A sucker punch to the gut.

The second bell rang. She shoved her backpack and the board into her locker, barely getting the door closed around them. It didn't make sense. Any of it. There was no way that Black could be responsible. And he especially wouldn't hurt her brother.

She walked into her homeroom, unprepared for the day. Just as she'd been unprepared for Seth's breakdown. And all that Jules threw at her. The attacks. The ashes.

The rest of the school day was a blur.

Olivia took a deep breath at her locker, turned the dial to the final number and felt it click. She yanked downward on the handle. The door clanged on its hinge as it ricocheted against the next locker, hitting the back of her hand in the process. It stung and dug up a chunk of skin. She sucked on the wound as she wrapped the fingers of her other hand in the loop of her backpack and pulled. It snagged her jacket as it freed itself from the small space, dropping it to her feet.

The locker was empty. No board. Her brow furrowed. Were they all delusional? Mass hysteria in a group of three? She'd seen the board. Held it in her hands. And Jules wasn't joking. The entire day she'd been an outsider, passing her friends in the halls, sitting alone at lunch. Phys. Ed. had been a joke, if only she knew who was laughing. Jules and Christie sat together on the bleachers, thick as thieves and eyeing her like she'd killed their best friend. They hadn't changed into their blue and white gym uniforms and weren't allowed to participate, but they watched her as she jogged the track. Every lap she completed, their eyes were on her.

It ached to be alone. Ached to not know what was going on. She'd lost Seth and her best friends overnight. She blinked hard but wouldn't give them the satisfaction of seeing her cry. The satisfaction of knowing they'd pulled the rug out from under her. Cut off her life support.

She'd talk to Black. He'd get to the bottom of it all.

Chapter 26

The dining hall was large and sunny, with high windows and long tables. It reminded Seth of his school, but whiter. Sanitized. Some of the inmates, he corrected himself, *patients*, sat with friends. Roommates, maybe. Others were alone, like him. Men and women in white jackets weaved through the room, a touch here and there, a good morning. All the *patients* were in pajamas. He shuffled his slippers under the table. It'd have been more degrading if everyone else didn't have on the same thing. Maybe they should be fluffy and pink.

He poked at the eggs on his plate with the plastic fork they had given him. You can't kill yourself when the tines bend, but you can't stab a piece of sausage, either.

"Hey, is this seat taken?" Dr. Ryan was holding a tray of his own, balancing a cup of coffee, his laptop tucked under one arm.

"Sure. I mean, no one's sitting there."

"Great, great." The man set his meal on the table and slid the laptop to the chair beside him without spilling a drop.

He must've done this a lot.

"How was your night?" He took off his jacket, the kind with the patches on the elbows, and hung it across the back of his chair. Sitting down, he picked up the three sugar packets at the corner of his tray and shook them before tearing them open.

"Okay."

"Don't let your eggs get cold. Eggs never taste good once they get cold." Tapping the sugar into his coffee, he looked toward the counter. "Forgot the creamer. Ah, well. I guess it's black and sweet this morning." The red plastic stirrer spun in his paper cup, scratching the bottom. "These things never do much."

Seth tried to size up the man. "Is this our session?"

The doctor paused. "This," he waved his hand over his tray, "is breakfast. I'm hungry and I thought we could chat."

"Okay." Seth, again, pushed the fork through his eggs, piling them up in the corner of the Styrofoam plate.

"If you'd prefer to wait until 9:00 am, that's fine. I don't want to make you uncomfortable." He half-stood, gathering his things.

"No, no. Stay."

"You're sure?"

"Yeah. You're the one comfortable thing in this place."

Dr. Ryan smiled and slid his chair closer to the table. "Good, good." He bit his roll and said, "Tomorrow is pancake day."

The corners of Seth's mouth raised a bit. "Cool."

"At least they give good portions." Dr. Ryan took a long sip of his coffee and made a face. "Never hot enough." He went back to his plate. They ate in silence.

"How's your room?"

Seth glanced up. "Small talk?"

"Breakfast talk. Harder stuff later."

"Well, it's not a hotel."

"True," Dr. Ryan agreed. "And it's not home."

Seth's expression clouded, anxiety reminding him why he hadn't been hungry this morning. "It's okay." Home was where he wanted to be and the last place on Earth he wanted to go. He shifted in his seat. "How long am I here? A few months, a lifetime?"

The doctor wiped his mouth on his napkin. "Nowhere near any of that. A few days. A week or so at the outside."

Seth's shoulders relaxed as obvious relief washed over him. "Really?" He was alert now and focused fully on the man across from him. "Really." He rested his elbows on the table and leaned forward on his arms.

Dr. Ryan pushed his tray to the side. Nothing was between them but his cup of cold coffee. "You're here to regroup. Get a grasp on what happened and why. Stabilize. Your mood, emotions. Tweak the meds that help you the most and get you home again." He took a last swig from the cup and tossed it onto the tray, then picked up his laptop and stood.

"You're leaving? I thought we were having our session."

"This was breakfast." He scanned the clock on the wall behind them, squinting. "I'll see you in about twenty minutes in my office."

Seth nodded and, as Dr. Ryan walked away, he said, "Can I get some regular clothes?"

The man called over his shoulder, "Probably not, but I'll see if anything can be arranged."

9:03 am. Seth walked the hallway to his therapist's office. Hemingway Hospital. What a joy. The doctors must see their committed patients on particular days or see the out-patient appointments when everyone else is off watching television or playing basketball or whatever activity they were going to want him to join. Not that he was sure he'd want to join, and not that he wanted to take part wearing pajamas or the scrubs they'd given him.

"Seth, come in," Dr. Ryan greeted him. "I see they upped your wardrobe."

Seth twirled, arms wide. White scrub top and pants, same slippers.

"Well, it's not the pajamas. They do have a firm policy on what patients can wear. Mainly for comfort."

"Mainly for not running away." Seth sat on the sofa opposite Dr. Ryan.

"Did you want to run away?"

"Where would I go?"

"You'd have to tell me."

Seth shook his head. "Nowhere. This is where I need to be."

"Interesting statement." Dr. Ryan took a moment to set up his laptop and get his clipboard ready. He pulled a pen from his pocket protector. "And pretty levelheaded, if you ask me."

Seth shrugged, folded his hands. He wished he had pockets.

"Let's get down to business. Why you're here. Why it's where you 'need' to be."

His stomach tightened.

"You had a meltdown the other night."

"That's an understatement."

"Seems so, from the way you sounded on the phone. And your mental state when you arrived."

"Yeah." Seth slouched. "It was pretty bad."

"What happened?"

"You know," Seth said. He felt like a mouse in the middle of a field, a vast expanse of choices and no idea which way to turn. "We talked on the phone."

"And you were in the throes of emotion. Turmoil. I want to dissect this rationally. Throw a little logic and calm perspective on it. Peel back the layers."

"Like an onion."

Dr. Ryan smiled. "My favorite analogy."

Seth crossed his legs. Uncrossed them.

The doctor waited.

"I lost it on the kid."

"And what was at the root of it. What caused you to 'lose it on the kid'?"

Seth took a deep breath. "He wouldn't stop. Wouldn't quit tormenting me. Over and over, on and on. I had this fierce headache, and he just wouldn't stop."

"Another migraine?"

Seth nodded.

Dr. Ryan made a note as he spoke. "How often are they coming on?"

"I don't know. A few times a week." He ran his hands through his hair and stood, walking to the window, back.

"Seth, that's significant."

"Tell me about it."

"What are you taking for them?"

"Tylenol. A lot of Tylenol."

"Okay, well, I can prescribe something specifically for migraines. We can clear up that issue, for sure."

"That would be awesome if it worked."

Dr. Ryan jotted another note. "Absolutely. I think we can definitely manage them, if not eradicate them all together."

Seth sat once more. "So why do you think I lost it? Am I crazy?"

"Do you think you are?"

He sat against the firm back of the sofa. "Sometimes. But not really."

Dr. Ryan shook his head. "You're not. This could all be an extreme emotional reaction to the stress of your friend's death, coupled with a chemical imbalance in your brain. That could easily lend itself to impulsive behavior. Plus, the pain of the migraines and whammo." He hit the edge of the table for emphasis. "You lashed out. We're here to help you get back in control again."

"Whammo. A technical term?"

"Whammo. Yes." Dr. Ryan chuckled.

"Then why am I on the schedule for group therapy later? Can't you just adjust my meds and let me chill? A little vacation in a padded cell for a few days?"

"First, it's not padded." The doctor checked the laptop, then searched the floor beside his chair for the charging cord. "Or a cell. But group is actually really helpful. It gets you to recognize your symptoms so you can learn how to manage them. It also gives you a network. Helps you to see, feel, that you're not alone."

Seth stared into the corner of the room. He absolutely was alone. More alone than anyone could understand. Singled out. Manipulated. Set on a plank over the ocean and it's do or die or do and die and the only possible shot at peace is to get rid of that kid. A claw squeezed his shoulder, and his blood ran cold.

"Seth?"

"Yes?" Back to reality. Whatever this was. The reality of a demon bound to his soul, exacting its hell-bent vendetta on some kid. And he was its tool.

"Are you still having hallucinations? Auditory? Visual?"

"If that's what you want to call it," he scoffed.

"Seth, the mind is an amazing and resourceful tool. It will come up with what it needs at the time to keep a person safe." Dr. Ryan leaned in closer. "For example. A little girl moves into a house in a new neighborhood. She has no friends. All of a sudden, she has a friend. It's imaginary, but very real to her. She sees it. Hears it. But it's not there, it's just a mechanism to help her cope with the loneliness."

"I wasn't lonely, and this isn't a friend. Let me make that clear."

"And I get that." He waved his hand as if erasing chalk from a blackboard. "Just an example. But I have to examine all the possible root causes and how likely they may be. If I didn't, I wouldn't be doing my job . . . and doing my patients a huge disservice. I'm not saying demons don't exist or that what you're experiencing isn't demon related. What I am saying is we need to exhaust the very real possibility that it's your mind convincing itself of something that may not be in the tangible reality."

Seth slid to the edge of the sofa. "I tried to believe that. But walking back into my house, even with meds, convinced me otherwise."

"And that's totally understandable. We haven't had enough time yet to get a handle on it all."

"So why is it trying to hurt me?"

Dr. Ryan set the clipboard between the chair leg and the table. "You and your friend were dabbling in darker things, probably scaring each other going down that path, feeding off the horror of it all. When he died, in front of you," Seth averted his eyes, "the trauma of it all seeped deep into your emotional being. In one of our sessions, you said you didn't have survivor's guilt, but I bet it's wrapped up in you so hard that it's almost unrecognizable. The demon your buddy was trying to summon would be what your mind is turning against you."

"I want to believe you. I do. It would make everything so much easier." Seth was sweating now. His heart beating a steady race he wasn't running.

"It's okay. You're safe here. Tell me, are you religious?"

Seth was confused. "My mom is. We used to go to church."

"Well, if there are demons, then there must be a God, yes?"

"Sure. I mean, it would seem so?"

"I'm just trying to take some layers off with a little logic. God, devil. Good, evil. If there's a negative, there's a positive."

"Okay."

Dr. Ryan held up his index finger. "Does what you're experiencing happen around others? Do they see it?"

"Well, no, they don't. But I can sense it. I know it's here with me now."

"And I get that." He paused. "Do you think you're possessed?"

"Not at all." A half-lie. At least for the moment his tormentor was letting him think on his own.

"Good. That's good."

"I wish you believed me." He let out a despondent sigh and closed his eyes, leaning his head back against the sofa.

"It's not that I don't believe you. But I also believe your destiny is in your own hands. That you have the power to change this. And I want to hit every natural explanation before I jump to supernatural. Those are the steps I have to follow. And, if we do that and it doesn't solve or explain what's going on, well, then I'll have to dive in where others fear to tread."

"Would you?" Seth tugged at a thread at the hem of his shirt.

"I would do everything in my power to help you."

Seth doubted there was anything in Dr. Ryan's arsenal that could send a demon back to hell.

# # #

Dom stood in front of the large glass windows of the pet shop beside Books and More. Cats and kittens were lounging in the sunbeam, soaking up what they could from the January afternoon. He tucked his bag tighter under his arm and gazed at the Russian blue sprawled across a carpeted stand. The sign beside it read: Johnny. Adult male, seven to eight years old. Affectionate. Found November second. Looking for a loving home.

Dom rested a palm against the glass. The cat stretched and meowed, a glint of recognition in its eyes.

"Sorry, man," he said under his breath. "There's too much coming." He wanted to rescue the poor guy. Barnes' cat. Amanda's adopted buddy. There was just no way. He couldn't take him in, only to be the next person to leave him behind when the coming shit hit the proverbial fan. It was going to be him or the demonic bastard that killed the cat's owner. "But I can do this."

He went inside the shop and rang the bell on the counter. A girl in a green "Montgomery Pets" shirt stepped from an aisle.

"Can I help you?" She propped her broom against the shelves and wiped her hands on her apron.

"The cat in the window? The blue? His name is Caesar."

"What?"

"The Russian blue. In the window. His name is Caesar." He tapped the sign. "Not Johnny."

"Oh! Are you the owner?"

"No. Just a friend." He turned to leave.

"Wait," she took a Sharpie from under the counter. "Do you know who the owner is?"

Dom paused. "The owner's dead." He pulled out his money clip and pressed a hundred-dollar bill into the girl's hand. "Treat him like a king."

Chapter 27

Olivia tripped over a break in the sidewalk and cursed. It'd be her luck to drop her phone onto concrete. She hit send again. It immediately dinged. Not delivered. "Damn it, Jules." She clicked to her recent calls and then on Christie's name but got the "half-ring into voicemail" bit. She was blocked. Entirely shut out by her two supposedly best friends.

Her sneaker skidded over a slick spot, and she caught herself, but not before getting an ankle full of slush. "Great," she said, shaking her foot. "Just great." She'd had enough of people jumping to conclusions, not listening to her, and avoiding her like she was some pariah. She kicked a mound of snow.

And what Jules said about Seth was like an itch in her brain. *Maybe this thing got him, too. You might want to consult those ashes again.*

A truck shifted gears as it went past and she braced herself for a spray of ice bits, a splash of brown snow, or any mix of the two, but all she got was a face full of exhaust. Her cheeks were flushed from the cold, and she wiped her nose on the edge of her glove, hoping no one saw.

"With the day I've had, I shouldn't give a damn," she said, stomping up her driveway. At least she could pretend she was knocking snow off her shoes.

Elaine was sitting on the sofa when she walked in. There were large boxes littering the floor and Tommy was playing among them with his trucks.

"How was your day?"

Olivia slid off her coat, turning to hang it on the rack. "Eh. Not great." She stepped on the back of her sneaker, took her foot out and rolled off her wet sock. "Jules and Christie are mad at me." She tilted her head toward the tree. "Taking it down?"

"Trying," Elaine sighed. "What happened with the girls?"

She slipped off the other sneaker. "I don't know. I didn't *do* anything."

"Well, I'm sure it'll blow over in a couple of days. Girl stuff usually does." Elaine rested her hands on her knees, smoothing the hem of her dress. "Want to help me with this?"

"Honestly?"

Elaine half-smiled. "Yes."

"Does it have to be done now?"

Tommy crawled on his belly as he ran his truck along the trunk of the Christmas tree, then turned onto his back to drive it upside down under the lowest branches.

Elaine watched him drive between ornaments, leaving them swinging. "No, it doesn't."

Olivia held the carry strap on her backpack. "I've got some homework, but I can help you after."

"You know what? That sounds like a plan. I'll put some stew on the stove, and this," she waved her hand with flourish, "can wait. It'll be our evening's entertainment."

"Rah, rah." Olivia gave a thumbs up, feigning enthusiasm.

"Believe me," Elaine said as she rounded the corner into the kitchen. "I feel the same."

Olivia continued to her bedroom and let the door shut behind her. She dropped her backpack onto her bed. There was no homework. She'd finished it in study hall. It was amazing what you could get done when you weren't sitting with your friends, passing notes and giggling at the substitute teacher. At first, she'd just skimmed the papers on her desk. But they proved to be a great distraction from Jules and Christie sitting three rows ahead of her.

If they were trying to hurt her, they were doing exactly that. How long were they going to treat her like this? Without them, she was alone.

I am here

She pulled off her jeans, flung them into the hamper and wrestled a pair of pajama pants out of her bureau. She barely noticed the chill in the air.

Alone. It was sinking in. No Jules. No Christie.

No Seth. That twisted her stomach, made her cheeks hot. Yanking her sweater over her head, she dropped that into the hamper, too, and pulled on an oversized, long sleeve tee shirt. Alone. Iggy wasn't even there for some comic relief or puppy kisses.

The rug had been pulled out from under her feet. Like four years ago, when she entered the foster system with a suitcase full of broken promises. *I'll be back. Rehab just takes a few months and we'll be together again.* Yeah. Sure.

You are not alone

"Well, it feels that way." She paused, taking some comfort from her spirit-friend. "You're like the only one I can count on."

I am

Olivia sat at her desk, her gaze falling to the Ouija board. She touched it, lifting its edge. It was real. Solid. "What's the deal with the board, anyway?" The shadow enveloped her and settled. She could feel her awareness widening.

The deal

"Jules said I left it at her house, but I know I bought it home.

It's here, it's always been here, and I don't get what she's talking about."

She is mistaken

"Jules said she was attacked. That something was in her house. Christie, too." Olivia spun her chair in a circle. The shadow moved through her, setting her veins on fire.

They are jealous of your abilities
Of me

"But they're my best friends. Without them, I'm," the word caught in her throat, "alone."

Black poured himself into her willing mind, expanding the pathways he'd been building.

Petty children
You don't need them

He stretched, expanding her knowledge, her desire, her need for him.

"I don't . . ."

You are not

"Alone."

You will never be alone again

She knew in her heart he was right, and a cool relief flooded her. She would be fine as long as Black was in her life and she knew, *knew*, he wouldn't leave her. They were bound in a way she couldn't put into words. Yet. She wasn't alone. She'd never be alone.

But Seth.

If her blood could have frozen, it did at that moment.

Seth was alone and losing his mind. He was being driven to the edge. Pushed into mental oblivion by that thing. He wasn't crazy. Olivia remembered Jules' words, and each one cut a little deeper than the last. *You might want to consult those ashes again.*

"Black? Can ashes predict the future?"

No response.

"Black. Did I predict the future with those ashes or was it some weird coincidence?"

The shadow coalesced in the corner by her door; the buzzing of ten thousand flies coming together in a seven-foot-tall darkness. There were just the two of them, her peripheral vision fading to gray. They were separate, yet one, and she struggled to keep the thought that was like an ice pick to the gut.

"Will Seth be okay?"

A knocking at her door pulled her back to the physical reality surrounding her. Her room, desk, chair. Backpack. Bed. It was like waking from a dream when she hadn't been asleep.

"Olivia!" Tommy yelled.

"What do you want?" she called, not stirring from her seat.

"I want to come in."

"Not now, Tommy."

"Come on," he whined, running his truck across the door. She cringed at the sound of plastic wheels grinding into the wood.

"I want to be alone right now."

The truck noise stopped. "That's not true."

"What?" She couldn't contain her annoyance. "What's not true?"

"New Mommy says lying is wrong."

"What are you talking about?"

"You aren't alone."

Olivia tipped backward in her chair. "Not now, little man."

The shadow waved its wrist, and she heard Tommy's truck slam into the opposite wall.

"Hey!"

She listened to him scramble to retrieve it. She covered her mouth with her hand as her shoulders shook with laughter and she heard her foster mother's footsteps come down the hallway.

"What's going on out here?"

Olivia peeked through her doorway, keeping hold of the knob. Tommy was rubbing his eyes.

"I told him he couldn't come in now. I'm doing homework and need to concentrate."

"I see." Elaine turned to Tommy. "If Olivia needs some time, you have to respect that. I'm sure when she's done with her homework, she'll be happy to play with you for a little while. Right, O.?"

"You bet. After dinner, when we're doing the tree."

Elaine took Tommy by the hand and led him away. "Why don't you help me make the stew, Tommy?"

He scowled at Olivia over his shoulder, eyes narrowed to slits.

She closed the door and locked it. "Tell me."

I do not make predictions

She concentrated, furrowing her brow, trying to focus to see what she could pull from the recesses of his mind, but was nowhere near strong enough. Experience of a millennia versus that of a neophyte, even though she knew it wouldn't work. But he had no reason to lie.

"You may not make predictions, but I do." She paced. "I don't know if the ashes told the truth, if I saw what my mind thought it should see or what, but I'm going to find out."

Your proposal

"I'm going to the church tonight. Try my own version of St. Mark's Eve. I'm assuming it takes intent. Focus. Like everything else you've shown me. I'll do the ritual and see what happens. If you can't tell me about Seth, then I'll see what I can find out myself."

Dinner came and went, stew with biscuits and Tommy chatter. Olivia helped Elaine put the Christmas ornaments away, one by one, and then unwound the lights. She stacked the loops of green cords in plastic grocery bags as her foster mother squashed the branches and tried to cram everything into the cardboard tree box.

"It never does fit the way it did when you bought it, you know?"

They maneuvered the boxes to the back of her closet and Elaine exhaled. "Another holiday over." She looked at Olivia. "The rest of the decorations can wait till tomorrow, eh?"

"Yeah."

"Me, me! It's time to play with me!" Tommy lunged at Olivia's legs, nearly knocking her over.

She managed to smile. "What do you want to play, buddy?"

"Trouble!"

That figures, she thought. All she wanted was for everyone to be asleep so she could get to the church and see what she could find out about Seth. At least the clock kept ticking. All she had to do was wait it out.

"Sure. Get the box."

They played a few rounds, but Tommy was more interested in pushing the bubble down and watching it pop up than anything else. Every time it snapped and flipped the dice, he belly laughed.

"I think someone's a little tired tonight," Elaine said, taking her turn. She hopped her piece around the board.

"Who?" Tommy reached in and hit the bubble one more time. He erupted in a laugh that was infectious.

Elaine had to catch her breath before she could respond. "A certain little boy who shall remain nameless."

He eyed her for a moment, then reached for the bubble.

"I think you're done, mister," she said.

His hand hovered over the board, waiting. He shot a hopeful glance at Olivia.

"Okay."

He held the bubble down as long as he could stand it before letting go, the suspense thrilling him.

Elaine chuckled and slid the board into its box. "Pajama time, little man. Say goodnight to Olivia."

"Aww. Okay. 'Night, Olivia."

"Night, Tommy."

She was happy to watch him head down the hallway, happy to be two hours closer to her mission. Debunk or prove. Debunk or death? No. Not on her watch.

The house was quiet. Dark. Olivia walked in her socks to the mudroom, carrying her boots. She stood beside the boiler, gently pulling her jacket over her sweatshirt. She'd zip it up outside. She slipped her right foot into its boot and tugged.

"Where are you going?"

She hadn't noticed Tommy wandering in. He was standing next to the washing machine, watching her.

"Damn it," she whispered. "Nowhere. Go back to bed."

"I want to go with you." He yawned, stretched.

"No, it's too late." She pulled on her left boot.

"But you're going."

"I'm older."

"Does New Mommy know?"

She hesitated a moment. He had her. She couldn't lie and say yes. He'd bring it up to her foster mother and blow everything. She'd be grounded till she was fifty. "No."

"I'll be good. I can keep a secret." He clamped a hand over his mouth and looked at her with wide, bright eyes. "Please." It was a muffled plea.

"It's cold out."

"I'll bundle!" He ran out before she could answer.

Olivia half-considered leaving him, heading out the mudroom door, but knew he'd either follow or make a fuss and get her into a ton of trouble. He had her over a barrel. She stepped across to his doorway. "Okay, I guess. But you have to be good. And quiet."

She helped him into a sweatshirt, socks and snowpants.

"It's a long walk, too. I don't want you getting cold or scared."

"I told you. Nothing scares me."

"Okay." She wondered what she was doing, taking this little boy out of the house to sit on church steps in the middle of the night. "And you can't tell anyone."

"I won't."

Olivia unlocked the door, turned the knob until it clicked. She realized she was holding her breath when her lungs started to burn. *Breathe*, she told herself. The house remained silent and still. She ushered Tommy through ahead of her, then eased the door shut behind them.

As they crunched through the snow, staying close to the bushes, he asked, "Is it far to the church?"

"What?" She tried to see his eyes in the moonlight.

"What?" he answered.

She let it go. "It is." There was too much at stake to worry about the things Tommy knew that he shouldn't.

They trudged along. Olivia kept them to the shadows, past the curbs and closest to shrubs and edges of sidewalks, away from streetlights as much as possible. Some houses had the glow of a television on, most didn't. She was glad it was a small town that folded up at night. An occasional car would hum by, and they'd duck behind a bush or tree before the headlights panned near them.

As they passed Mrs. Harper's house, she scanned every window for a glimpse of her friend. She picked up a faint sense of her, but then it was gone. She didn't understand why the woman had pulled away. It was ever since . . . Olivia squinted at Tommy, then focused forward. Ever since.

Olivia's attention returned to keeping them safe, away from cars and the prying eyes of neighbors, and tried to convince herself that Seth was okay, and nothing would happen. That St. Mark's was an old wives' tale and ashes could lie.

"It's up the next street," she said. "We're almost there."

Tommy watched, stepping over snowy patches.

At the corner, they could see the church. It was dark except for a small bulb above one of the side entrances. The front steps leading to the large, wooden double doors were shoveled, with small mounds of snow along the iron railings. She led Tommy to the top of the stairs.

"Sit next to me, where it's darkest."

They settled, the freezing chill of the cement seeping through Olivia's jeans. She was glad she'd put Tommy in snowpants.

"All right," she said, taking in the street to town, then shifting her gaze toward the more residential end. "I need you to be quiet. I need to focus."

Tommy tucked his chin into his jacket and pulled the drawstring on his hood. Only his eyes peeked out.

She closed her eyes, cleared her mind. Steadied her breathing. Her cheeks burned in the January air, but they soon numbed as her other senses clawed to the forefront. An awareness ran through her mind, the edge that Black had been providing. Enhancing her abilities. Empowering them. She had a strength of direction and a growing control. And she liked it.

She concentrated. *Show me the future dead*, she willed. *Show me St. Mark's message.* It became her mantra. *Show me show me show me.* She opened her eyes. In the distance, the faint sound of horseshoes clip-clopping on the street caught her attention. As the sound got closer, the image solidified. A horse and bier, a rider. A single coffin was carried, and the rider silently pulled the reins in front of the church.

He jumped to the ground and waited.

Olivia held her breath.

Three knocks came from within. The rider, in a rumpled vest and worn jacket, rested a hand on the wood, then shoved the top open. He took off his hat and held it to his chest.

A hand appeared. It gripped the edge of its confines and a man climbed out. He shuffled past the horse without notice and made his way to the steps of the church, taking them one by one. She couldn't make out his features. When he reached the top, he stepped through the closed church doors. Olivia gasped as quietly as she could. She recognized the wraith. The spirit in the church was her elderly next-door neighbor. A stunned sadness gripped her.

The horse pawed the ground, and she could see steam rise from its nostrils.

Movement. Another spirit was on the ground beside the rider. A woman. Younger. Her twenties, Olivia surmised. She squinted, unmoving, as the ghost moved through the darkness toward them. But ghost was the wrong word. That would be the spirit of someone deceased. What did you call the future dead? The woman adjusted her pencil skirt as she stood before the church doors and then moved through them as if they weren't there.

Olivia breathed through her pursed lips. Waiting.

A third spirit crawled out of the coffin. It hesitated beside the horseman, then began the trek toward the church. The build was familiar, and the stride. Olivia could feel the tremors of her heart against her ribs, an anxious flutter. The hooded figure took the steps by two and hesitated at the top. Its hood dropped back to reveal exactly what Olivia wanted to avoid. Or confront. Her face went white as her stomach lurched.

Seth.

He looked through her and followed the others into the building.

Olivia mouthed the word, "No," and gripped the hem of her jacket with all her might. "No." It all came crashing in on her in that moment. The ashes hadn't lied and now this proved what fate was lying in wait for her brother. A damned destiny because of that malignant spirit.

She forced herself to stare into the eyes of the horseman. "No more," she said. She poured all her will into the command. "Show me no more."

The man bowed in her direction. He returned his hat to his head, climbed onto the horse and drove, fading into oblivion.

"What'd you see, Olivia?"

She had forgotten that Tommy was with her, had negated his existence. Swallowing, she dragged him to his feet and brushed the snow off his pants. "Nothing." Her hands were shaking as she took his. "We have to go. It's late."

A light snow was falling, and she wiped her eyes, taking as deep a breath as the searing cold would allow.

Tommy smiled. "Was it Seth?"

They locked eyes and she stopped dead in her tracks.

"Why would you say that? What do you know?"

The little boy shrugged. "He's mean. I don't like him," he said. "I want to go home now. I'm tired." He drifted into her, clinging to her leg.

"He's not mean. He's trou-," she stopped mid-word. He wasn't troubled. Or mentally ill. There was a demon attached to him and she was bound and determined it wasn't going to take him down. Her mind raced as she said, "You're right, Tommy. Let's get home."

Seth kicked off his blankets. He knew he was dreaming. Knew there was something off in his room. The scratchiness of the sheets, the damp chill in the air. Even the moonlight streaming through his window seemed eerie. Too yellow. Too bright. He couldn't put his finger on what was wrong. Couldn't determine the issue. But it set his teeth on edge. He braced himself and waited.

Bang.

The sound startled him, and he tensed for the next assault. The next blow that would come out of the night.

Bang.

Bang.

The shutters! He lay against his pillow, reveling in its softness, relieved. He sat up. He'd been so tired lately, he never thought to close the shutters before he laid down.

He regretted ever opening windows in the dead of winter and, shaking his head, went to close them. The smack of wood slats on cement walls stopped when he reached the window. Reaching out, he touched the cool glass. The windows were closed. Locked. And the air was still. No leaves swaying in any breeze. No branches moving. The moon was clear and there were stars shining. No storm. No clouds littering the sky.

As he assessed the night, a crow landed on the windowsill.

"Hey, Milo," he said, tapping the glass. "How'd you get here?"

The bird cocked its head to the side to peer into the room. Out of nowhere, a larger bird appeared, swooping in and attacking the crow. The larger bird grasped the smaller with its talons, fiercely pecking at its head until it was a lifeless, bloody mess.

And then it grew. Its red eyes were glowing orbs that expanded with its body until it blocked out the sky. There was no light. The stars were gone. Blotted out by darkness. And, as Seth stood by the window, laughter began. A shrill, crowing laughter that made him grip the sides of his head. Cover his ears.

He fell onto his bed.

When he woke, he could still hear crowing in the distance.

Olivia helped Tommy off with his jacket and got him back into his red footie pajamas. "Scoot off to bed, little man," she said, giving him a shove. "And remember, no word to anyone about this." She clasped her hand over her mouth.

He did the same and climbed into bed.

Olivia stood statue-still. No movement, no sound. She envisioned herself a ninja as she made her way to her room. Stealth was key. There was no way she wanted her foster mother to notice and start questioning where she'd been. That'd go over like a lead balloon in a downdraft.

She let relief wash over her as she shut her bedroom door. Dropping her jacket at the end of her bed, she peeled off her outdoor clothes and donned a pair of pajamas. Sliding under the covers, she scooched to the corner of her bed, her back against the wall. Closing her eyes, she let her senses take over.

"Black, I think it's time."

Chapter 28

Olivia watched the clock tick down the seconds to the final bell. Eighth period study hall was a blessing and a curse. She could usually knock out her homework without an issue, but the days without homework dragged on. Especially Fridays. Even the book she'd been reading, *Breaking Evil*, didn't keep her attention. It was more a novel to her than non-fiction. Black had more knowledge of evil in his little finger, if he had fingers, than all the books in all the world. She wouldn't need a paranormal library as long as he was around.

The buzzer sounded, signaling the beginning of the weekend. Olivia gathered her books and joined the mass of students headed toward freedom. She didn't hesitate today. Didn't wait to fall behind Christie and Jules to see what they were doing or hope they would notice her. For a day, it felt awkward and ached her heart to see them walking together.

A day.

But now, she realized, she didn't need them the way she thought she had. It wasn't so bad leaving them behind. She was destined for greater things.

She arrived home, dropped her backpack by the coat rack. The smell of chicken roasting made her mouth water.

"Did you walk home with your jacket flapping like that?" Elaine peered out of the kitchen, wiping her hands on a dish towel. "It's twenty degrees."

"I'm fine. Didn't even feel the cold."

"I don't want you getting sick."

Tommy was watching cartoons. "Don't get sick." He had his toys surrounding him in a little fort he'd made with the sofa cushions.

Olivia winked at him, hooked her jacket on the rack and followed her foster mother into the kitchen. She took an apple from a bowl on the table. "I have the constitution of a horse." She bit the apple. Juice dripped into her palm and she wiped it on her jeans.

"I'll get you some sugar cubes at the store. In the meantime, zip up your jacket when it's bitter outside."

"Okay, Mother." She sat at the table.

Elaine's eyes crinkled at the corners. "I got some good news today. From Dr. Ryan."

Olivia perked up. "Spill it."

Elaine pulled out the chair across from Olivia. She leaned in, her arms resting on the tablecloth. "Seth is coming home Monday." She patted the table and sat back.

"Oh, my God! That's fabulous."

"It is. I'm excited. Relieved." She lowered her voice. "We'll have to make an extra effort to make sure Tommy knows it's okay. That things are better. That Seth is better."

Olivia took her hand. "Mom, I think it'll all be all right. We'll make sure everything will be good again."

Elaine's eyes welled up with tears. "I thought maybe we could clean his room. You know, really tear it apart and make it fresh."

"I'm in but do you think he'll be okay with that?"

It was Elaine's turn to shrug. "Maybe?" She paused. "Personally, if I was so unhappy, depressed and anxious, coming home to a dark dungeon of a room wouldn't help. If I was starting to improve, I'd appreciate coming home to something that echoed that mood. If not, he can change it into whatever makes him happy. But at least it'll be clean."

"Let's do it." Olivia walked over to the cabinet with the cleaning supplies.

"Not now. Tomorrow. It's going to be a job and you just got

home. Take tonight to relax and we'll hit it first thing in the morning."

She swung the cabinet door closed. "Sounds like a plan."

Olivia bounced out of bed at 7:30 am, ready to start her day. It was time for a fresh start. Time to get her brother home and rid him of everything negative. And, she had Black on her side to make sure that would happen.

She ate her breakfast while her foster mother gathered the supplies to clean Seth's room.

"Bucket, sponge." Elaine was saying as she reached to the back of the cabinet. "Lysol, Pledge. Garbage bags."

"Can I help?" Tommy asked.

"You can be in charge of the garbage bags. If I need one, you bring it. Also, if there's anything I forgot, you're my runner."

"What's that?"

"If there's anything I need, you run and get it. A very important job."

"Yay!" He looked proudly at Olivia. "I'm the runner."

"Good for you."

"You can play or watch cartoons until we need you to run, okay?"

"Okay." He left for the living room.

"I'm ready when you are," Olivia said, depositing her plate in the sink. "Let's do this thing."

Elaine opened Seth's bedroom door and flipped on the light switch.

"Did you bring rubber gloves?" Olivia said. "I'm not sure there aren't mushrooms growing in this tomb."

"Geez-oh-whiz." Elaine let out a whistle, shaking her head. She took a step inside the room and sized it up, floor to ceiling. "I guess the first thing we do is get some light in here."

They flanked the window and peeled the duct tape he'd stuck

from the molding to the shade. It left a sticky residue.

"This might tear the shade."

"Here." Elaine grabbed the cardboard roll at the top of the window and pulled downward. It yanked the shade free from the duct tape and let the sun pour in. "I'll buy a new one. For now," she tossed it to the side, "we need light."

Dust and cobwebs were everywhere, except the corner of the room near the ceiling that kept taking Olivia's attention. She could feel what had taken up residence there, although it wasn't in the room now. She had to guess that when Seth went to the hospital, it went along for the ride. She hurt for what he was going through. But things would be better soon. She'd make sure of it.

Seth's bed was bare. His sheets and blanket were balled up in the corner of the room, giving every indication he'd been sleeping on the bare mattress. If he slept at all. Dirty dishes were piled beside his computer. Old glasses that had contained who-knows-what were everywhere, moldy.

"Where do we start?"

Elaine was deep in thought, wondering how her child got so lost. So deep and dark.

"Mom?"

"Hmm? Oh. Start. How about you grab the sheets and laundry and I'll take the dishes to the kitchen? Meet you in the mudroom?"

"Sure." Olivia piled every piece of clothing she saw into the middle of the sheet and wrapped it up like a hobo tote, dragging it down the hallway.

Elaine picked up the plates and silverware, balancing three glasses in the crook of her elbow. Tommy cut off her exit from the room.

"Whoa, there. Careful. I almost dropped these. Then, we'd really have a mess to clean up."

"Do you need me to get something?"

"Not officially. Not quite yet. But you can run back to the living room so I can see how fast you are."

The boy zipped into the living room, circled it and returned.

"Nice job. I know I can count on you. Now go play a bit till we're ready."

"Okay!"

Olivia smirked as she stood at the washing machine sorting the clothes. She winced when she got down to his sheets. Elaine appeared in the doorway.

"These are bad, Mom. Will this wash?"

"What is it?" She stepped forward. "He spilled something?"

"It's pee. And it's strong." She held it at arm's length.

Elaine sniffed and coughed. "Could it have been Iggy?"

"I don't know. I don't think so, or Sy would've complained."

"That's nasty."

"Will it wash out?"

Elaine considered it. "Throw them out. I'll go to the store tomorrow and buy new. He shouldn't come home to that, either as a smell or a memory."

Olivia agreed. "Runner!"

The sound of little footsteps came down the hallway. "Here!" He slid to a stop in front of her.

"I need one of the big garbage bags from under the sink. Maybe two."

"Okay!" Tommy sped off.

"Silly kid."

Elaine swept while Olivia wiped down the computer desk. "Be careful where you step," Elaine said. "His phone's here and the screen's shattered. I don't know if there are any shards on the floor. Best to be careful."

They scrubbed and Lysol'd everything they wouldn't ruin by spraying, then wiped it all down. The sun flowing in did the most good. It changed the entire mood of the space.

"I hope he likes it," Elaine said when they were done. She folded her arms and took in all they had accomplished. "I just hope he likes it."

Chapter 29

Seth was waiting when he saw his mother's Camry pull along the bend to the main doors of Hemmingway. It'd taken half the morning to do his discharge paperwork, to set therapy appointments and have Dr. Ryan write out his new scripts. At least they'd fed him lunch. A turkey sandwich and bowl of tomato soup were worth the wait.

His mother got out of the car and held out her arms when she saw him. She seemed as if she'd aged while he was gone. Appeared a little more cautious, concerned. She hugged him, hard, and she held back tears when she said, "Oh, Seth, it's so good to see you!"

"Missed you, Mom." He waited until she let go, careful not to let his papers scatter.

She noted his file. "Is there anything I need to do? See anyone, sign?"

"All taken care of. I'm free as a bird."

Elaine clicked the key fob to unlock the car and opened the door for him. She closed it and ducked to the driver's side.

"You know I'm not sick, right? This wasn't a typical hospital stay. It's not like I broke my leg or something."

With both hands on the steering wheel, she said, "You're right. Sorry." She shouldn't feel uncomfortable around her son, but she was. Eggshells. She was walking on them. As she drove out of the lot, she searched for light conversation to make. Small talk. "Weatherman says there's a storm on the horizon. I think it's supposed to blow through in the next day or so."

Seth cocked his head to the side, squinted one eye closed and put on his best old man voice. "Is that so? You don't say."

They laughed.

"You know you don't have to treat me differently. Things got to be too much emotionally, and I exploded. In a bad way. And I'm really sorry it happened, Mom." He was sorry, but more than that, he knew it was what she needed to hear. Acknowledge what had happened so she could chill. "I'm fine. New meds, more therapy." But he wasn't fine. The demon-thing wanted to destroy him, but not until he finished its bidding. Not until he got rid of Tommy and whatever larger evil had come with him.

But he had a plan.

"It'll be okay."

"Oh, hon. I know. And I'm sorry I wasn't there for you. Didn't see it coming. You know I would do anything for you. Anything."

"I know." For now, he would concentrate on Dr. Ryan's words of wisdom and keep everything positive. For his mother.

They rode in silence, staring at bare trees and mounds of dirty snow plowed onto the sides of the road. "Olive didn't want to skip school to meet me?"

"She would've if I mentioned it. I figured we needed a little alone time."

"Yeah. We do. Where's the kid?"

"Bev came over to babysit. Do you need lunch? Should I stop somewhere? I know most hospital food is like what you'd get from a prison lunch line."

Seth stretched, his fingertips tapping the ceiling of the car. "Nah, thanks. That was the one thing I enjoyed about Hemmingway. They fed me pretty well." He patted his stomach. "A turkey sandwich and tomato soup about an hour ago."

The corners of Elaine's lips turned upward. "Well, you should be ready for another in about," she glanced at her watch, "fifteen minutes."

"Yeah, yeah," he said. "Wait a minute. What are you implying?"

Elaine held up her palm. "I plead the fifth." She signaled and took exit twelve for Aliton.

"Just so you know, Dr. Ryan called in the new meds to Pop's."

Elaine took her foot off the accelerator. "Should I have gotten off at Montgomery? Do you need them tonight?"

"Oh, no, no." He sat up, adjusting the shoulder belt and letting it slide into position. "I just want to get home."

"Okay."

"He gave me a med specifically for my migraines. Seems to be helping." A lie. They still hit like an axe to his frontal lobe, or a talon to his cortex, but she didn't need to know that. Let her believe all was on the mend.

Elaine's tension visibly eased. Her shoulders, tight as they had been, lowered. "I'm so glad, hon." In the next moment, she furrowed her brow, took a breath and said, "There is one thing, Seth."

"What?"

"Olivia and I cleaned your room." She said it quickly, like ripping off a Band-Aid. "I know you didn't want anyone in there, but this seemed like it might really help. A fresh start. New beginning. And it needed it."

At the mention of his room, he tensed. A knot grew in his stomach, and he tried to logic-force it away, but in his reality, there was no logic.

"It's fine."

"It was quite a mess and so dark. There were stacks of dishes and the laundry, wow."

"I know. Mom, it's all right."

She exhaled.

"Hope you left my porn."

Again, the laughter came. A little louder, a little longer. But it felt good to joke and feel alive, even for a short while. Seth appreciated the levity, especially since he knew it couldn't last.

He was sitting on the sofa when Olivia walked in from school. She contained her smile as best she could and slowly took off her jacket.

"Sy." She dropped her backpack.

"Olive." He nodded in her direction.

"You're looking well." She circled him like a cat.

"As are you, dear sister."

"Nice to have you back."

"Pleasant to be back."

"Did Mom tell you what we did to your room?"

"You mean with the flame thrower or the holy water and priest?"

Neither could contain it any longer. Olivia snorted and Seth's shoulders shook as he laughed.

"You know, either would have taken less time."

"I'm sure. I do appreciate it, though. You both did a great job."

She finger-gunned him. "Keep it that way."

He threw a pillow, hitting her in the legs. "Ah, it's good to be home." And he almost meant it.

Olivia bent to take off her boots and saw Tommy peeking from the hallway. "Hey, Tom Tom. What's up?"

Seth met the boy's eyes. "Hey, Tommy."

The boy stared at him without answering.

Seth got up and walked over to him, bending onto one knee. The thing on his shoulder woke, piercing his brain with its fangs and sending poison through his mind. In that instant he hated the child with every ounce of his being, every molecule, but spit out the words, "I'm sorry." He steadied himself and went back to the sofa.

Tommy nodded.

"Just give me some space and we'll be okay."

The boy took a step backward.

Olivia held in a giggle. "Good try, kid."

The boy picked up his trucks and ran into the kitchen.

Seth's migraine began. Flashes of shimmering light invaded his vision, and the pain wasn't far behind. Damn. They shouldn't have skipped stopping for the meds. He'd try to make it through dinner and go lie down. Yeah. Lie down in the newly freshened pit of hell. Fear, anger, despair flooded him. He felt manipulated. Singled out. Alone. Set to walk the plank over an ocean of ravenous sharks and the kid had to go. The seething hatred of the beast on his shoulder was overwhelming.

He knew he'd have to break the connection between himself and the demon or he was going to end up killing the kid. That was a fact. And he'd have to act soon.

Seth rubbed his eyes, stealing a furtive glance at the fireplace. Of course, it wasn't lit. It probably wouldn't be for a very long time.

Olivia watched her brother through new eyes. More intuitive, alert. Aware. She settled into the recliner near him, opened her senses. She could see the thing attached to him now. It was huge, dark and she could sense its claws sunk deep into Seth's flesh, its tentacles curled through his heart and mind. And she could feel it breathe. A toxic evil.

No wonder he couldn't cope and was losing his shit. She wondered if it knew she could see it and that its days were numbered. Black would help in that regard. Take the reins. Black would take care of everything.

"Dinner's ready!" Elaine called. "Seth, would you carry the pot for me?"

He rounded the corner to see that his mother had placed four potholders in the middle of the table and was standing at the stove holding a ladle. He lifted the pot as the oven timer went off.

"Sweet potato fries on the way." She rested the ladle beside the pot and muttered about having to get more potholders. She used a kitchen towel to take the cookie sheet out of the oven.

Tommy climbed into his chair. "What's in there?"

Olivia took the lid off and breathed in the delicious steam. "Split pea soup with bits of ham. Yum." She took the chair opposite him.

"O., would you dish it up, please?" Elaine slid the fries into a large green bowl.

Olivia picked up Tommy's dish first, depositing a heaping ladleful of soup and putting it in front of him.

"Eww."

Seth tugged his chair closer to Olivia and sat, trying not to pay attention to Tommy. "Be polite." It wasn't what he wanted to say. He wanted to backhand the asshole. Take the ladle and smash it into his face. But he didn't. There still a small part of him keeping control.

But there was something else now. An additional hatred pouring out of him centered around Olivia. He slid the chair away from his sister and tried to understand the war raging in his mind.

Olivia took his bowl and filled it with soup, her arm crossing in front of him as she set it down. He wanted to break it. Snap it in two. And then her neck.

He leaned backward in his chair, trying to put some distance between himself and them.

"Don't sit like that, hon," Elaine said. "It's bad for the chair legs."

He let the chair fall into place and slid it halfway between Olivia and Tommy. The hideous throbbing in his mind was almost too much. A talon raked down the middle of his back and he felt the warm blood welling. He scooped up his bowl and stood by the sink. Maybe a little distance would help. Ease it enough that he could make it through dinner without destroying his family.

He needed to kill this thing. Or die trying. He had to save them before he snapped. It was coming. He wouldn't be strong enough to keep up this fight much longer. And he knew what he had to do. He'd have to go back to where it all started. Where he already tried to end it once. And where he'd make his final stand. To save Olivia. Maybe himself. Dr. Ryan said his destiny was in his own hands and it seemed pretty apparent now.

Elaine's brow furrowed. She wiped her mouth with a napkin. "You okay?"

"It's the light, Mom. I feel a migraine coming on and that light is just too bright." Another lie. He had to move away. Get farther from Olivia. Get the thing in his mind and soul to ease up, if only for a short while. Keep his sanity just a little longer.

"Oh, hon. I'm sorry. Is there anything I can do?"

He looked at the floor. "There is, and I hate to ask."

"What?"

"I actually don't have any more migraine meds. I'm so sorry. We should have stopped at Pop's. I really thought they had given me some before I left Hemmingway."

She checked the clock over the stove and pushed away from the table. "It's only six. They don't close until at least eight-thirty. I can go."

"Eat first. Please, Mom. I'd feel awful if you didn't."

"If you're sure."

Seth nodded. He took a mouthful of the soup but didn't taste it. "Really."

"Okay. But then I'll head right out. I don't want you in pain."

He stepped over and squeezed her shoulder. She rested her head on his hand for a moment and then continued eating.

Elaine wiggled her fingers into her gloves and straightened the collar of her pea coat. "I'll be home in about forty-five minutes," she said. "You're sure you're good until then?"

"Yes, Mom." Seth was lying on the sofa, arm over his eyes. "It'll be fine."

"All right. Olivia, you've got Tommy. I'm sure he'll be good until I get back." She glanced between her son and Olivia, the worry apparent in her eyes.

"I've got it," Olivia said. "We'll play in my room so Seth can rest."

Elaine mouthed the words *thank you* and walked out the door. It shut with a thud against the wind.

"Yay, what are we playing?" Tommy asked, skittering into the hallway.

"Anything you want."

Seth waited until he heard the car start and pull away, then watched the headlights move down the street before he sprang into action. He went into the garage, almost tripping over the rake, to grab two red gas cans. He was done. Done with pain. Done with something commanding his life, controlling his actions. Turning his dreams into nightmares, and his waking life into a living hell. It was time to break his covenant with evil. Their covenant. His and Blake's. He wondered for a second if dying had been his friend's release. It didn't matter. He'd burn their covenant tonight and either he or the demon would be dead before morning. It was his last chance to keep his soul and send this thing back to Hades.

He hefted the cans, one in each hand, and was satisfied that they were full. With his elbow, he hit the button to open the garage door and walked the cans to the back of the house. Setting them down, he slid the door aside and went in to find a lighter.

Olivia was at the sink, washing a glass. "What's doing, Sy?"

"Nothing you need to concern yourself with." He saw the lighter they used for the jack-o-lanterns and grabbed it. He spun the spark wheel and it lit, sending up a long, yellow flame.

Olivia followed him to the sliding door, stepping through. A blast of cold hit her in the face. "Sy, what's going on?"

He picked up the gas cans and strode away from her.

"Seth!"

"Not now, Olivia."

She started after him, her bare feet frigid in the snow and ice. There was a faint whistling in the distance. "What are you doing?" She ran up to him and grabbed his wrist.

He whipped to face her, burning from her touch. The beast writhed in his mind, enraged him. "Go inside. There's something I have to take care of." He winced from the pain that descended on him, claws shredding his flesh. It wanted her dead. It wanted her gone. Gone. Gone! He stumbled backward. "Please. Go. You're not safe out here."

"Seth, we can get rid of it!"

"What?" A look of confusion spread across his face. "What?"

"That thing on you. Twisting your mind. We can get rid of it. I know you're not crazy. I can see it's killing you!"

"We? No. This is mine alone. I have to do this on my own."

Olivia shook her head hard. "No. We. Me and . . . it's too long a story. A spirit I found through the board. He's strong, Seth. He can help me get rid of that thing."

Seth watched a tall darkness form beside his sister, and he recognized a greater evil. His demon scrambled up his back, tearing his arms and neck. Olivia saw its gaping maw and razor teeth, hovering above him, like a demented cobra ready to strike.

"No, Olivia. No, no, no!" How did this happen? Why didn't he see this coming? "You need to get away from that thing," he said. "For the love of God, Olivia, it's a demon." His eyes went wild. His sanity was thinning and soon he wouldn't be able to protect her. But she was in league with a demon and how could he fight that, too? His mind swam.

"Seth, I've got this. I swear!"

The whistling grew louder, but neither noticed.

"Oh, don't fucking even tell me that." The gas cans swayed in his hands as he staggered. "Haven't you learned anything from this? From seeing me? It's evil. This isn't a fucking walk in the park. It's the road to hell."

"And what's that on you? I can handle this, Sy. Don't think I can't. My abilities are so ramped up right now and Black's opened my eyes to so much more. He can get rid of the piece of shit that's been riding you." She took a few steps closer, feet and ankles numb with the cold.

"At what cost?!" She was thwarting his plan, and his mother would be back from the pharmacy soon. He'd lose himself and his sister and probably his entire family would go down on this sinking ship. And it was all his fault. He'd let them down. Every last one. He stared into her eyes, and it felt like razor wire tightening around his skull, sending excruciating pain through his eyeballs. It took all of his strength not to fall to his knees.

"None. Seth, just let us help you."

"He's lying to you. Like demons do. There's always a cost. Look at me! Do you think this was random? Oh, my God, Olivia," he shifted the cans, hands aching. "Blake and I pulled this shitstorm out of hell. And it worked for a while. Why do you think Blake is dead?"

And then it was clear. It was the board he and Blake had used that created their portal to this hell. It was the board Olivia had that brought this other thing in. He had to burn it. Destroy it. Close the damn portal that was leading them to destruction. Damnation. At least he could save his sister. Maybe there'd be some redemption in that.

His attachment latched onto his thought and dug deeper into his soul. It spurred him on.

Burn it burn it burn it send its master back to hell burn it burn it destroy the board destroy the maker burn it burn it burn it

The wretched, frantic, frenetic screaming in his head was almost too much to bear. Seth dropped one gas can and rushed toward the house, shoving past Olivia. The gas glugged out onto the snow.

Seth dug in his pocket for the lighter as he went for the sliding door.

She saw what was in his mind and screamed, "No!" With a strength not her own, she grabbed him and spun him back, digging her fingernails into his arm. "Not the board!" The lighter fell to the ground at their feet.

His rage took over, his demon driving him. Their thoughts mixing. He would get the board and destroy its maker, the commander of flies . . . it was the forefront of their thoughts, their screaming insanity. He'd save his sister, kill the master, burn the board, kill his sister . . . all thoughts melded, indistinguishable, and he struggled with her, dragging her to the ground. She could smell the puddle of gas a few feet away.

His demon pulled itself away from him and leapt to attack Olivia.

She thrashed, at the air, at Seth, digging her fingers into his face. And then she screamed, "Black!"

The shadow demon shielded its charge, opening its maw and sending forth a gravelly bellow that shattered the lesser ghoul into puke-green shards that melted into the earth, mixing with the gas from the can. It then poured into Olivia fully, with a force and power she hadn't realized she could command. She saw through its eyes and it through hers, and it turned their intent on the lighter. With a twist of her wrist, Black's wrist, their wrist, the lighter lit and the gas can exploded, the blaze engulfing everything it touched.

Including her brother.

The whistling stopped.

It was Seth's turn to scream.

With one last shred of compassion, Olivia focused on his heart, stopping it. His body lay burning in the melted snow, the ground scorched beneath him.

With muted emotion, she said, "He was my brother."

In another life
We need to leave this place
There is much work ahead

Olivia went inside, leaving wet footprints in the hallway. Tommy was sitting on her bed with the Trouble board set up.

"Ready to play?"

She ignored him as she grabbed the survival pack from her closet, shoving clothes into it. She reached into her desk drawer and took out the small handful of gift cards her grandmother had sent over the years, along with the money she'd saved from babysitting. She turned off her cell phone and dropped it into the trash.

"Are you going to play with me?" He jumped off the bed and stood by her chair, spinning it in circles. "What are you doing?"

She sat on the edge of the bed to pull on a pair of thick socks, then shoved her feet into her hiking boots, lacing them tightly. She picked up the spirit board to slide it into the pack and Tommy grabbed it.

"That's mine!" he shouted.

She yanked it out of his hands, knocking him to the floor.

"Hey!"

She threw on a jacket, slung the pack onto her back and picked up the walking stick, the weight of it right in her hand. There'd be uneven terrain to traverse. Grabbing her top hat, she strode toward the living room. Tommy found his footing and ran after her.

"Stop! That's mine!"

Black waved a shadow arm. The dart board fell from the wall as the metal darts dislodged and drove into Tommy's right leg.

He dropped to the floor, writhing and screaming.

Without breaking stride, Olivia asked, "What happened?"

I stopped him

She paused in the living room to adjust the pack and gazed into the mirror. Her eyes were entirely black. She shook her head. "Not the eyes."

They returned to normal.

"Good."

When she slung the pack onto her shoulder, she noticed a small black mark on the inside of her right wrist. A mark that bound them. Branded her soul.

She left in the direction of the woods, two minutes before Elaine pulled into the driveway, saw the flames and collapsed.

EPILOGUE

Dom cracked a second egg over the frying pan, letting it sizzle in the butter. The satisfying smell of frying eggs filled the kitchen. His toast popped up as the Keurig finished. A perfect winter breakfast in the making. It'd been a while since he had hot cocoa, and he was going to relax and enjoy it.

He laid his plate on the coffee table and reached for the remote, turning on the television and clicking until he found the local news. A press conference was being held and there, behind the podium, was the woman from the blue Camry. He hit the volume up three, four times.

"Please," she was saying. "Olivia is not just my foster child. I love her like my own daughter. Please," she stumbled on the words, throat tight, "anyone with any information, I beg you to come forward. I've lost my son. Please don't make me lose my daughter, too."

The woman stepped back from the podium and the media specialist took over. To Dom he looked like the police chief.

"Thank you, Mrs. Resnick." He turned to the cameras. "Again, this has been what we believe to be a murder-kidnapping, and we have reason to believe the perpetrator or perpetrators are on the move toward higher terrain as outdoor items are missing from the home. However, an Amber alert has been issued and we will follow up on every tip we receive on our hotline."

Dom finished his eggs, eyes unwavering from the screen. In the background he recognized some search and rescue personnel, confirming to him that they were taking to the woods behind Aliton. He gulped his cocoa, grabbed his cane and went into the bedroom.

He pulled an old backpack and sleeping bag from under the bed. It was time to act.

He dressed. Thermal underwear, flannel lined jeans, sweatshirt. Hunting socks. And he threw into his pack a couple of days' worth of changes. Dry socks were imperative. His wallet. $130 in cash, plus cards. Camping gear was already stowed in the pack's inner pockets. Flint, firestarter, jackknife. Canteen, compass. Phone, remote charger. Grabbing his winter jacket and gloves, he moved to the living room. At his desk, he added the blessed water. Protection pouches. One he tucked into his shirt pocket. He put on a necklace he'd found at a yard sale that had a pendant of a pentacle and cross.

His mind could have been spinning; he could have rushed. But all was quiet. He knew what he had to do, and the time had come to follow through. Tucking his keys into his pocket, he wondered where he'd end up leaving the car. There had to be a parking lot where he could hide it in a back corner somewhere. But that didn't matter, either. Let them find it. Let it be towed.

He picked up the knife. It slid perfectly into the side pocket of his pack, along with the stone. He was ready. He was the demon killer. He would be Amanda's redeemer. Jacket on, gloves. He threw the pack and bag onto his back and left the apartment.

Stepping outside he paused, breathing in the fresh air. A crow cawed to the west. Aliton. Black was on the move, and he'd be right behind. There was no turning back from destiny.

Coming Soon:

Cult of Darkness

ABOUT THE AUTHOR

Barb Shadow is a paranormal investigator and researcher, living with her family on the East Coast. She founded the Sullivan Paranormal Society, an investigative team in upstate New York, and has appeared on numerous radio shows to discuss her experiences. Barb has kept a journal of her ghostly encounters for the last thirty years.

Her horror series, From the Darkness, began as a challenge to write a novel in a month. With the first draft penned, Barb won the challenge, combining her flair for storytelling with her passion for the paranormal. The series caught fire. Her readers have said they read with the lights on and only when they're not alone. When not writing spine-tingling tales, you can find Barb with headphones on, listening for EVPs from her team's latest investigations.

To find out more and get updates on upcoming titles, visit **barbshadow.com**. There you can follow her blog on the paranormal and contact her with any comments or questions you have. She is always happy to connect with fans and those interested in the unexplained.

You can find her team's Facebook page at Sullivan Paranormal Society (and listen to some of the amazing EVPs they've recorded). Not for the faint of heart!

Barb can also be found on Instagram at **barbshadowwrites**.

If you've had a paranormal experience and would like to share it with Barb or have it considered for inclusion in her upcoming anthology, *True Ghost Stories and Hauntings, vol. 3,* you can submit it on the From the Shadows Publishing website, **fromtheshadowspublishing.com**.

www.ingramcontent.com/pod-product-compliance
Lightning Source LLC
Chambersburg PA
CBHW030531270626
47155CB00024B/2715